Men's Wives

Men's Wives

William Makepeace
Thackeray

MINT EDITIONS

Men's Wives was first published in 1852.

This edition published by Mint Editions 2021.

ISBN 9781513271996 | E-ISBN 9781513276991

Published by Mint Editions®

 MINT
EDITIONS

minteditionbooks.com

Publishing Director: Jennifer Newens
Design & Production: Rachel Lopez Metzger
Project Manager: Micaela Clark
Typesetting: Westchester Publishing Services

Contents

MR. AND MRS. FRANK BERRY

THE RAVENSWING

I

WHICH IS ENTIRELY INTRODUCTORY—
CONTAINS AN ACCOUNT OF MISS CRUMP,
HER SUITORS, AND HER FAMILY CIRCLE

In a certain quiet and sequestered nook of the retired village of
London—perhaps in the neighbourhood of Berkeley Square, or at
any rate somewhere near Burlington Gardens—there was once a house
of entertainment called the "Bootjack Hotel." Mr. Crump, the landlord,
had, in the outset of life, performed the duties of Boots in some inn
even more frequented than his own, and, far from being ashamed of
his origin, as many persons are in the days of their prosperity, had thus
solemnly recorded it over the hospitable gate of his hotel.

Crump married Miss Budge, so well known to the admirers of the
festive dance on the other side of the water as Miss Delancy; and they had
one daughter, named Morgiana, after that celebrated part in the "Forty
Thieves" which Miss Budge performed with unbounded applause both
at the "Surrey" and "The Wells." Mrs. Crump sat in a little bar, profusely
ornamented with pictures of the dancers of all ages, from Hillisberg,
Rose, Parisot, who plied the light fantastic toe in 1805, down to the
Sylphides of our day. There was in the collection a charming portrait
of herself, done by De Wilde; she was in the dress of Morgiana, and in
the act of pouring, to very slow music, a quantity of boiling oil into one
of the forty jars. In this sanctuary she sat, with black eyes, black hair, a
purple face and a turban, and morning, noon, or night, as you went
into the parlour of the hotel, there was Mrs. Crump taking tea (with a
little something in it), looking at the fashions, or reading Cumberland's
"British Theatre." The Sunday Times was her paper, for she voted the
Dispatch, that journal which is taken in by most ladies of her profession,
to be vulgar and Radical, and loved the theatrical gossip in which the
other mentioned journal abounds.

The fact is, that the "Royal Bootjack," though a humble, was a very
genteel house; and a very little persuasion would induce Mr. Crump, as
he looked at his own door in the sun, to tell you that he had himself
once drawn off with that very bootjack the top-boots of His Royal
Highness the Prince of Wales and the first gentleman in Europe. While,

then, the houses of entertainment in the neighbourhood were loud in their pretended Liberal politics, the "Bootjack" stuck to the good old Conservative line, and was only frequented by such persons as were of that way of thinking. There were two parlours, much accustomed, one for the gentlemen of the shoulder-knot, who came from the houses of their employers hard by; another for some "gents who used the 'ouse," as Mrs. Crump would say (Heaven bless her!) in her simple Cockniac dialect, and who formed a little club there.

I forgot to say that while Mrs. C. was sipping her eternal tea or washing up her endless blue china, you might often hear Miss Morgiana employed at the little red-silk cottage piano, singing, "Come where the haspens quiver," or "Bonny lad, march over hill and furrow," or "My art and lute," or any other popular piece of the day. And the dear girl sang with very considerable skill, too, for she had a fine loud voice, which, if not always in tune, made up for that defect by its great energy and activity; and Morgiana was not content with singing the mere tune, but gave every one of the roulades, flourishes, and ornaments as she heard them at the theatres by Mrs. Humby, Mrs. Waylett, or Madame Vestris. The girl had a fine black eye like her mamma, a grand enthusiasm for the stage, as every actor's child will have, and, if the truth must be known, had appeared many and many a time at the theatre in Catherine Street, in minor parts first, and then in Little Pickle, in Desdemona, in Rosina, and in Miss Foote's part where she used to dance: I have not the name to my hand, but think it is Davidson. Four times in the week, at least, her mother and she used to sail off at night to some place of public amusement, for Mrs. Crump had a mysterious acquaintance with all sorts of theatrical personages; and the gates of her old haunt "The Wells," of the "Cobourg" (by the kind permission of Mrs. Davidge), nay, of the "Lane" and the "Market" themselves, flew open before her "Open sesame," as the robbers' door did to her colleague, Ali Baba (Hornbuckle), in the operatic piece in which she was so famous.

Beer was Mr. Crump's beverage, diversified by a little gin, in the evenings; and little need be said of this gentleman, except that he discharged his duties honourably, and filled the president's chair at the club as completely as it could possibly be filled; for he could not even sit in it in his greatcoat, so accurately was the seat adapted to him. His wife and daughter, perhaps, thought somewhat slightingly of him, for he had no literary tastes, and had never been at a theatre since he took his bride from one. He was valet to Lord Slapper at the time, and certain it is that his lordship set him up in the "Bootjack," and that stories HAD been told. But what are such to you or me? Let bygones be bygones; Mrs. Crump was quite as honest as her neighbours, and Miss had five hundred pounds to be paid down on the day of her wedding.

Those who know the habits of the British tradesman are aware that he has gregarious propensities like any lord in the land; that he loves a joke, that he is not averse to a glass; that after the day's toil he is happy to consort with men of his degree; and that as society is not so far advanced among us as to allow him to enjoy the comforts of splendid club-houses, which are open to many persons with not a tenth part of his pecuniary means, he meets his friends in the cosy tavern parlour, where a neat sanded floor, a large Windsor chair, and a glass of hot something and water, make him as happy as any of the clubmen in their magnificent saloons.

At the "Bootjack" was, as we have said, a very genteel and select society, called the "Kidney Club," from the fact that on Saturday evenings a little graceful supper of broiled kidneys was usually discussed by the members of the club. Saturday was their grand night; not but that they met on all other nights in the week when inclined for festivity: and indeed some of them could not come on Saturdays in the summer having elegant villas in the suburbs, where they passed the six-and-thirty hours of recreation that are happily to be found at the end of every week.

There was Mr. Balls, the great grocer of South Audley Street, a warm man, who, they say, had his twenty thousand pounds; Jack Snaffle, of the mews hard by, a capital fellow for a song; Clinker, the ironmonger: all married gentlemen, and in the best line of business; Tressle, the undertaker, etc. No liveries were admitted into the room, as may be imagined, but one or two select butlers and major-domos joined the circle; for the persons composing it knew very well how important it was to be on good terms with these gentlemen and many a time my lord's account would never have been paid, and my lady's large order never have been given, but for the conversation which took place at the "Bootjack," and the friendly intercourse subsisting between all the members of the society.

The tiptop men of the society were two bachelors, and two as fashionable tradesmen as any in the town: Mr. Woolsey, from Stultz's, of the famous house of Linsey, Woolsey and Co. of Conduit Street, Tailors; and Mr. Eglantine, the celebrated perruquier and perfumer of Bond Street, whose soaps, razors, and patent ventilating scalps are know throughout Europe. Linsey, the senior partner of the tailors' firm had his handsome mansion in Regent's Park, drove his buggy, and did little more than lend his name to the house. Woolsey lived in it, was the working man of the firm, and it was said that his cut was as magnificent as that of any man in the profession. Woolsey and Eglantine were rivals in many ways—rivals in fashion, rivals in wit, and, above all, rivals for the hand of an amiable young lady whom we have already mentioned, the dark-eyed songstress Morgiana Crump. They were both desperately in love with her, that was the truth; and each, in the absence of the other, abused his rival heartily. Of the hairdresser Woolsey said, that as for Eglantine being his real name, it was all his (Mr. Woolsey's) eye; that he was in the hands of the Jews, and his stock and grand shop eaten up by usury. And with regard to Woolsey, Eglantine remarked, that his pretence of being descended from the Cardinal was all nonsense; that he was a partner, certainly, in the firm, but had only a sixteenth share; and that the firm could never get their moneys in, and had an immense number of bad debts in their books. As is usual, there was a great deal of truth and a great deal of malice in these tales; however, the gentlemen were, take them all in all, in a very fashionable way of business, and had their claims to Miss Morgiana's hand backed by the parents. Mr. Crump was a partisan of the tailor; while Mrs. C. was a strong advocate for the claims of the enticing perfumer.

Now, it was a curious fact, that these two gentlemen were each in need of the other's services—Woolsey being afflicted with premature baldness, or some other necessity for a wig still more fatal—Eglantine being a very fat man, who required much art to make his figure at all decent. He wore a brown frock-coat and frogs, and attempted by all sorts of contrivances to hide his obesity; but Woolsey's remark, that, dress as he would, he would always look like a snob, and that there was only one man in England who could make a gentleman of him, went to the perfumer's soul; and if there was one thing on earth he longed for (not including the hand of Miss Crump) it was to have a coat from Linsey's, in which costume he was sure that Morgiana would not resist him.

If Eglantine was uneasy about the coat, on the other hand he attacked Woolsey atrociously on the score of his wig; for though the latter went to the best makers, he never could get a peruke to sit naturally upon him and the unhappy epithet of Mr. Wiggins, applied to him on one occasion by the barber, stuck to him ever after in the club, and made him writhe when it was uttered. Each man would have quitted the "Kidneys" in disgust long since, but for the other—for each had an attraction in the place, and dared not leave the field in possession of his rival.

To do Miss Morgiana justice, it must be said, that she did not encourage one more than another; but as far as accepting eau-de-Cologne and hair-combs from the perfumer—some opera tickets, a treat to Greenwich, and a piece of real Genoa velvet for a bonnet (it had originally been intended for a waistcoat), from the admiring tailor, she had been equally kind to each, and in return had made each a present of a lock of her beautiful glossy hair. It was all she had to give, poor girl! and what could she do but gratify her admirers by this cheap and artless testimony of her regard? A pretty scene and quarrel took place between the rivals on the day when they discovered that each was in possession of one of Morgiana's ringlets.

Such, then, were the owners and inmates of the little "Bootjack," from whom and which, as this chapter is exceedingly discursive and descriptive, we must separate the reader for a while, and carry him—it is only into Bond Street, so no gentleman need be afraid—carry him into Bond Street, where some other personages are awaiting his consideration.

Not far from Mr. Eglantine's shop in Bond Street, stand, as is very well known, the Windsor Chambers. The West Diddlesex Association (Western Branch), the British and Foreign Soap Company, the celebrated attorneys Kite and Levison, have their respective offices here; and as the names of the other inhabitants of the chambers are not only painted on the walls, but also registered in Mr. Boyle's "Court Guide," it is quite unnecessary that they should be repeated here. Among them, on the entresol (between the splendid saloons of the Soap Company on the first floor, with their statue of Britannia presenting a packet of the soap to Europe, Asia, Africa, and America, and the West Diddlesex Western Branch on the basement)—lives a gentleman by the name of Mr. Howard Walker. The brass plate on the door of that gentleman's chambers had the word "Agency" inscribed beneath his name; and we are therefore at liberty to imagine that he followed that mysterious occupation. In person Mr. Walker was very genteel; he had large whiskers, dark eyes (with a slight cast in them), a cane, and a velvet waistcoat. He was a member of a club; had an admission to the opera, and knew every face behind the scenes; and was in the habit of using a number of French phrases in his conversation, having picked up a smattering of that language during a residence "on the Continent;" in fact, he had found it very convenient at various times of his life to dwell in the city of Boulogne, where he acquired a knowledge of smoking, ecarte, and billiards, which was afterwards of great service to him. He knew all the best tables in town, and the marker at Hunt's could only give him ten. He had some fashionable acquaintances too, and you might see him walking arm-in-arm with such gentlemen as my Lord Vauxhall, the Marquess of Billingsgate, or Captain Buff; and at the same time nodding to young Moses, the dandy bailiff; or Loder, the gambling-house keeper; or Aminadab, the cigar-seller in the Quadrant. Sometimes he wore a pair of moustaches, and was called Captain Walker; grounding his claim to that title upon the fact of having once held a commission in the service of Her Majesty the Queen of Portugal. It scarcely need be said that he had been through the Insolvent Court many times. But to those who did not know his history intimately there was some difficulty in identifying him with the individual who had so taken the benefit of the law, inasmuch as in his schedule his name appeared as Hooker Walker, wine-merchant, commission-agent, music-seller, or what not. The fact is, that though he preferred to call himself Howard, Hooker was his Christian name, and it had been bestowed on him by his worthy old father, who was a clergyman, and had intended his son for that profession. But as the old gentleman died in York gaol, where he was a prisoner for debt, he was never able to put his pious intentions with regard to his son into execution; and the young fellow (as he was wont with many oaths to assert) was thrown on his own resources, and became a man of the world at a very early age.

What Mr. Howard Walker's age was at the time of the commencement of this history, and, indeed, for an indefinite period before or afterwards, it is impossible to determine. If he were eight-and-twenty, as he asserted himself, Time had dealt hardly with him: his hair was thin, there were many crows'-feet about his eyes, and other signs in his countenance of the progress of decay. If, on the contrary, he were forty, as Sam Snaffle declared, who himself had misfortunes in early life, and vowed he knew Mr. Walker in Whitecross Street Prison in 1820, he was a very young-looking person considering his age. His figure was active and slim, his leg neat, and he had not in his whiskers a single white hair.

It must, however, be owned that he used Mr. Eglantine's Regenerative Unction (which will make your whiskers as black as your boot), and, in fact, he was a pretty constant visitor at that gentleman's emporium; dealing with him largely for soaps and articles of perfumery, which he had at an exceedingly low rate. Indeed, he was never known to pay Mr. Eglantine one single shilling for those objects of luxury, and, having them on such moderate terms, was enabled to indulge in them pretty copiously. Thus Mr. Walker was almost as great a nosegay as Mr. Eglantine himself: his handkerchief was scented with verbena, his hair with jessamine, and his coat had usually a fine perfume of cigars, which rendered his presence in a small room almost instantaneously remarkable. I have described Mr. Walker thus accurately, because, in truth, it is more with characters than with astounding events that this little history deals, and Mr. Walker is one of the principal of our dramatis personae.

And so, having introduced Mr. W., we will walk over with him to Mr. Eglantine's emporium, where that gentleman is in waiting, too, to have his likeness taken.

There is about an acre of plate glass under the Royal arms on Mr. Eglantine's shop-window; and at night, when the gas is lighted, and the washballs are illuminated, and the lambent flame plays fitfully over numberless bottles of vari-coloured perfumes—now flashes on a case of razors, and now lightens up a crystal vase, containing a hundred thousand of his patent tooth-brushes—the effect of the sight may be imagined. You don't suppose that he is a creature who has those odious, simpering wax figures in his window, that are called by the vulgar dummies? He is above such a wretched artifice; and it is my belief that he would as soon have his own head chopped off, and placed as a trunkless decoration to his shop-window, as allow a dummy to figure there. On one pane you read in elegant gold letters "Eglantinia"—'tis his essence for the handkerchief; on the other is written "Regenerative Unction"—'tis his invaluable pomatum for the hair.

There is no doubt about it: Eglantine's knowledge of his profession amounts to genius. He sells a cake of soap for seven shillings, for which another man would not get a shilling, and his tooth-brushes go off like wildfire at half-a-guinea apiece. If he has to administer rouge or pearl-powder to ladies, he does it with a mystery and fascination which there is no resisting, and the ladies believe there are no cosmetics like his. He gives his wares unheard-of names, and obtains for them sums equally prodigious. He CAN dress hair—that is a fact—as few men in this age can; and has been known to take twenty pounds in a single night from as many of the first ladies of England when ringlets were in fashion. The introduction of bands, he says, made a difference of two thousand pounds a year in his income; and if there is one thing in the world he hates and despises, it is a Madonna. "I'm not," says he, "a tradesman—I'm a HARTIST"

(Mr. Eglantine was born in London)—"I'm a hartist; and show me a fine 'ead of air, and I'll dress it for nothink." He vows that it was his way of dressing Mademoiselle Sontag's hair, that caused the count her husband to fall in love with her; and he has a lock of it in a brooch, and says it was the finest head he ever saw, except one, and that was Morgiana Crump's.

With his genius and his position in the profession, how comes it, then, that Mr. Eglantine was not a man of fortune, as many a less clever has been? If the truth must be told, he loved pleasure, and was in the hands of the Jews. He had been in business twenty years: he had borrowed a thousand pounds to purchase his stock and shop; and he calculated that he had paid upwards of twenty thousand pounds for the use of the one thousand, which was still as much due as on the first day when he entered business. He could show that he had received a thousand dozen of champagne from the disinterested money-dealers with whom he usually negotiated his paper. He had pictures all over his "studios," which had been purchased in the same bargains. If he sold his goods at an enormous price, he paid for them at a rate almost equally exorbitant. There was not an article in his shop but came to him through his Israelite providers; and in the very front shop itself sat a gentleman who was the nominee of one of them, and who was called Mr. Mossrose. He was there to superintend the cash account, and to see that certain instalments were paid to his principals, according to certain agreements entered into between Mr. Eglantine and them.

Having that sort of opinion of Mr. Mossrose which Damocles may have had of the sword which hung over his head, of course Mr. Eglantine hated his foreman profoundly. "He an artist," would the former gentleman exclaim; "why, he's only a disguised bailiff! Mossrose indeed! The chap's name's Amos, and he sold oranges before he came here." Mr. Mossrose, on his side, utterly despised Mr. Eglantine, and looked forward to the day when he would become the proprietor of the shop, and take Eglantine for a foreman; and then it would His turn to sneer and bully, and ride the high horse.

Thus it will be seen that there was a skeleton in the great perfumer's house, as the saying is: a worm in his heart's core, and though to all appearance prosperous, he was really in an awkward position.

What Mr. Eglantine's relations were with Mr. Walker may be imagined from the following dialogue which took place between the two gentlemen at five o'clock one summer's afternoon, when Mr. Walker, issuing from his chambers, came across to the perfumer's shop:—

"Is Eglantine at home, Mr. Mossrose?" said Walker to the foreman, who sat in the front shop.

"Don't know—go and look" (meaning go and be hanged); for Mossrose also hated Mr. Walker.

"If you're uncivil I'll break your bones, Mr. Amos," says Mr. Walker, sternly.

"I should like to see you try, Mr. Hooker Walker," replies the undaunted shopman; on which the Captain, looking several tremendous canings at him, walked into the back room or "studio."

"How are you, Tiny my buck?" says the Captain. "Much doing?"

"Not a soul in town. I 'aven't touched the hirons all day," replied Mr. Eglantine, in rather a desponding way.

"Well, just get them ready now, and give my whiskers a turn. I'm going to dine with Billingsgate and some out-and-out fellows at the 'Regent,' and so, my lad, just do your best."

"I can't," says Mr. Eglantine. "I expect ladies, Captain, every minute."

"Very good; I don't want to trouble such a great man, I'm sure. Good-bye, and let me hear from you This Day Week, Mr. Eglantine." "This day week" meant that at seven days from that time a certain bill accepted by Mr. Eglantine would be due, and presented for payment.

"Don't be in such a hurry, Captain—do sit down. I'll curl you in one minute. And, I say, won't the party renew?"

"Impossible—it's the third renewal."

"But I'll make the thing handsome to you;—indeed I will."

"How much?"

"Will ten pounds do the business?"

"What! offer my principal ten pounds? Are you mad, Eglantine?—A little more of the iron to the left whisker."

"No, I meant for commission."

"Well, I'll see if that will do. The party I deal with, Eglantine, has power, I know, and can defer the matter no doubt. As for me, you know, I've nothing to do in the affair, and only act as a friend between you and him. I give you my honour and soul, I do."

"I know you do, my dear sir." The last two speeches were lies. The perfumer knew perfectly well that Mr. Walker would pocket the ten pounds; but he was too easy to care for paying it, and too timid to quarrel with such a powerful friend. And he had on three different occasions already paid ten pounds' fine for the renewal of the bill in question, all of which bonuses he knew went to his friend Mr. Walker.

Here, too, the reader will perceive what was, in part, the meaning of the word "Agency" on Mr. Walker's door. He was a go-between between money-lenders and borrowers in this world, and certain small sums always remained with him in the course of the transaction. He was an agent for wine, too; an agent for places to be had through the influence of great men; he was an agent for half-a-dozen theatrical people, male and female, and had the interests of the latter especially, it was said, at heart. Such were a few of the means by which this worthy gentleman contrived to support himself, and if, as he was fond of high living, gambling, and pleasures of all kinds, his revenue was not large enough for his expenditure—why, he got into debt, and settled his bills that way. He was as much at home in the Fleet as in Pall Mall, and quite as happy in the one place as in the other. "That's the way I take things," would this philosopher say. "If I've money, I spend; if I've credit, I borrow; if I'm dunned, I whitewash; and so you can't beat me down." Happy elasticity of temperament! I do believe that, in spite of his misfortunes and precarious position, there was no man in England whose conscience was more calm, and whose slumbers were more tranquil, than those of Captain Howard Walker.

As he was sitting under the hands of Mr. Eglantine, he reverted to "the ladies," whom the latter gentleman professed to expect; said he was a sly dog, a lucky ditto, and asked him if the ladies were handsome.

Eglantine thought there could be no harm in telling a bouncer to a gentleman with whom he was engaged in money transactions; and so, to give the Captain an idea of his solvency and the brilliancy of his future prospects, "Captain," said he, "I've got a hundred and eighty pounds out with you, which you were obliging enough to negotiate for me. Have I, or have I not, two bills out to that amount?"

"Well, my good fellow, you certainly have; and what then?"

"What then? Why, I bet you five pounds to one, that in three months those bills are paid."

"Done! five pounds to one. I take it."

This sudden closing with him made the perfumer rather uneasy; but he was not to pay for three months, and so he said, "Done!" too, and went on: "What would you say if your bills were paid?"

"Not mine; Pike's."

"Well, if Pike's were paid; and the Minories' man paid, and every single liability I have cleared off; and that Mossrose flung out of winder, and me and my emporium as free as hair?"

"You don't say so? Is Queen Anne dead? and has she left you a fortune? or what's the luck in the wind now?"

"It's better than Queen Anne, or anybody dying. What should you say to seeing in that very place where Mossrose now sits (hang him!)— seeing the FINEST HEAD OF 'AIR NOW IN EUROPE? A woman, I tell you—a slap-up lovely woman, who, I'm proud to say, will soon be called Mrs. Heglantine, and will bring me five thousand pounds to her fortune."

"Well, Tiny, this Is good luck indeed. I say, you'll be able to do a bill or two for ME then, hay? You won't forget an old friend?"

"That I won't. I shall have a place at my board for you, Capting; and many's the time I shall 'ope to see you under that ma'ogany."

"What will the French milliner say? She'll hang herself for despair, Eglantine."

"Hush! not a word about 'ER. I've sown all my wild oats, I tell you. Eglantine is no longer the gay young bachelor, but the sober married man. I want a heart to share the feelings of mine. I want repose. I'm not so young as I was: I feel it."

"Pooh! pooh! you are—you are—"

"Well, but I sigh for an 'appy fireside; and I'll have it."

"And give up that club which you belong to, hay?"

"'The Kidneys?' Oh! of course, no married man should belong to such places: at least, I'LL not; and I'll have my kidneys broiled at home. But be quiet, Captain, if you please; the ladies appointed to—"

"And is it THE lady you expect? eh, you rogue!"

"Well, get along. It's her and her Ma."

But Mr. Walker determined he wouldn't get along, and would see these lovely ladies before he stirred.

The operation on Mr. Walker's whiskers being concluded, he was arranging his toilet before the glass in an agreeable attitude: his neck out, his enormous pin settled in his stock to his satisfaction, his eyes complacently directed towards the reflection of his left and favourite whisker. Eglantine was laid on a settee, in an easy, though melancholy posture; he was twiddling the tongs with which he had just operated on Walker with one hand, and his right-hand ringlet with the other, and he was thinking—thinking of Morgiana; and then of the bill which was to become due on the 16th; and then of a light-blue velvet waistcoat with gold sprigs, in which he looked very killing, and so was trudging round in his little circle of loves, fears, and vanities. "Hang it!" Mr. Walker was thinking, "I Am a handsome man. A pair of whiskers like mine are not met with every day. If anybody can see that my tuft is dyed, may I be—" When the door was flung open, and a large lady with a curl on her forehead, yellow shawl, a green-velvet bonnet with feathers, half-boots, and a drab gown with tulips and other large exotics painted on it—when, in a word, Mrs. Crump and her daughter bounced into the room.

"Here we are, Mr. E," cries Mrs. Crump, in a gay folatre confidential air. "But law! there's a gent in the room!"

"Don't mind me, ladies," said the gent alluded to, in his fascinating way. "I'm a friend of Eglantine's; ain't I, Egg? a chip of the old block, hay?"

"That you are," said the perfumer, starting up.

"An 'air-dresser?" asked Mrs. Crump. "Well, I thought he was; there's something, Mr. E., in gentlemen of your profession so exceeding, so uncommon distangy."

"Madam, you do me proud," replied the gentleman so complimented, with great presence of mind. "Will you allow me to try my skill upon you, or upon Miss, your lovely daughter? I'm not so clever as Eglantine, but no bad hand, I assure you."

"Nonsense, Captain," interrupted the perfumer, who was uncomfortable somehow at the rencontre between the Captain and the object of his affection. "He's not in the profession, Mrs. C. This is my friend Captain Walker, and proud I am to call him my friend." And then aside to Mrs. C., "One of the first swells on town, ma'am—a regular tiptopper."

Humouring the mistake which Mrs. Crump had just made, Mr. Walker thrust the curling-irons into the fire in a minute, and looked round at the ladies with such a fascinating grace, that both, now made acquainted with his quality, blushed and giggled, and were quite pleased. Mamma looked at 'Gina, and 'Gina looked at mamma; and then mamma gave 'Gina a little blow in the region of her little waist, and then both burst out laughing, as ladies will laugh, and as, let us trust, they may laugh for ever and ever. Why need there be a reason for laughing? Let us laugh when we are laughy, as we sleep when we are sleepy. And so Mrs. Crump and her demoiselle laughed to their hearts' content; and both fixed their large shining black eyes repeatedly on Mr. Walker.

"I won't leave the room," said he, coming forward with the heated iron in his hand, and smoothing it on the brown paper with all the dexterity of a professor (for the fact is, Mr. W. every morning curled his own immense whiskers with the greatest skill and care)—"I won't leave the room, Eglantine my boy. My lady here took me for a hairdresser, and so, you know, I've a right to stay."

"He can't stay," said Mrs. Crump, all of a sudden, blushing as red as a peony.

"I shall have on my peignoir, Mamma," said Miss, looking at the gentleman, and then dropping down her eyes and blushing too.

"But he can't stay, 'Gina, I tell you: do you think that I would, before a gentleman, take off my—"

"Mamma means her FRONT!" said Miss, jumping up, and beginning to laugh with all her might; at which the honest landlady of the "Bootjack," who loved a joke, although at her own expense, laughed too, and said that no one, except Mr. Crump and Mr. Eglantine, had ever seen her without the ornament in question.

"Do go now, you provoking thing, you!" continued Miss C. to Mr. Walker; "I wish to hear the hoverture, and it's six o'clock now, and we shall never be done against then:" but the way in which Morgiana said "Do go," clearly indicated "don't" to the perspicacious mind of Mr. Walker.

"Perhaps you 'ad better go," continued Mr. Eglantine, joining in this sentiment, and being, in truth, somewhat uneasy at the admiration which his "swell friend" excited.

"I'll see you hanged first, Eggy my boy! Go I won't, until these ladies have had their hair dressed: didn't you yourself tell me that Miss Crump's was the most beautiful hair in Europe? And do you think that I'll go away without seeing it? No, here I stay."

"You naughty wicked odious provoking man!" said Miss Crump. But, at the same time, she took off her bonnet, and placed it on one of the side candlesticks of Mr. Eglantine's glass (it was a black-velvet bonnet, trimmed with sham lace, and with a wreath of nasturtiums, convolvuluses, and wallflowers within), and then said, "Give me the peignoir, Mr. Archibald, if you please;" and Eglantine, who would do anything for her when she called him Archibald, immediately produced that garment, and wrapped round the delicate shoulders of the lady, who, removing a sham gold chain which she wore on her forehead, two brass hair-combs set with glass rubies, and the comb which kept her back hair together—removing them, I say, and turning her great eyes towards the stranger, and giving her head a shake, down let tumble such a flood of shining waving heavy glossy jetty hair, as would have done Mr. Rowland's heart good to see. It tumbled down Miss Morgiana's back, and it tumbled over her shoulders, it tumbled over the chair on which she sat, and from the midst of it her jolly bright-eyed rosy face beamed out with a triumphant smile, which said, "A'n't I now the most angelic being you ever saw?"

"By Heaven! it's the most beautiful thing I ever saw!" cried Mr. Walker, with undisguised admiration.

"Isn't it?" said Mrs. Crump, who made her daughter's triumph her own. "Heigho! when I acted at 'The Wells' in 1820, before that dear girl was born, *I* had such a head of hair as that, to a shade, sir, to a shade. They called me Ravenswing on account of it. I lost my head of hair when that dear child was born, and I often say to her, 'Morgiana, you came into the world to rob your mother of her 'air.' Were you ever at 'The Wells,' sir, in 1820? Perhaps you recollect Miss Delancy? I am that Miss Delancy. Perhaps you recollect,—

> *"'Tink-a-tink, tink-a-tink,*
> *By the light of the star,*
> *On the blue river's brink,*
> *I heard a guitar.*

> *"'I heard a guitar,*
> *On the blue waters clear,*
> *And knew by its mu-u-sic,*
> *That Selim was near!'*

You remember that in the 'Bagdad Bells'? Fatima, Delancy; Selim, Benlomond (his real name was Bunnion: and he failed, poor fellow, in the public line afterwards). It was done to the tambourine, and dancing between each verse,—

> *"'Tink-a-tink, tink-a-tink,*
> *How the soft music swells,*
> *And I hear the soft clink*
> *Of the minaret bells!*

> *"'Tink-a—'"*

"Oh!" here cried Miss Crump, as if in exceeding pain (and whether Mr. Eglantine had twitched, pulled, or hurt any one individual hair of that lovely head I don't know)—"Oh, you are killing me, Mr. Eglantine!"

And with this mamma, who was in her attitude, holding up the end of her boa as a visionary tambourine, and Mr. Walker, who was looking at her, and in his amusement at the mother's performances had almost forgotten the charms of the daughter—both turned round at once, and looked at her with many expressions of sympathy, while Eglantine, in a voice of reproach, said, "KILLED you, Morgiana! I kill You?"

"I'm better now," said the young lady, with a smile—"I'm better, Mr. Archibald, now." And if the truth must be told, no greater coquette than Miss Morgiana existed in all Mayfair—no, not among the most fashionable mistresses of the fashionable valets who frequented the "Bootjack." She believed herself to be the most fascinating creature that the world ever produced; she never saw a stranger but she tried these fascinations upon him; and her charms of manner and person were of that showy sort which is most popular in this world, where people are wont to admire most that which gives them the least trouble to see; and so you will find a tulip of a woman to be in fashion when a little humble violet or daisy of creation is passed over without remark. Morgiana was a tulip among women, and the tulip fanciers all came flocking round her.

Well, the said "Oh" and "I'm better now, Mr. Archibald," thereby succeeded in drawing everybody's attention to her lovely self. By the latter words Mr. Eglantine was specially inflamed; he glanced at Mr. Walker, and said, "Capting! didn't I tell you she was a CREECHER? See her hair, sir: it's as black and as glossy as satting. It weighs fifteen pound, that hair, sir; and I wouldn't let my apprentice—that blundering Mossrose, for instance (hang him!)—I wouldn't let anyone but myself dress that hair for five hundred guineas! Ah, Miss Morgiana, remember that you MAY ALWAYS have Eglantine to dress your hair!—remember that, that's all." And with this the worthy gentleman began rubbing delicately a little of the Eglantinia into those ambrosial locks, which he loved with all the love of a man and an artist.

And as for Morgiana showing her hair, I hope none of my readers will entertain a bad opinion of the poor girl for doing so. Her locks were her pride; she acted at the private theatre "hair parts," where she could appear on purpose to show them in a dishevelled state; and that her modesty was real, and not affected may be proved by the fact that when Mr. Walker, stepping up in the midst of Eglantine's last speech, took hold of a lock of her hair very gently with his hand, she cried "Oh!" and started with all her might. And Mr. Eglantine observed very gravely, "Capting! Miss Crump's hair is to be seen and not to be touched, if you please."

"No more it is, Mr. Eglantine!" said her mamma. "And now, as it's come to my turn, I beg the gentleman will be so obliging as to go."

"MUST I?" cried Mr. Walker; and as it was half-past six, and he was engaged to dinner at the "Regent Club," and as he did not wish to make Eglantine jealous, who evidently was annoyed by his staying, he took his hat just as Miss Crump's coiffure was completed, and saluting her and her mamma, left the room.

"A tip-top swell, I can assure you," said Eglantine, nodding after him: "a regular bang-up chap, and no MISTAKE. Intimate with the Marquess of Billingsgate, and Lord Vauxhall, and that set."

"He's very genteel," said Mrs. Crump.

"Law! I'm sure I think nothing of him," said Morgiana.

And Captain Walker walked towards his club, meditating on the beauties of Morgiana. "What hair," said he, "what eyes the girl has! they're as big as billiard-balls; and five thousand pounds. Eglantine's in luck! five thousand pounds—she can't have it, it's impossible!"

No sooner was Mrs. Crump's front arranged, during the time of which operation Morgiana sat in perfect contentment looking at the last French fashions in the Courrier des Dames, and thinking how her pink satin slip would dye, and make just such a mantilla as that represented in the engraving—no sooner was Mrs. Crump's front arranged, than both ladies, taking leave of Mr. Eglantine, tripped back to the "Bootjack Hotel" in the neighbourhood, where a very neat green fly was already in waiting, the gentleman on the box of which (from a livery-stable in the neighbourhood) gave a knowing touch to his hat, and a salute with his whip, to the two ladies, as they entered the tavern.

"Mr. W.'s inside," said the man—a driver from Mr. Snaffle's establishment; "he's been in and out this score of times, and looking down the street for you." And in the house, in fact, was Mr. Woolsey, the tailor, who had hired the fly, and was engaged to conduct the ladies that evening to the play.

It was really rather too bad to think that Miss Morgiana, after going to one lover to have her hair dressed, should go with another to the play; but such is the way with lovely woman! Let her have a dozen admirers, and the dear coquette will exercise her power upon them all: and as a lady, when she has a large wardrobe, and a taste for variety in dress, will appear every day in a different costume, so will the young and giddy beauty wear her lovers, encouraging now the black whiskers, now smiling on the brown, now thinking that the gay smiling rattle of an admirer becomes her very well, and now adopting the sad sentimental melancholy one, according as her changeful fancy prompts her. Let us not be too angry with these uncertainties and caprices of beauty; and depend on it that, for the most part, those females who cry out loudest against the flightiness of their sisters, and rebuke their undue encouragement of this man or that, would do as much themselves if they had the chance, and are constant, as I am to my coat just now, because I have no other.

"Did you see Doubleyou, 'Gina dear?" said her mamma, addressing that young lady. "He's in the bar with your Pa, and has his military coat with the king's buttons, and looks like an officer."

This was Mr. Woolsey's style, his great aim being to look like an army gent, for many of whom he in his capacity of tailor made those splendid red and blue coats which characterise our military. As for the royal button, had not he made a set of coats for his late Majesty, George IV.? and he would add, when he narrated this circumstance, "Sir, Prince Blucher and Prince Swartzenberg's measure's in the house now; and what's more, I've cut for Wellington." I believe he would have gone to St. Helena to make a coat for Napoleon, so great was his ardour. He wore a blue-black wig, and his whiskers were of the same hue. He was brief and stern in conversations; and he always went to masquerades and balls in a field-marshal's uniform.

"He looks really quite the thing to-night," continued Mrs. Crump.

"Yes," said 'Gina; "but he's such an odious wig, and the dye of his whiskers always comes off on his white gloves."

"Everybody has not their own hair, love," continued Mrs. Crump with a sigh; "but Eglantine's is beautiful."

"Every hairdresser's is," answered Morgiana, rather contemptuously; "but what I can't bear is that their fingers is always so very fat and pudgy."

In fact, something had gone wrong with the fair Morgiana. Was it that she had but little liking for the one pretender or the other? Was it that young Glauber, who acted Romeo in the private theatricals, was far younger and more agreeable than either? Or was it, that seeing a REAL GENTLEMAN, such as Mr. Walker, with whom she had had her first interview, she felt more and more the want of refinement in her other declared admirers? Certain, however, it is, that she was very reserved all the evening, in spite of the attentions of Mr. Woolsey; that she repeatedly looked round at the box-door, as if she expected someone to enter; and that she partook of only a very few oysters, indeed, out of the barrel which the gallant tailor had sent down to the "Bootjack," and off which the party supped.

"What is it?" said Mr. Woolsey to his ally, Crump, as they sat together after the retirement of the ladies. "She was dumb all night. She never once laughed at the farce, nor cried at the tragedy, and you know she laughs and cries uncommon. She only took half her negus, and not above a quarter of her beer."

"No more she did!" replied Mr. Crump, very calmly. "I think it must be the barber as has been captivating her: he dressed her hair for the play."

"Hang him, I'll shoot him!" said Mr. Woolsey. "A fat foolish effeminate beast like that marry Miss Morgiana? Never! I WILL shoot him. I'll provoke him next Saturday—I'll tread on his toe—I'll pull his nose."

"No quarrelling at the 'Kidneys!'" answered Crump sternly; "there shall be no quarrelling in that room as long as I'm in the chair!"

"WELL, AT ANY RATE YOU'LL stand my friend?"

"You know I will," answered the other. "You are honourable, and I like you better than Eglantine. I trust you more than Eglantine, sir. You're more of a man than Eglantine, though you ARE a tailor; and I wish with all my heart you may get Morgiana. Mrs. C. goes the other way, I know: but I tell you what, women will go their own ways, sir, and Morgy's like her mother in this point, and depend upon it, Morgy will decide for herself."

Mr. Woolsey presently went home, still persisting in his plan for the assassination of Eglantine. Mr. Crump went to bed very quietly, and snored through the night in his usual tone. Mr. Eglantine passed some feverish moments of jealousy, for he had come down to the club in the evening, and had heard that Morgiana was gone to the play with his rival. And Miss Morgiana dreamed, of a man who was—must we say it?—exceedingly like Captain Howard Walker. "Mrs. Captain So-and-so!" thought she. "Oh, I do love a gentleman dearly!"

And about this time, too, Mr. Walker himself came rolling home from the "Regent," hiccupping. "Such hair!—such eyebrows!—such eyes! like b-b-billiard-balls, by Jove!"

II

In which Mr. Walker makes three attempts to ascertain the dwelling of Morgiana

The day after the dinner at the "Regent Club," Mr. Walker stepped over to the shop of his friend the perfumer, where, as usual, the young man, Mr. Mossrose, was established in the front premises.

For some reason or other, the Captain was particularly good-humoured; and, quite forgetful of the words which had passed between him and Mr. Eglantine's lieutenant the day before, began addressing the latter with extreme cordiality.

"A good morning to you, Mr. Mossrose," said Captain Walker. "Why, sir, you look as fresh as your namesake—you do, indeed, now, Mossrose."

"You look ash yellow ash a guinea," responded Mr. Mossrose, sulkily. He thought the Captain was hoaxing him.

"My good sir," replies the other, nothing cast down, "I drank rather too freely last night."

"The more beast you!" said Mr. Mossrose.

"Thank you, Mossrose; the same to you," answered the Captain.

"If you call me a beast, I'll punch your head off!" answered the young man, who had much skill in the art which many of his brethren practise.

"I didn't, my fine fellow," replied Walker. "On the contrary, you—"

"Do you mean to give me the lie?" broke out the indignant Mossrose, who hated the agent fiercely, and did not in the least care to conceal his hate.

In fact, it was his fixed purpose to pick a quarrel with Walker, and to drive him, if possible, from Mr. Eglantine's shop. "Do you mean to give me the lie, I say, Mr. Hooker Walker?"

"For Heaven's sake, Amos, hold your tongue!" exclaimed the Captain, to whom the name of Hooker was as poison; but at this moment a customer stepping in, Mr. Amos exchanged his ferocious aspect for a bland grin, and Mr. Walker walked into the studio.

When in Mr. Eglantine's presence, Walker, too, was all smiles in a minute, sank down on a settee, held out his hand to the perfumer, and began confidentially discoursing with him.

"Such a dinner, Tiny my boy," said he; "such prime fellows to eat it, too! Billingsgate, Vauxhall, Cinqbars, Buff of the Blues, and half-a-dozen more of the best fellows in town. And what do you think the dinner cost a head? I'll wager you'll never guess."

"Was it two guineas a head?—In course I mean without wine," said the genteel perfumer.

"Guess again!"

"Well, was it ten guineas a head? I'll guess any sum you please," replied Mr. Eglantine: "for I know that when you Nobs are together, you don't spare your money. I myself, at the "Star and Garter" at Richmond, once paid—"

"Eighteenpence?"

"Heighteenpence, sir!—I paid five-and-thirty shillings per 'ead. I'd have you to know that I can act as a gentleman as well as any other gentleman, sir," answered the perfumer with much dignity.

"Well, eighteenpence was what We paid, and not a rap more, upon my honour."

"Nonsense, you're joking. The Marquess of Billinsgate dine for eighteenpence! Why, hang it, if I was a marquess, I'd pay a five-pound note for my lunch."

"You little know the person, Master Eglantine," replied the Captain, with a smile of contemptuous superiority; "you little know the real man of fashion, my good fellow. Simplicity, sir—simplicity's the characteristic of the real gentleman, and so I'll tell you what we had for dinner."

"Turtle and venison, of course:—no nob dines without Them."

"Psha! we're sick of 'em! We had pea soup and boiled tripe! What do you think of That? We had sprats and herrings, a bullock's heart, a baked shoulder of mutton and potatoes, pig's-fry and Irish stew. I ordered the dinner, sir, and got more credit for inventing it than they ever gave to Ude or Soyer. The Marquess was in ecstasies, the Earl devoured half a bushel of sprats, and if the Viscount is not laid up with a surfeit of bullock's heart, my name's not Howard Walker. Billy, as I call him, was in the chair, and gave my health; and what do you think the rascal proposed?"

"What Did his Lordship propose?"

"That every man present should subscribe twopence, and pay for my share of the dinner. By Jove! it is true, and the money was handed to me in a pewter-pot, of which they also begged to make me a present. We afterwards went to Tom Spring's, from Tom's to the 'Finish,' from the

'Finish' to the watch-house—that is, THEY did—and sent for me, just as I was getting into bed, to bail them all out."

"They're happy dogs, those young noblemen," said Mr. Eglantine; "nothing but pleasure from morning till night; no affectation neither—no HOTURE; but manly downright straightforward good fellows."

"Should you like to meet them, Tiny my boy?" said the Captain.

"If I did sir, I hope I should show myself to be gentleman," answered Mr. Eglantine.

"Well, you SHALL meet them, and Lady Billingsgate shall order her perfumes at your shop. We are going to dine, next week, all our set, at Mealy-faced Bob's, and you shall be my guest," cried the Captain, slapping the delighted artist on the back. "And now, my boy, tell me how YOU spent the evening."

"At my club, sir," answered Mr. Eglantine, blushing rather.

"What! not at the play with the lovely black-eyed Miss—What is her name, Eglantine?

"Never mind her name, Captain," replied Eglantine, partly from prudence and partly from shame. He had not the heart to own it was Crump, and he did not care that the Captain should know more of his destined bride.

"You wish to keep the five thousand to yourself—eh, you rogue?" responded the Captain, with a good-humoured air, although exceedingly mortified; for, to say the truth, he had put himself to the trouble of telling the above long story of the dinner, and of promising to introduce Eglantine to the lords, solely that he might elicit from that gentleman's good-humour some further particulars regarding the young lady with the billiard-ball eyes. It was for the very same reason, too, that he had made the attempt at reconciliation with Mr. Mossrose which had just so signally failed. Nor would the reader, did he know Mr. W. better, at all require to have the above explanation; but as yet we are only at the first chapter of his history, and who is to know what the hero's motives can be unless we take the trouble to explain?

Well, the little dignified answer of the worthy dealer in bergamot, "NEVER MIND HER NAME, CAPTAIN!" threw the gallant Captain quite aback; and though he sat for a quarter of an hour longer, and was exceedingly kind; and though he threw out some skilful hints, yet the perfumer was quite unconquerable; or, rather, he was too frightened to tell: the poor fat timid easy good-natured gentleman was always the prey of rogues,—panting and floundering in one rascal's snare or another's.

He had the dissimulation, too, which timid men have; and felt the presence of a victimiser as a hare does of a greyhound. Now he would be quite still, now he would double, and now he would run, and then came the end. He knew, by his sure instinct of fear, that the Captain had, in asking these questions, a scheme against him, and so he was cautious, and trembled, and doubted. And oh! how he thanked his stars when Lady Grogmore's chariot drove up, with the Misses Grogmore, who wanted their hair dressed, and were going to a breakfast at three o'clock!

"I'll look in again, Tiny," said the Captain, on hearing the summons.

"Do, Captain," said the other: "Thank You;" and went into the lady's studio with a heavy heart.

"Get out of the way, you infernal villain!" roared the Captain, with many oaths, to Lady Grogmore's large footman, with ruby-coloured tights, who was standing inhaling the ten thousand perfumes of the shop; and the latter, moving away in great terror, the gallant agent passed out, quite heedless of the grin of Mr. Mossrose.

Walker was in a fury at his want of success, and walked down Bond Street in a fury. "I Will know where the girl lives!" swore he. "I'll spend a five-pound note, by Jove! rather than not know where she lives!"

"That You Would—I Know You Would!" said a little grave low voice, all of a sudden, by his side. "Pooh! what's money to you?"

Walker looked down: it was Tom Dale.

Who in London did not know little Tom Dale? He had cheeks like an apple, and his hair curled every morning, and a little blue stock, and always two new magazines under his arm, and an umbrella and a little brown frock-coat, and big square-toed shoes with which he went Papping down the street. He was everywhere at once. Everybody met him every day, and he knew everything that everybody ever did; though nobody ever knew what He did. He was, they say, a hundred years old, and had never dined at his own charge once in those hundred years. He looked like a figure out of a waxwork, with glassy clear meaningless eyes: he always spoke with a grin; he knew what you had for dinner the day before he met you, and what everybody had had for dinner for a century back almost. He was the receptacle of all the scandal of all the world, from Bond Street to Bread Street; he knew all the authors, all the actors, all the "notorieties" of the town, and the private histories of each. That is, he never knew anything really, but supplied deficiencies of truth and memory with ready-coined, never-failing lies. He was the most benevolent man in the universe, and never saw you without telling you everything most cruel of your neighbour, and when he left you he went to do the same kind turn by yourself.

"Pooh! what's money to you, my dear boy?" said little Tom Dale, who had just come out of Ebers's, where he had been filching an opera-ticket. "You make it in bushels in the City, you know you do—in thousands. I saw you go into Eglantine's. Fine business that; finest in London. Five-shilling cakes of soap, my dear boy. I can't wash with such. Thousands a year that man has made—hasn't he?"

"Upon my word, Tom, I don't know," says the Captain.

"You not know? Don't tell me. You know everything—you agents. You KNOW he makes five thousand a year—ay, and might make ten, but you know why he don't."

"Indeed I don't."

"Nonsense. Don't humbug a poor old fellow like me. Jews—Amos—fifty per cent., ay? Why can't he get his money from a good Christian?"

"I HAVE heard something of that sort," said Walker, laughing. "Why, by Jove, Tom, you know everything!"

"You know everything, my dear boy. You know what a rascally trick that opera creature served him, poor fellow. Cashmere shawls—Storr and Mortimer's—'Star and Garter.' Much better dine quiet off pea-soup and sprats—ay? His betters have, as you know very well."

"Pea-soup and sprats! What! have you heard of that already?"

"Who bailed Lord Billingsgate, hey, you rogue?" and here Tom gave a knowing and almost demoniacal grin. "Who wouldn't go to the 'Finish'? Who had the piece of plate presented to him filled with sovereigns? And you deserved it, my dear boy—you deserved it. They said it was only halfpence, but I know better!" and here Tom went off in a cough.

"I say, Tom," cried Walker, inspired with a sudden thought, "you, who know everything, and are a theatrical man, did you ever know a Miss Delancy, an actress?"

"At 'Sadler's Wells' in '16? Of course I did. Real name was Budge. Lord Slapper admired her very much, my dear boy. She married a man by the name of Crump, his Lordship's black footman, and brought him five thousand pounds; and they keep the 'Bootjack' public-house in Bunker's Buildings, and they've got fourteen children. Is one of them handsome, eh, you sly rogue—and is it that which you will give five pounds to know? God bless you, my dear dear boy. Jones, my dear friend, how are you?"

And now, seizing on Jones, Tom Dale left Mr. Walker alone, and proceeded to pour into Mr. Jones's ear an account of the individual whom he had just quitted; how he was the best fellow in the world, and Jones KNEW it; how he was in a fine way of making his fortune; how he had been in the Fleet many times, and how he was at this moment employed in looking out for a young lady of whom a certain great marquess (whom Jones knew very well, too) had expressed an admiration.

But for these observations, which he did not hear, Captain Walker, it may be pronounced, did not care. His eyes brightened up, he marched quickly and gaily away; and turning into his own chambers opposite Eglantine's, shop, saluted that establishment with a grin of triumph. "You wouldn't tell me her name, wouldn't you?" said Mr. Walker. "Well, the luck's with me now, and here goes."

Two days after, as Mr. Eglantine, with white gloves and a case of eau-de-Cologne as a present in his pocket, arrived at the "Bootjack Hotel," Little Bunker's Buildings, Berkeley Square (for it must out— that was the place in which Mr. Crump's inn was situated), he paused for a moment at the threshold of the little house of entertainment, and listened, with beating heart, to the sound of delicious music that a well-known voice was uttering within.

The moon was playing in silvery brightness down the gutter of the humble street. A "helper," rubbing down one of Lady Smigsmag's carriage-horses, even paused in his whistle to listen to the strain. Mr. Tressle's man, who had been professionally occupied, ceased his tap-tap upon the coffin which he was getting in readiness. The greengrocer (there is always a greengrocer in those narrow streets, and he goes out in white Berlin gloves as a supernumerary footman) was standing charmed at his little green gate; the cobbler (there is always a cobbler too) was drunk, as usual, of evenings, but, with unusual subordination, never sang except when the refrain of the ditty arrived, when he hiccupped it forth with tipsy loyalty; and Eglantine leaned against the chequers painted on the door-side under the name of Crump, and looked at the red illumined curtain of the bar, and the vast well-known shadow of Mrs. Crump's turban within. Now and again the shadow of that worthy matron's hand would be seen to grasp the shadow of a bottle; then the shadow of a cup would rise towards the turban, and still the strain proceeded. Eglantine, I say, took out his yellow bandanna, and brushed the beady drops from his brow, and laid the contents of his white kids on his heart, and sighed with ecstatic sympathy. The song began,—

"Come to the greenwood tree,
Come where the dark woods be,
Dearest, O come with me!
Let us rove—O my love—O my love!
O my-y love!

(Drunken Cobbler without)

O my-y love!"

"Beast!" says Eglantine.

"Come—'tis the moonlight hour,
Dew is on leaf and flower,
Come to the linden bower,
Let us rove—O my love—O my love!
Let us ro-o-ove, lurlurliety; yes, we'll rove, lurlurliety,
Through the gro-o-ove, lurlurliety—lurlurli-e-i-e-i-e-i!

(Cobbler, as usual)—

Let us ro-o-ove," etc.

"You here?" says another individual, coming clinking up the street, in a military-cut dress-coat, the buttons whereof shone very bright in the moonlight. "You here, Eglantine?—You're always here."

"Hush, Woolsey," said Mr. Eglantine to his rival the tailor (for he was the individual in question); and Woolsey, accordingly, put his back against the opposite door-post and chequers, so that (with poor Eglantine's bulk) nothing much thicker than a sheet of paper could pass out or in. And thus these two amorous caryatides kept guard as the song continued:—

"Dark is the wood, and wide,
Dangers, they say, betide;
But, at my Albert's side,
Nought, I fear, O my love—O my love!
"Welcome the greenwood tree,
Welcome the forest tree,
Dearest, with thee, with thee,
Nought I fear, O my love—O ma-a-y love!"

Eglantine's fine eyes were filled with tears as Morgiana passionately uttered the above beautiful words. Little Woolsey's eyes glistened, as he clenched his fist with an oath, and said, "Show me any singing that can beat THAT. Cobbler, shut your mouth, or I'll break your head!"

But the cobbler, regardless of the threat, continued to perform the "Lurlurliety" with great accuracy; and when that was ended, both on his part and Morgiana's, a rapturous knocking of glasses was heard in the little bar, then a great clapping of hands, and finally somebody shouted "Brava!"

"Brava!"

At that word Eglantine turned deadly pale, then gave a start, then a rush forward, which pinned, or rather cushioned, the tailor against the wall; then twisting himself abruptly round, he sprang to the door of the bar, and bounced into that apartment.

"HOW ARE YOU, MY NOSEGAY?" exclaimed the same voice which had shouted "Brava!" It was that of Captain Walker.

At ten o'clock the next morning, a gentleman, with the King's button on his military coat, walked abruptly into Mr. Eglantine's shop, and, turning on Mr. Mossrose, said, "Tell your master I want to see him."

"He's in his studio," said Mr. Mossrose.

"Well, then, fellow, go and fetch him!"

And Mossrose, thinking it must be the Lord Chamberlain, or Doctor Praetorius at least, walked into the studio, where the perfumer was seated in a very glossy old silk dressing-gown, his fair hair hanging over his white face, his double chin over his flaccid whity-brown shirt-collar, his pea-green slippers on the hob, and on the fire the pot of chocolate which was simmering for his breakfast. A lazier fellow than poor Eglantine it would be hard to find; whereas, on the contrary, Woolsey was always up and brushed, spick-and-span, at seven o'clock; and had gone through his books, and given out the work for the journeymen, and eaten a hearty breakfast of rashers of bacon, before Eglantine had put the usual pound of grease to his hair (his fingers were always as damp and shiny as if he had them in a pomatum-pot), and arranged his figure for the day.

"Here's a gent wants you in the shop," says Mr. Mossrose, leaving the door of communication wide open.

"Say I'm in bed, Mr. Mossrose; I'm out of sperrets, and really can see nobody."

"It's someone from Vindsor, I think; he's got the royal button," says Mossrose.

"It's me—Woolsey," shouted the little man from the shop.

Mr. Eglantine at this jumped up, made a rush to the door leading to his private apartment, and disappeared in a twinkling. But it must not be imagined that he fled in order to avoid Mr. Woolsey. He only went away for one minute just to put on his belt, for he was ashamed to be seen without it by his rival.

This being assumed, and his toilet somewhat arranged, Mr. Woolsey was admitted into his private room. And Mossrose would have heard every word of the conversation between those two gentlemen, had not Woolsey, opening the door, suddenly pounced on the assistant, taken him by the collar, and told him to disappear altogether into the shop: which Mossrose did; vowing he would have his revenge.

The subject on which Woolsey had come to treat was an important one. "Mr. Eglantine," says he, "there's no use disguising from one another that we are both of us in love with Miss Morgiana, and that our chances up to this time have been pretty equal. But that Captain whom you introduced, like an ass as you were—"

"An ass, Mr. Woolsey! I'd have you to know, sir, that I'm no more a hass than you are, sir; and as for introducing the Captain, I did no such thing."

"Well, well, he's got a-poaching into our preserves somehow. He's evidently sweet upon the young woman, and is a more fashionable chap than either of us two. We must get him out of the house, sir—we must circumvent him; and THEN, Mr. Eglantine, will be time enough for you and me to try which is the best man."

"HE the best man?" thought Eglantine; "the little bald unsightly tailor-creature! A man with no more soul than his smoothing-hiron!" The perfumer, as may be imagined, did not utter this sentiment aloud, but expressed himself quite willing to enter into any HAMICABLE arrangement by which the new candidate for Miss Crump's favour must be thrown over. It was accordingly agreed between the two gentlemen that they should coalesce against the common enemy; that they should, by reciting many perfectly well-founded stories in the Captain's disfavour, influence the minds of Miss Crump's parents, and of herself, if possible, against this wolf in sheep's clothing; and that, when they were once fairly rid of him, each should be at liberty, as before, to prefer his own claim.

"I have thought of a subject," said the little tailor, turning very red, and hemming and hawing a great deal. "I've thought, I say, of a pint, which may be resorted to with advantage at the present juncture, and in which each of us may be useful to the other. An exchange, Mr. Eglantine: do you take?"

"Do you mean an accommodation-bill?" said Eglantine, whose mind ran a good deal on that species of exchange.

"Pooh, nonsense, sir! The name of OUR firm is, I flatter myself, a little more up in the market than some other people's names."

"Do you mean to insult the name of Archibald Eglantine, sir? I'd have you to know that at three months—"

"Nonsense!" says Mr. Woolsey, mastering his emotion. "There's no use a-quarrelling, Mr. E.: we're not in love with each other, I know that. You wish me hanged, or as good, I know that!"

"Indeed I don't, sir!"

"You do, sir; I tell you, you do! and what's more, I wish the same to you—transported, at any rate! But as two sailors, when a boat's a-sinking, though they hate each other ever so much, will help and bale the boat out; so, sir, let Us act: let us be the two sailors."

"Bail, sir?" said Eglantine, as usual mistaking the drift of the argument. "I'll bail no man! If you're in difficulties, I think you had better go to your senior partner, Mr. Woolsey." And Eglantine's cowardly little soul was filled with a savage satisfaction to think that his enemy was in distress, and actually obliged to come to HIM for succour.

"You're enough to make Job swear, you great fat stupid lazy old barber!" roared Mr. Woolsey, in a fury.

Eglantine jumped up and made for the bell-rope. The gallant little tailor laughed.

"There's no need to call in Betsy," said he. "I'm not a-going to eat you, Eglantine; you're a bigger man than me: if you were just to fall on me, you'd smother me! Just sit still on the sofa and listen to reason."

"Well, sir, pro-ceed," said the barber with a gasp.

"Now, listen! What's the darling wish of your heart? I know it, sir! you've told it to Mr. Tressle, sir, and other gents at the club. The darling wish of your heart, sir, is to have a slap-up coat turned out of the ateliers of Messrs. Linsey, Woolsey and Company. You said you'd give twenty guineas for one of our coats, you know you did! Lord Bolsterton's a fatter man than you, and look what a figure we turn HIM out. Can any firm in England dress Lord Bolsterton but us, so as to make his Lordship look decent? I defy 'em, sir! We could have given Daniel Lambert a figure!"

"If I want a coat, sir," said Mr. Eglantine, "and I don't deny it, there's some people want a HEAD OF HAIR!"

"That's the very point I was coming to," said the tailor, resuming the violent blush which was mentioned as having suffused his countenance at the beginning of the conversation. "Let us have terms of mutual accommodation. Make me a wig, Mr. Eglantine, and though I never yet cut a yard of cloth except for a gentleman, I'll pledge you my word I'll make you a coat."

"WILL you, honour bright?" says Eglantine.

"Honour bright," says the tailor. "Look!" and in an instant he drew from his pocket one of those slips of parchment which gentlemen of his profession carry, and putting Eglantine into the proper position, began to take the preliminary observations. He felt Eglantine's heart thump with happiness as his measure passed over that soft part of the perfumer's person.

Then pulling down the window-blind, and looking that the door was locked, and blushing still more deeply than ever, the tailor seated himself in an arm-chair towards which Mr. Eglantine beckoned him, and, taking off his black wig, exposed his head to the great perruquier's gaze. Mr. Eglantine looked at it, measured it, manipulated it, sat for three minutes with his head in his hand and his elbow on his knee, gazing at the tailor's cranium with all his might, walked round it twice or thrice, and then said, "It's enough, Mr. Woolsey. Consider the job as done. And now, sir," said he, with a greatly relieved air—"and now, Woolsey, let us 'ave a glass of curacoa to celebrate this hauspicious meeting."

The tailor, however, stiffly replied that he never drank in a morning, and left the room without offering to shake Mr. Eglantine by the hand: for he despised that gentleman very heartily, and himself, too, for coming to any compromise with him, and for so far demeaning himself as to make a coat for a barber.

Looking from his chambers on the other side of the street, that inevitable Mr. Walker saw the tailor issuing from the perfumer's shop, and was at no loss to guess that something extraordinary must be in progress when two such bitter enemies met together.

III

WHAT CAME OF MR. WALKER'S DISCOVERY OF THE "BOOTJACK"

It is very easy to state how the Captain came to take up that proud position at the "Bootjack" which we have seen him occupy on the evening when the sound of the fatal "Brava!" so astonished Mr. Eglantine.

The mere entry into the establishment was, of course, not difficult. Any person by simply uttering the words "A pint of beer," was free of the "Bootjack;" and it was some such watchword that Howard Walker employed when he made his first appearance. He requested to be shown into a parlour, where he might repose himself for a while, and was ushered into that very sanctum where the "Kidney Club" met. Then he stated that the beer was the best he had ever tasted, except in Bavaria, and in some parts of Spain, he added; and professing to be extremely "peckish," requested to know if there were any cold meat in the house whereof he could make a dinner.

"I don't usually dine at this hour, landlord," said he, flinging down a half-sovereign for payment of the beer; "but your parlour looks so comfortable, and the Windsor chairs are so snug, that I'm sure I could not dine better at the first club in London."

"ONE of the first clubs in London is held in this very room," said Mr. Crump, very well pleased; "and attended by some of the best gents in town, too. We call it the 'Kidney Club'."

"Why, bless my soul! it is the very club my friend Eglantine has so often talked to me about, and attended by some of the tip-top tradesmen of the metropolis!"

"There's better men here than Mr. Eglantine," replied Mr. Crump, "though he's a good man—I don't say he's not a good man—but there's better. Mr. Clinker, sir; Mr. Woolsey, of the house of Linsey, Woolsey and Co—"

"The great army-clothiers!" cried Walker; "the first house in town!" and so continued, with exceeding urbanity, holding conversation with Mr. Crump, until the honest landlord retired delighted, and told Mrs. Crump in the bar that there was a tip-top swell in the "Kidney" parlour, who was a-going to have his dinner there.

Fortune favoured the brave Captain in every way. It was just Mr. Crump's own dinner-hour; and on Mrs. Crump stepping into the parlour to ask the guest whether he would like a slice of the joint to which the family were about to sit down, fancy that lady's start of astonishment at recognising Mr. Eglantine's facetious friend of the day before. The Captain at once demanded permission to partake of the joint at the family table; the lady could not with any great reason deny this request; the Captain was inducted into the bar; and Miss Crump, who always came down late for dinner, was even more astonished than her mamma, on beholding the occupier of the fourth place at the table. Had she expected to see the fascinating stranger so soon again? I think she had. Her big eyes said as much, as, furtively looking up at Mr. Walker's face, they caught his looks; and then bouncing down again towards her plate, pretended to be very busy in looking at the boiled beef and carrots there displayed. She blushed far redder than those carrots, but her shining ringlets hid her confusion together with her lovely face.

Sweet Morgiana! the billiard-ball eyes had a tremendous effect on the Captain. They fell plump, as it were, into the pocket of his heart; and he gallantly proposed to treat the company to a bottle of champagne, which was accepted without much difficulty.

Mr. Crump, under pretence of going to the cellar (where he said he had some cases of the finest champagne in Europe), called Dick, the boy, to him, and despatched him with all speed to a wine merchant's, where a couple of bottles of the liquor were procured.

"Bring up two bottles, Mr. C.," Captain Walker gallantly said when Crump made his move, as it were, to the cellar and it may be imagined after the two bottles were drunk (of which Mrs. Crump took at least nine glasses to her share), how happy, merry, and confidential the whole party had become. Crump told his story of the "Bootjack," and whose boot it had drawn; the former Miss Delancy expatiated on her past theatrical life, and the pictures hanging round the room. Miss was equally communicative; and, in short, the Captain had all the secrets of the little family in his possession ere sunset. He knew that Miss cared little for either of her suitors, about whom mamma and papa had a little quarrel. He heard Mrs. Crump talk of Morgiana's property, and fell more in love with her than ever. Then came tea, the luscious crumpet, the quiet game at cribbage, and the song—the song which poor Eglantine heard, and which caused Woolsey's rage and his despair.

At the close of the evening the tailor was in a greater rage, and the perfumer in greater despair than ever. He had made his little present of eau-de-Cologne. "Oh fie!" says the Captain, with a horse-laugh, "it SMELLS OF THE SHOP!" He taunted the tailor about his wig, and the honest fellow had only an oath to give by way of repartee. He told his stories about his club and his lordly friends. What chance had either against the all-accomplished Howard Walker?

Old Crump, with a good innate sense of right and wrong, hated the man; Mrs. Crump did not feel quite at her ease regarding him; but Morgiana thought him the most delightful person the world ever produced.

Eglantine's usual morning costume was a blue satin neck-cloth embroidered with butterflies and ornamented with a brandy-ball brooch, a light shawl waistcoat, and a rhubarb-coloured coat of the sort which, I believe, are called Taglionis, and which have no waist-buttons, and made a pretence, as it were, to have no waists, but are in reality adopted by the fat in order to give them a waist. Nothing easier for an obese man than to have a waist; he has but to pinch his middle part a little, and the very fat on either side pushed violently forward MAKES a waist, as it were, and our worthy perfumer's figure was that of a bolster cut almost in two with a string.

Walker presently saw him at his shop-door grinning in this costume, twiddling his ringlets with his dumpy greasy fingers, glittering with oil and rings, and looking so exceedingly contented and happy that the estate-agent felt assured some very satisfactory conspiracy had been planned between the tailor and him. How was Mr. Walker to learn what the scheme was? Alas! the poor fellow's vanity and delight were such, that he could not keep silent as to the cause of his satisfaction; and rather than not mention it at all, in the fulness of his heart he would have told his secret to Mr. Mossrose himself.

"When I get my coat," thought the Bond Street Alnaschar, "I'll hire of Snaffle that easy-going cream-coloured 'oss that he bought from Astley's, and I'll canter through the Park, and WON'T I pass through Little Bunker's Buildings, that's all? I'll wear my grey trousers with the velvet stripe down the side, and get my spurs lacquered up, and a French polish to my boot; and if I don't DO for the Captain, and the tailor too, my name's not Archibald. And I know what I'll do: I'll hire the small clarence, and invite the Crumps to dinner at the 'Gar and Starter'" (this was his facetious way of calling the "Star and Garter"), "and I'll ride by them all the way to Richmond. It's rather a long ride, but with Snaffle's soft saddle I can do it pretty easy, I dare say." And so the honest fellow built castles upon castles in the air; and the last most beautiful vision of all was Miss Crump "in white satting, with a horange flower in her 'air," putting him in possession of "her lovely 'and before the haltar of St. George's, 'Anover Square." As for Woolsey, Eglantine determined that he should have the best wig his art could produce; for he had not the least fear of his rival.

These points then being arranged to the poor fellow's satisfaction, what does he do but send out for half a quire of pink note-paper, and in a filagree envelope despatch a note of invitation to the ladies at the "Bootjack":—

BOWER OF BLOOM, BOND STREET:
Thursday.

"MR. ARCHIBALD EGLANTINE presents his compliments to Mrs. and Miss Crump, and requests the HONOUR AND PLEASURE of their company at the 'Star and Garter' at Richmond to an early dinner on Sunday next.

"IF AGREEABLE, Mr. Eglantine's carriage will be at your door at three o'clock, and I propose to accompany them on horseback, if agreeable likewise."

This note was sealed with yellow wax, and sent to its destination; and of course Mr. Eglantine went himself for the answer in the evening: and of course he told the ladies to look out for a certain new coat he was going to sport on Sunday; and of course Mr. Walker happens to call the next day with spare tickets for Mrs. Crump and her daughter, when the whole secret was laid bare to him—how the ladies were going to Richmond on Sunday in Mr. Snaffle's clarence, and how Mr. Eglantine was to ride by their side.

Mr. Walker did not keep horses of his own; his magnificent friends at the "Regent" had plenty in their stables, and some of these were at livery at the establishment of the Captain's old "college" companion, Mr. Snaffle. It was easy, therefore, for the Captain to renew his acquaintance with that individual. So, hanging on the arm of my Lord Vauxhall, Captain Walker next day made his appearance at Snaffle's livery-stables, and looked at the various horses there for sale or at bait, and soon managed, by putting some facetious questions to Mr. Snaffle regarding the "Kidney Club," etc. to place himself on a friendly footing with that gentleman, and to learn from him what horse Mr. Eglantine was to ride on Sunday.

The monster Walker had fully determined in his mind that Eglantine should FALL off that horse in the course of his Sunday's ride.

"That sing'lar hanimal," said Mr. Snaffle, pointing to the old horse, "is the celebrated Hemperor that was the wonder of Hastley's some years back, and was parted with by Mr. Ducrow honly because his feelin's wouldn't allow him to keep him no longer after the death of the first Mrs. D., who invariably rode him. I bought him, thinking that p'raps ladies and Cockney bucks might like to ride him (for his haction is wonderful, and he canters like a harm-chair); but he's not safe on any day except Sundays."

"And why's that?" asked Captain Walker. "Why is he safer on Sundays than other days?"

"BECAUSE THERE'S NO MUSIC in the streets on Sundays. The first gent that rode him found himself dancing a quadrille in Hupper Brook Street to an 'urdy-gurdy that was playing 'Cherry Ripe,' such is the natur of the hanimal. And if you reklect the play of the 'Battle of Hoysterlitz,' in which Mrs. D. hacted 'the female hussar,' you may remember how she and the horse died in the third act to the toon of 'God preserve the Emperor,' from which this horse took his name. Only play that toon to him, and he rears hisself up, beats the hair in time with his forelegs, and then sinks gently to the ground as though he were carried off by a cannon-ball. He served a lady hopposite Hapsley 'Ouse so one day, and since then I've never let him out to a friend except on Sunday, when, in course, there's no danger. Heglantine Is a friend of mine, and of course I wouldn't put the poor fellow on a hanimal I couldn't trust."

After a little more conversation, my lord and his friend quitted Mr. Snaffle's, and as they walked away towards the "Regent," his Lordship might be heard shrieking with laughter, crying, "Capital, by jingo! exthlent! Dwive down in the dwag! Take Lungly. Worth a thousand pound, by Jove!" and similar exclamations, indicative of exceeding delight.

On Saturday morning, at ten o'clock to a moment, Mr. Woolsey called at Mr. Eglantine's with a yellow handkerchief under his arm. It contained the best and handsomest body-coat that ever gentleman put on. It fitted Eglantine to a nicety—it did not pinch him in the least, and yet it was of so exquisite a cut that the perfumer found, as he gazed delighted in the glass, that he looked like a manly portly high-bred gentleman—a lieutenant-colonel in the army, at the very least.

WILLIAM MAKEPEACE THACKERAY

"You're a full man, Eglantine," said the tailor, delighted, too, with his own work; "but that can't be helped. You look more like Hercules than Falstaff now, sir, and if a coat can make a gentleman, a gentleman you are. Let me recommend you to sink the blue cravat, and take the stripes off your trousers. Dress quiet, sir; draw it mild. Plain waistcoat, dark trousers, black neckcloth, black hat, and if there's a better-dressed man in Europe to-morrow, I'm a Dutchman."

"Thank you, Woolsey—thank you, my dear sir," said the charmed perfumer. "And now I'll just trouble you to try on this here."

The wig had been made with equal skill; it was not in the florid style which Mr. Eglantine loved in his own person, but, as the perfumer said, a simple straightforward head of hair. "It seems as if it had grown there all your life, Mr. Woolsey; nobody would tell that it was not your nat'ral colour" (Mr. Woolsey blushed)—"it makes you look ten year younger; and as for that scarecrow yonder, you'll never, I think, want to wear that again."

Woolsey looked in the glass, and was delighted too. The two rivals shook hands and straightway became friends, and in the overflowing of his heart the perfumer mentioned to the tailor the party which he had arranged for the next day, and offered him a seat in the carriage and at the dinner at the "Star and Garter." "Would you like to ride?" said Eglantine, with rather a consequential air. "Snaffle will mount you, and we can go one on each side of the ladies, if you like."

But Woolsey humbly said he was not a riding man, and gladly consented to take a place in the clarence carriage, provided he was allowed to bear half the expenses of the entertainment. This proposal was agreed to by Mr. Eglantine, and the two gentlemen parted to meet once more at the "Kidneys" that night, when everybody was edified by the friendly tone adopted between them.

Mr. Snaffle, at the club meeting, made the very same proposal to Mr. Woolsey that the perfumer had made; and stated that as Eglantine was going to ride Hemperor, Woolsey, at least, ought to mount too. But he was met by the same modest refusal on the tailor's part, who stated that he had never mounted a horse yet, and preferred greatly the use of a coach.

Eglantine's character as a "swell" rose greatly with the club that evening.

Two o'clock on Sunday came: the two beaux arrived punctually at the door to receive the two smiling ladies.

"Bless us, Mr. Eglantine!" said Miss Crump, quite struck by him, "I never saw you look so handsome in your life." He could have flung his arms around her neck at the compliment. "And law, Ma! what has happened to Mr. Woolsey? doesn't he look ten years younger than yesterday?" Mamma assented, and Woolsey bowed gallantly, and the two gentlemen exchanged a nod of hearty friendship.

The day was delightful. Eglantine pranced along magnificently on his cantering armchair, with his hat on one ear, his left hand on his side, and his head flung over his shoulder, and throwing under-glances at Morgiana whenever the "Emperor" was in advance of the clarence. The "Emperor" pricked up his ears a little uneasily passing the Ebenezer chapel in Richmond, where the congregation were singing a hymn, but beyond this no accident occurred; nor was Mr. Eglantine in the least stiff or fatigued by the time the party reached Richmond, where he arrived time enough to give his steed into the charge of an ostler, and to present his elbow to the ladies as they alighted from the clarence carriage.

What this jovial party ate for dinner at the "Star and Garter" need not here be set down. If they did not drink champagne I am very much mistaken. They were as merry as any four people in Christendom; and between the bewildering attentions of the perfumer, and the manly courtesy of the tailor, Morgiana very likely forgot the gallant Captain, or, at least, was very happy in his absence.

At eight o'clock they began to drive homewards. "Won't you come into the carriage?" said Morgiana to Eglantine, with one of her tenderest looks; "Dick can ride the horse." But Archibald was too great a lover of equestrian exercise. "I'm afraid to trust anybody on this horse," said he with a knowing look; and so he pranced away by the side of the little carriage. The moon was brilliant, and, with the aid of the gas-lamps, illuminated the whole face of the country in a way inexpressibly lovely.

Presently, in the distance, the sweet and plaintive notes of a bugle were heard, and the performer, with great delicacy, executed a religious air. "Music, too! heavenly!" said Morgiana, throwing up her eyes to the stars. The music came nearer and nearer, and the delight of the company was only more intense. The fly was going at about four miles an hour, and the "Emperor" began cantering to time at the same rapid pace.

"This must be some gallantry of yours, Mr. Woolsey," said the romantic Morgiana, turning upon that gentleman. "Mr. Eglantine treated us to the dinner, and you have provided us with the music."

Now Woolsey had been a little, a very little, dissatisfied during the course of the evening's entertainment, by fancying that Eglantine, a much more voluble person than himself, had obtained rather an undue share of the ladies' favour; and as he himself paid half of the expenses, he felt very much vexed to think that the perfumer should take all the credit of the business to himself. So when Miss Crump asked if he had provided the music, he foolishly made an evasive reply to her query, and rather wished her to imagine that he HAD performed that piece of gallantry. "If it pleases YOU, Miss Morgiana," said this artful Schneider, "what more need any man ask? wouldn't I have all Drury Lane orchestra to please you?"

The bugle had by this time arrived quite close to the clarence carriage, and if Morgiana had looked round she might have seen whence the music came. Behind her came slowly a drag, or private stage-coach, with four horses. Two grooms with cockades and folded arms were behind; and driving on the box, a little gentleman, with a blue bird's-eye neckcloth, and a white coat. A bugleman was by his side, who performed the melodies which so delighted Miss Crump. He played very gently and sweetly, and "God save the King" trembled so softly out of the brazen orifice of his bugle, that the Crumps, the tailor, and Eglantine himself, who was riding close by the carriage, were quite charmed and subdued.

"Thank you, DEAR Mr. Woolsey," said the grateful Morgiana; which made Eglantine stare, and Woolsey was just saying, "Really, upon my word, I've nothing to do with it," when the man on the drag-box said to the bugleman, "Now!"

The bugleman began the tune of—

> "Heaven preserve our Emperor Fra-an-cis,
> Rum tum-ti-tum-ti-titty-ti."

At the sound, the "Emperor" reared himself (with a roar from Mr. Eglantine)—reared and beat the air with his fore-paws. Eglantine flung his arms round the beast's neck; still he kept beating time with his fore-paws. Mrs. Crump screamed: Mr. Woolsey, Dick, the clarence coachman, Lord Vauxhall (for it was he), and his Lordship's two grooms, burst into a shout of laughter; Morgiana cries "Mercy! mercy!" Eglantine yells "Stop!"—"Wo!"—"Oh!" and a thousand exclamations of hideous terror; until, at last, down drops the "Emperor" stone dead in the middle of the road, as if carried off by a cannon-ball.

Fancy the situation, ye callous souls who laugh at the misery of humanity, fancy the situation of poor Eglantine under the "Emperor"! He had fallen very easy, the animal lay perfectly quiet, and the perfumer was to all intents and purposes as dead as the animal. He had not fainted, but he was immovable with terror; he lay in a puddle, and thought it was his own blood gushing from him; and he would have lain there until Monday morning, if my Lord's grooms, descending, had not dragged him by the coat-collar from under the beast, who still lay quiet.

"Play 'Charming Judy Callaghan,' will ye?" says Mr. Snaffle's man, the fly-driver; on which the bugler performed that lively air, and up started the horse, and the grooms, who were rubbing Mr. Eglantine down against a lamp-post, invited him to remount.

But his heart was too broken for that. The ladies gladly made room for him in the clarence. Dick mounted "Emperor" and rode homewards. The drag, too, drove away, playing "Oh dear, what can the matter be?" and with a scowl of furious hate, Mr. Eglantine sat and regarded his rival. His pantaloons were split, and his coat torn up the back.

"Are you hurt much, dear Mr. Archibald?" said Morgiana, with unaffected compassion.

"N-not much," said the poor fellow, ready to burst into tears.

"Oh, Mr. Woolsey," added the good-natured girl, "how could you play such a trick?"

"Upon my word," Woolsey began, intending to plead innocence; but the ludicrousness of the situation was once more too much for him, and he burst out into a roar of laughter.

"You! you cowardly beast!" howled out Eglantine, now driven to fury—"You laugh at me, you miserable cretur! Take THAT, sir!" and he fell upon him with all his might, and well-nigh throttled the tailor, and pummelling his eyes, his nose, his ears, with inconceivable rapidity, wrenched, finally, his wig off his head, and flung it into the road.

Morgiana saw that Woolsey had red hair.

IV

IN WHICH THE HEROINE HAS A NUMBER
MORE LOVERS, AND CUTS A VERY DASHING
FIGURE IN THE WORLD

Two years have elapsed since the festival at Richmond, which, begun so peaceably, ended in such general uproar. Morgiana never could be brought to pardon Woolsey's red hair, nor to help laughing at Eglantine's disasters, nor could the two gentlemen be reconciled to one another. Woolsey, indeed, sent a challenge to the perfumer to meet him with pistols, which the latter declined, saying, justly, that tradesmen had no business with such weapons; on this the tailor proposed to meet him with coats off, and have it out like men, in the presence of their friends of the "Kidney Club". The perfumer said he would be party to no such vulgar transaction; on which, Woolsey, exasperated, made an oath that he would tweak the perfumer's nose so surely as he ever entered the club-room; and thus ONE member of the "Kidneys" was compelled to vacate his armchair.

Woolsey himself attended every meeting regularly, but he did not evince that gaiety and good-humour which render men's company agreeable in clubs. On arriving, he would order the boy to "tell him when that scoundrel Eglantine came;" and, hanging up his hat on a peg, would scowl round the room, and tuck up his sleeves very high, and stretch, and shake his fingers and wrists, as if getting them ready for that pull of the nose which he intended to bestow upon his rival. So prepared, he would sit down and smoke his pipe quite silently, glaring at all, and jumping up, and hitching up his coat-sleeves, when anyone entered the room.

The "Kidneys" did not like this behaviour. Clinker ceased to come. Bustard, the poulterer, ceased to come. As for Snaffle, he also disappeared, for Woolsey wished to make him answerable for the misbehaviour of Eglantine, and proposed to him the duel which the latter had declined. So Snaffle went. Presently they all went, except the tailor and Tressle, who lived down the street, and these two would sit and pug their tobacco, one on each side of Crump, the landlord, as silent as Indian chiefs in a wigwam. There grew to be more and more room for poor old Crump in his chair and in his clothes; the "Kidneys" were gone, and why should he remain? One Saturday he did not come down to preside at the club (as he still fondly called it), and the Saturday following Tressle had made a coffin for him; and Woolsey, with the undertaker by his side, followed to the grave the father of the "Kidneys."

Mrs. Crump was now alone in the world. "How alone?" says some innocent and respected reader. Ah! my dear sir, do you know so little of human nature as not to be aware that, one week after the Richmond affair, Morgiana married Captain Walker? That did she privately, of course; and, after the ceremony, came tripping back to her parents, as young people do in plays, and said, "Forgive me, dear Pa and Ma, I'm married, and here is my husband the Captain!" Papa and mamma did forgive her, as why shouldn't they? and papa paid over her fortune to her, which she carried home delighted to the Captain. This happened several months before the demise of old Crump; and Mrs. Captain Walker was on the Continent with her Howard when that melancholy event took place; hence Mrs. Crump's loneliness and unprotected condition. Morgiana had not latterly seen much of the old people; how could she, moving in her exalted sphere, receive at her genteel new residence in the Edgware Road the old publican and his wife?

Being, then, alone in the world, Mrs. Crump could not abear, she said, to live in the house where she had been so respected and happy: so she sold the goodwill of the "Bootjack," and, with the money arising from this sale and her own private fortune, being able to muster some sixty pounds per annum, retired to the neighbourhood of her dear old "Sadler's Wells," where she boarded with one of Mrs. Serle's forty pupils. Her heart was broken, she said; but, nevertheless, about nine months after Mr. Crump's death, the wallflowers, nasturtiums, polyanthuses, and convolvuluses began to blossom under her bonnet as usual; in a year she was dressed quite as fine as ever, and now never missed "The Wells," or some other place of entertainment, one single night, but was as regular as the box-keeper. Nay, she was a buxom widow still, and an old flame of hers, Fisk, so celebrated as pantaloon in Grimaldi's time, but now doing the "heavy fathers" at "The Wells," proposed to her to exchange her name for his.

But this proposal the worthy widow declined altogether. To say truth, she was exceedingly proud of her daughter, Mrs. Captain Walker. They did not see each other much at first; but every now and then Mrs. Crump would pay a visit to the folks in Connaught Square; and on the days when "the Captain's" lady called in the City Road, there was not a single official at "The Wells," from the first tragedian down to the call-boy, who was not made aware of the fact.

It has been said that Morgiana carried home her fortune in her own reticule, and, smiling, placed the money in her husband's lap; and hence the reader may imagine, who knows Mr. Walker to be an extremely selfish fellow, that a great scene of anger must have taken place, and many coarse oaths and epithets of abuse must have come from him, when he found that five hundred pounds was all that his wife had, although he had expected five thousand with her. But, to say the truth, Walker was at this time almost in love with his handsome rosy good-humoured simple wife. They had made a fortnight's tour, during which they had been exceedingly happy; and there was something so frank and touching in the way in which the kind creature flung her all into his lap, saluting him with a hearty embrace at the same time, and wishing that it were a thousand billion billion times more, so that her darling Howard might enjoy it, that the man would have been a ruffian indeed could he have found it in his heart to be angry with her; and so he kissed her in return, and patted her on the shining ringlets, and then counted over the notes with rather a disconsolate air, and ended by locking them up in his portfolio. In fact, SHE had never deceived him; Eglantine had, and he in return had out-tricked Eglantine and so warm were his affections for Morgiana at this time that, upon my word and honour, I don't think he repented of his bargain. Besides, five hundred pounds in crisp bank-notes was a sum of money such as the Captain was not in the habit of handling every day; a dashing sanguine fellow, he fancied there was no end to it, and already thought of a dozen ways by which it should increase and multiply into a plum. Woe is me! Has not many a simple soul examined five new hundred-pound notes in this way, and calculated their powers of duration and multiplication?

This subject, however, is too painful to be dwelt on. Let us hear what Walker did with his money. Why, he furnished the house in the Edgware Road before mentioned, he ordered a handsome service of plate, he sported a phaeton and two ponies, he kept a couple of smart maids and a groom foot-boy—in fact, he mounted just such a neat unpretending gentleman-like establishment as becomes a respectable young couple on their outset in life. "I've sown my wild oats," he would say to his acquaintances; "a few years since, perhaps, I would have longed to cut a dash, but now prudence is the word; and I've settled every farthing of Mrs. Walker's fifteen thousand on herself." And the best proof that the world had confidence in him is the fact, that for the articles of plate, equipage, and furniture, which have been mentioned as being in his possession, he did not pay one single shilling; and so prudent was he, that but for turnpikes, postage-stamps, and king's taxes, he hardly had occasion to change a five-pound note of his wife's fortune.

To tell the truth, Mr. Walker had determined to make his fortune. And what is easier in London? Is not the share-market open to all? Do not Spanish and Columbian bonds rise and fall? For what are companies invented, but to place thousands in the pockets of shareholders and directors? Into these commercial pursuits the gallant Captain now plunged with great energy, and made some brilliant hits at first starting, and bought and sold so opportunely, that his name began to rise in the City as a capitalist, and might be seen in the printed list of directors of many excellent and philanthropic schemes, of which there is never any lack in London. Business to the amount of thousands was done at his agency; shares of vast value were bought and sold under his management. How poor Mr. Eglantine used to hate him and envy him, as from the door of his emporium (the firm was Eglantine and Mossrose now) he saw the Captain daily arrive in his pony-phaeton, and heard of the start he had taken in life.

The only regret Mrs. Walker had was that she did not enjoy enough of her husband's society. His business called him away all day; his business, too, obliged him to leave her of evenings very frequently alone; whilst he (always in pursuit of business) was dining with his great friends at the club, and drinking claret and champagne to the same end.

She was a perfectly good-natured and simple soul, never made him a single reproach; but when he could pass an evening at home with her she was delighted, and when he could drive with her in the Park she was happy for a week after. On these occasions, and in the fulness of her heart, she would drive to her mother and tell her story. "Howard drove with me in the Park yesterday, Mamma;" and "Howard has promised to take me to the Opera," and so forth. And that evening the manager, Mr. Gawler, the first tragedian, Mrs. Serle and her forty pupils, all the box-keepers, bonnet-women—nay, the ginger-beer girls themselves at "The Wells," knew that Captain and Mrs. Walker were at Kensington Gardens, or were to have the Marchioness of Billingsgate's box at the Opera. One night—O joy of joys!—Mrs. Captain Walker appeared in a private box at "The Wells." That's she with the black ringlets and Cashmere shawl, smelling-bottle, and black-velvet gown, and bird of paradise in her hat. Goodness gracious! how they all acted at her, Gawler and all, and how happy Mrs. Crump was! She kissed her daughter between all the acts, she nodded to all her friends on the stage, in the slips, or in the real water; she introduced her daughter, Mrs. Captain Walker, to the box-opener; and Melvil Delamere (the first comic), Canterfield (the tyrant), and Jonesini (the celebrated Fontarabian Statuesque), were all on the steps, and shouted for Mrs. Captain Walker's carriage, and waved their hats, and bowed as the little pony-phaeton drove away. Walker, in his moustaches, had come in at the end of the play, and was not a little gratified by the compliments paid to himself and lady.

Among the other articles of luxury with which the Captain furnished his house we must not omit to mention an extremely grand piano, which occupied four-fifths of Mrs. Walker's little back drawing-room, and at which she was in the habit of practising continually. All day and all night during Walker's absences (and these occurred all night and all day), you might hear—the whole street might hear—the voice of the lady at No. 23, gurgling, and shaking, and quavering, as ladies do when they practise. The street did not approve of the continuance of the noise; but neighbours are difficult to please, and what would Morgiana have had to do if she had ceased to sing? It would be hard to lock a blackbird in a cage and prevent him from singing too. And so Walker's blackbird, in the snug little cage in the Edgware Road, sang and was not unhappy.

After the pair had been married for about a year, the omnibus that passes both by Mrs. Crump's house near "The Wells," and by Mrs. Walker's street off the Edgware Road, brought up the former-named lady almost every day to her daughter. She came when the Captain had gone to his business; she stayed to a two-o'clock dinner with Morgiana; she drove with her in the pony-carriage round the Park; but she never stopped later than six. Had she not to go to the play at seven? And, besides, the Captain might come home with some of his great friends, and he always swore and grumbled much if he found his mother-in-law on the premises. As for Morgiana, she was one of those women who encourage despotism in husbands. What the husband says must be right, because he says it; what he orders must be obeyed tremblingly. Mrs. Walker gave up her entire reason to her lord. Why was it? Before marriage she had been an independent little person; she had far more brains than her Howard. I think it must have been his moustaches that frightened her, and caused in her this humility.

Selfish husbands have this advantage in maintaining with easy-minded wives a rigid and inflexible behaviour, viz. that if they Do by any chance grant a little favour, the ladies receive it with such transports of gratitude as they would never think of showing to a lord and master who was accustomed to give them everything they asked for; and hence, when Captain Walker signified his assent to his wife's prayer that she should take a singing-master, she thought his generosity almost divine, and fell upon her mamma's neck, when that lady came the next day, and said what a dear adorable angel her Howard was, and what ought she not to do for a man who had taken her from her humble situation, and raised her to be what she was! What she was, poor soul! She was the wife of a swindling parvenu gentleman. She received visits from six ladies of her husband's acquaintances—two attorneys' ladies, his bill-broker's lady, and one or two more, of whose characters we had best, if you please, say nothing; and she thought it an honour to be so distinguished: as if Walker had been a Lord Exeter to marry a humble maiden, or a noble prince to fall in love with a humble Cinderella, or a majestic Jove to come down from heaven and woo a Semele. Look through the world, respectable reader, and among your honourable acquaintances, and say if this sort of faith in women is not very frequent? They WILL believe in their husbands, whatever the latter do. Let John be dull, ugly, vulgar, and a humbug, his Mary Ann never finds it out; let him tell his stories ever so many times, there is she always ready with her kind smile; let him be stingy, she says he is prudent; let him quarrel with his best friend, she says he is always in the right; let him be prodigal, she says he is generous, and that his health requires enjoyment; let him be idle, he must have relaxation; and she will pinch herself and her household that he may have a guinea for his club. Yes; and every morning, as she wakes and looks at the face, snoring on the pillow by her side—every morning, I say, she blesses that dull ugly countenance, and the dull ugly soul reposing there, and thinks both are something divine. I want to know how it is that women do not find out their husbands to be humbugs? Nature has so provided it, and thanks to her. When last year they were acting the "Midsummer Night's Dream," and all the boxes began to roar with great coarse heehaws at Titania hugging Bottom's long long ears—to me, considering these things, it seemed that there were a hundred other male brutes squatted round about, and treated just as reasonably as Bottom was. Their Titanias lulled them to sleep in their laps, summoned a hundred smiling delicate household fairies to tickle their gross intellects and minister to their vulgar pleasures; and (as the above remarks are only supposed to apply to honest women loving their own lawful spouses) a mercy it is that no wicked Puck is in the way to open their eyes, and point out their folly. Cui bono? let them live on in their deceit: I know two lovely ladies who will read this, and will say it is just very likely, and not see in the least, that it has been written regarding THEM.

Another point of sentiment, and one curious to speculate on. Have you not remarked the immense works of art that women get through? The worsted-work sofas, the counterpanes patched or knitted (but these are among the old-fashioned in the country), the bushels of pincushions, the albums they laboriously fill, the tremendous pieces of music they practise, the thousand other fiddle-faddles which occupy the attention of the dear souls—nay, have we not seen them seated of evenings in a squad or company, Louisa employed at the worsted-work before mentioned, Eliza at the pincushions, Amelia at card-racks or filagree matches, and, in the midst, Theodosia with one of the candles, reading out a novel aloud? Ah! my dear sir, mortal creatures must be very hard put to it for amusement, be sure of that, when they are forced to gather together in a company and hear novels read aloud! They only do it because they can't help it, depend upon it: it is a sad life, a poor pastime. Mr. Dickens, in his American book, tells of the prisoners at the silent prison, how they had ornamented their rooms, some of them with a frightful prettiness and elaboration. Women's fancy-work is of this sort often—only prison work, done because there was no other exercising-ground for their poor little thoughts and fingers; and hence these wonderful pincushions are executed, these counterpanes woven, these sonatas learned. By everything sentimental, when I see two kind innocent fresh-cheeked young women go to a piano, and sit down opposite to it upon two chairs piled with more or less music-books (according to their convenience), and, so seated, go through a set of double-barrelled variations upon this or that tune by Herz or Kalkbrenner—I say, far from receiving any satisfaction at the noise made by the performance, my too susceptible heart is given up entirely to bleeding for the performers. What hours, and weeks, nay, preparatory years of study, has that infernal jig cost them! What sums has papa paid, what scoldings has mamma administered ("Lady Bullblock does not play herself," Sir Thomas says, "but she has naturally the finest ear for music ever known!"); what evidences of slavery, in a word, are there! It is the condition of the young lady's existence. She breakfasts at eight, she does "Mangnall's Questions" with the governess till ten, she practises till one, she walks in the square with bars round her till two, then she practises again, then she sews or hems, or reads French, or Hume's "History," then she comes down to play to papa, because he likes music whilst he is asleep after dinner, and then it is bed-time, and the morrow is another day with what are called the same "duties" to be gone through. A friend of mine went to call at a nobleman's house the other day, and one of the young ladies of the house came into the room with a tray on her head; this tray was to give Lady Maria a graceful carriage. Mon Dieu! and who knows but at that moment Lady Bell was at work with a pair of her dumb namesakes, and Lady Sophy lying flat on a stretching-board? I could write whole articles on this theme but peace! we are keeping Mrs. Walker waiting all the while.

Well, then, if the above disquisitions have anything to do with the story, as no doubt they have, I wish it to be understood that, during her husband's absence, and her own solitary confinement, Mrs. Howard Walker bestowed a prodigious quantity of her time and energy on the cultivation of her musical talent; and having, as before stated, a very fine loud voice, speedily attained no ordinary skill in the use of it. She first had for teacher little Podmore, the fat chorus-master at "The Wells," and who had taught her mother the "Tink-a-tink" song which has been such a favourite since it first appeared. He grounded her well, and bade her eschew the singing of all those "Eagle Tavern" ballads in which her heart formerly delighted; and when he had brought her to a certain point of skill, the honest little chorus-master said she should have a still better instructor, and wrote a note to Captain Walker (enclosing his own little account), speaking in terms of the most flattering encomium of his lady's progress, and recommending that she should take lessons of the celebrated Baroski. Captain Walker dismissed Podmore then, and engaged Signor Baroski, at a vast expense; as he did not fail to tell his wife. In fact, he owed Baroski no less than two hundred and twenty guineas when he was—But we are advancing matters.

Little Baroski is the author of the opera of "Eliogabalo," of the oratorio of "Purgatorio," which made such an immense sensation, of songs and ballet-musics innumerable. He is a German by birth, and shows such an outrageous partiality for pork and sausages, and attends at church so constantly, that I am sure there cannot be any foundation in the story that he is a member of the ancient religion. He is a fat little man, with a hooked nose and jetty whiskers, and coal-black shining eyes, and plenty of rings and jewels on his fingers and about his person, and a very considerable portion of his shirtsleeves turned over his coat to take the air. His great hands (which can sprawl over half a piano, and produce those effects on the instrument for which he is celebrated) are encased in lemon-coloured kids, new, or cleaned daily. Parenthetically, let us ask why so many men, with coarse red wrists and big hands, persist in the white kid glove and wristband system? Baroski's gloves alone must cost him a little fortune; only he says with a leer, when asked the question, "Get along vid you; don't you know dere is a gloveress that lets me have dem very sheap?" He rides in the Park; has splendid lodgings in Dover Street; and is a member of the "Regent Club," where he is a great source of amusement to the members, to whom he tells astonishing stories of his successes with the ladies, and for whom he has always play and opera tickets in store. His eye glistens and his little heart beats when a lord speaks to him; and he has been known to spend large sums of money in giving treats to young sprigs of fashion at Richmond and elsewhere. "In my bolyticks," he says, "I am consarevatiff to de bag-bone." In fine, he is a puppy, and withal a man of considerable genius in his profession.

This gentleman, then, undertook to complete the musical education of Mrs. Walker. He expressed himself at once "enshanted vid her gababilities," found that the extent of her voice was "brodigious," and guaranteed that she should become a first-rate singer. The pupil was apt, the master was exceedingly skilful; and, accordingly, Mrs. Walker's progress was very remarkable: although, for her part, honest Mrs. Crump, who used to attend her daughter's lessons, would grumble not a little at the new system, and the endless exercises which she, Morgiana, was made to go through. It was very different in HER time, she said. Incledon knew no music, and who could sing so well now? Give her a good English ballad: it was a thousand times sweeter than your "Figaros" and "Semiramides."

In spite of these objections, however, and with amazing perseverance and cheerfulness, Mrs. Walker pursued the method of study pointed out to her by her master. As soon as her husband went to the City in the morning her operations began; if he remained away at dinner, her labours still continued: nor is it necessary for me to particularise her course of study, nor, indeed, possible; for, between ourselves, none of the male Fitz-Boodles ever could sing a note, and the jargon of scales and solfeggios is quite unknown to me. But as no man can have seen persons addicted to music without remarking the prodigious energies they display in the pursuit, as there is no father of daughters, however ignorant, but is aware of the piano-rattling and voice-exercising which go on in his house from morning till night, so let all fancy, without further inquiry, how the heroine of our story was at this stage of her existence occupied.

Walker was delighted with her progress, and did everything but pay Baroski, her instructor. We know why he didn't pay. It was his nature not to pay bills, except on extreme compulsion; but why did not Baroski employ that extreme compulsion? Because, if he had received his money, he would have lost his pupil, and because he loved his pupil more than money. Rather than lose her, he would have given her a guinea as well as her cachet. He would sometimes disappoint a great personage, but he never missed his attendance on HER; and the truth must out, that he was in love with her, as Woolsey and Eglantine had been before.

"By the immortel Chofe!" he would say, "dat letell ding sents me mad vid her big ice! But only vait avile: in six veeks I can bring any voman in England on her knees to me and you shall see vat I vill do vid my Morgiana." He attended her for six weeks punctually, and yet Morgiana was never brought down on her knees; he exhausted his best stock of "gomblimends," and she never seemed disposed to receive them with anything but laughter. And, as a matter of course, he only grew more infatuated with the lovely creature who was so provokingly good-humoured and so laughingly cruel.

Benjamin Baroski was one of the chief ornaments of the musical profession in London; he charged a guinea for a lesson of three-quarters of an hour abroad, and he had, furthermore, a school at his own residence, where pupils assembled in considerable numbers, and of that curious mixed kind which those may see who frequent these places of instruction. There were very innocent young ladies with their mammas, who would hurry them off trembling to the farther corner of the room when certain doubtful professional characters made their appearance. There was Miss Grigg, who sang at the "Foundling," and Mr. Johnson, who sang at the "Eagle Tavern," and Madame Fioravanti (a very doubtful character), who sang nowhere, but was always coming out at the Italian Opera. There was Lumley Limpiter (Lord Tweedledale's son), one of the most accomplished tenors in town, and who, we have heard, sings with the professionals at a hundred concerts; and with him, too, was Captain Guzzard, of the Guards, with his tremendous bass voice, which all the world declared to be as fine as Porto's, and who shared the applause of Baroski's school with Mr. Bulger, the dentist of Sackville Street, who neglected his ivory and gold plates for his voice, as every unfortunate individual will do who is bitten by the music mania. Then among the ladies there were a half-score of dubious pale governesses and professionals with turned frocks and lank damp bandeaux of hair under shabby little bonnets; luckless creatures these, who were parting with their poor little store of half-guineas to be enabled to say they were pupils of Signor Baroski, and so get pupils of their own among the British youths, or employment in the choruses of the theatres.

The prima donna of the little company was Amelia Larkins, Baroski's own articled pupil, on whose future reputation the eminent master staked his own, whose profits he was to share, and whom he had farmed, to this end, from her father, a most respectable sheriff's officer's assistant, and now, by his daughter's exertions, a considerable capitalist. Amelia is blonde and blue-eyed, her complexion is as bright as snow, her ringlets of the colour of straw, her figure—but why describe her figure? Has not all the world seen her at the Theatres Royal and in America under the name of Miss Ligonier?

Until Mrs. Walker arrived, Miss Larkins was the undisputed princess of the Baroski company—the Semiramide, the Rosina, the Tamina, the Donna Anna. Baroski vaunted her everywhere as the great rising genius of the day, bade Catalani look to her laurels, and questioned whether Miss Stephens could sing a ballad like his pupil. Mrs. Howard Walker arrived, and created, on the first occasion, no small sensation. She improved, and the little society became speedily divided into Walkerites and Larkinsians; and between these two ladies (as indeed between Guzzard and Bulger before mentioned, between Miss Brunck and Miss Horsman, the two contraltos, and between the chorus-singers, after their kind) a great rivalry arose. Larkins was certainly the better singer; but could her straw-coloured curls and dumpy high-shouldered figure bear any comparison with the jetty ringlets and stately form of Morgiana? Did not Mrs. Walker, too, come to the music-lesson in her carriage, and with a black velvet gown and Cashmere shawl, while poor Larkins meekly stepped from Bell Yard, Temple Bar, in an old print gown and clogs, which she left in the hall? "Larkins sing!" said Mrs. Crump, sarcastically; "I'm sure she ought; her mouth's big enough to sing a duet." Poor Larkins had no one to make epigrams in her behoof; her mother was at home tending the younger ones, her father abroad following the duties of his profession; she had but one protector, as she thought, and that one was Baroski. Mrs. Crump did not fail to tell Lumley Limpiter of her own former triumphs, and to sing him "Tink-a-tink," which we have previously heard, and to state how in former days she had been called the Ravenswing. And Lumley, on this hint, made a poem, in which he compared Morgiana's hair to the plumage of the Raven's wing, and Larkinissa's to that of the canary; by which two names the ladies began soon to be known in the school.

Ere long the flight of the Ravenswing became evidently stronger, whereas that of the canary was seen evidently to droop. When Morgiana sang, all the room would cry "Bravo!" when Amelia performed, scarce a hand was raised for applause of her, except Morgiana's own, and that the Larkinses thought was lifted in odious triumph, rather than in sympathy, for Miss L. was of an envious turn, and little understood the generosity of her rival.

At last, one day, the crowning victory of the Ravenswing came. In the trio of Baroski's own opera of "Eliogabalo," "Rosy lips and rosy wine," Miss Larkins, who was evidently unwell, was taking the part of the English captive, which she had sung in public concerts before royal dukes, and with considerable applause, and, from some reason, performed it so ill, that Baroski, slapping down the music on the piano in a fury, cried, "Mrs. Howard Walker, as Miss Larkins cannot sing to-day, will you favour us by taking the part of Boadicetta?" Mrs. Walker got up smilingly to obey—the triumph was too great to be withstood; and, as she advanced to the piano, Miss Larkins looked wildly at her, and stood silent for a while, and, at last, shrieked out, "BENJAMIN!" in a tone of extreme agony, and dropped fainting down on the ground. Benjamin looked extremely red, it must be confessed, at being thus called by what we shall denominate his Christian name, and Limpiter looked round at Guzzard, and Miss Brunck nudged Miss Horsman, and the lesson concluded rather abruptly that day; for Miss Larkins was carried off to the next room, laid on a couch, and sprinkled with water.

Good-natured Morgiana insisted that her mother should take Miss Larkins to Bell Yard in her carriage, and went herself home on foot; but I don't know that this piece of kindness prevented Larkins from hating her. I should doubt if it did.

Hearing so much of his wife's skill as a singer, the astute Captain Walker determined to take advantage of it for the purpose of increasing his "connection." He had Lumley Limpiter at his house before long, which was, indeed, no great matter, for honest Lum would go anywhere for a good dinner—and an opportunity to show off his voice afterwards, and Lumley was begged to bring any more clerks in the Treasury of his acquaintance; Captain Guzzard was invited, and any officers of the Guards whom he might choose to bring; Bulger received occasional cards:—in a word, and after a short time, Mrs. Howard Walker's musical parties began to be considerably suivies. Her husband had the satisfaction to see his rooms filled by many great personages; and once or twice in return (indeed, whenever she was wanted, or when people could not afford to hire the first singers) she was asked to parties elsewhere, and treated with that killing civility which our English aristocracy knows how to bestow on artists. Clever and wise aristocracy! It is sweet to mark your ways, and study your commerce with inferior men.

I was just going to commence a tirade regarding the aristocracy here, and to rage against that cool assumption of superiority which distinguishes their lordships' commerce with artists of all sorts: that politeness which, if it condescends to receive artists at all, takes care to have them altogether, so that there can be no mistake about their rank—that august patronage of art which rewards it with a silly flourish of knighthood, to be sure, but takes care to exclude it from any contact with its betters in society—I was, I say, just going to commence a tirade against the aristocracy for excluding artists from their company, and to be extremely satirical upon them, for instance, for not receiving my friend Morgiana, when it suddenly came into my head to ask, was Mrs. Walker fit to move in the best society?—to which query it must humbly be replied that she was not. Her education was not such as to make her quite the equal of Baker Street. She was a kind honest and clever creature; but, it must be confessed, not refined. Wherever she went she had, if not the finest, at any rate the most showy gown in the room; her ornaments were the biggest; her hats, toques, berets, marabouts, and other fallals, always the most conspicuous. She drops "h's" here and there. I have seen her eat peas with a knife (and Walker, scowling on the opposite side of the table, striving in vain to catch her eye); and I shall never forget Lady Smigsmag's horror when she asked for porter at dinner at Richmond, and began to drink it out of the pewter pot. It was a fine sight. She lifted up the tankard with one of the finest arms, covered with the biggest bracelets ever seen; and had a bird of paradise on her head, that curled round the pewter disc of the pot as she raised it, like a halo. These peculiarities she had, and has still. She is best away from the genteel world, that is the fact. When she says that "The weather is so 'ot that it is quite debiliating;" when she laughs, when she hits her neighbour at dinner on the side of the waistcoat (as she will if he should say anything that amuses her), she does what is perfectly natural and unaffected on her part, but what is not customarily done among polite persons, who can sneer at her odd manners and her vanity, but don't know the kindness, honesty, and simplicity which distinguish her. This point being admitted, it follows, of course, that the tirade against the aristocracy would, in the present instance, be out of place—so it shall be reserved for some other occasion.

The Ravenswing was a person admirably disposed by nature to be happy. She had a disposition so kindly that any small attention would satisfy it; was pleased when alone; was delighted in a crowd; was charmed with a joke, however old; was always ready to laugh, to sing, to dance, or to be merry; was so tender-hearted that the smallest ballad would make her cry: and hence was supposed, by many persons, to be extremely affected, and by almost all to be a downright coquette. Several competitors for her favour presented themselves besides Baroski. Young dandies used to canter round her phaeton in the park, and might be seen haunting her doors in the mornings. The fashionable artist of the day made a drawing of her, which was engraved and sold in the shops; a copy of it was printed in a song, "Black-eyed Maiden of Araby," the words by Desmond Mulligan, Esquire, the music composed and dedicated to MRS. HOWARD WALKER, by her most faithful and obliged servant, Benjamin Baroski; and at night her Opera-box was full. Her Opera-box? Yes, the heiress of the "Bootjack" actually had an Opera-box, and some of the most fashionable manhood of London attended it.

Now, in fact, was the time of her greatest prosperity; and her husband gathering these fashionable characters about him, extended his "agency" considerably, and began to thank his stars that he had married a woman who was as good as a fortune to him.

In extending his agency, however, Mr. Walker increased his expenses proportionably, and multiplied his debts accordingly. More furniture and more plate, more wines and more dinner-parties, became necessary; the little pony-phaeton was exchanged for a brougham of evenings; and we may fancy our old friend Mr. Eglantine's rage and disgust, as he looked from the pit of the Opera, to see Mrs. Walker surrounded by what he called "the swell young nobs" about London, bowing to my Lord, and laughing with his Grace, and led to carriage by Sir John.

The Ravenswing's position at this period was rather an exceptional one. She was an honest woman, visited by that peculiar class of our aristocracy who chiefly associate with ladies who are NOT honest. She laughed with all, but she encouraged none. Old Crump was constantly at her side now when she appeared in public, the most watchful of mammas, always awake at the Opera, though she seemed to be always asleep; but no dandy debauchee could deceive her vigilance, and for this reason Walker, who disliked her (as every man naturally will, must, and should dislike his mother-in-law), was contented to suffer her in his house to act as a chaperon to Morgiana.

None of the young dandies ever got admission of mornings to the little mansion in the Edgware Road; the blinds were always down; and though you might hear Morgiana's voice half across the Park as she was practising, yet the youthful hall-porter in the sugar-loaf buttons was instructed to deny her, and always declared that his mistress was gone out, with the most admirable assurance.

After some two years of her life of splendour, there were, to be sure, a good number of morning visitors, who came with SINGLE knocks, and asked for Captain Walker; but these were no more admitted than the dandies aforesaid, and were referred, generally, to the Captain's office, whither they went or not at their convenience. The only man who obtained admission into the house was Baroski, whose cab transported him thrice a week to the neighbourhood of Connaught Square, and who obtained ready entrance in his professional capacity.

But even then, and much to the wicked little music-master's disappointment, the dragon Crump was always at the piano, with her endless worsted work, or else reading her unfailing Sunday Times; and Baroski could only employ "de langvitch of de ice," as he called it, with his fair pupil, who used to mimic his manner of rolling his eyes about afterwards, and perform "Baroski in love" for the amusement of her husband and her mamma. The former had his reasons for overlooking the attentions of the little music-master; and as for the latter, had she not been on the stage, and had not many hundreds of persons, in jest or earnest, made love to her? What else can a pretty woman expect who is much before the public? And so the worthy mother counselled her daughter to bear these attentions with good humour, rather than to make them a subject of perpetual alarm and quarrel.

Baroski, then, was allowed to go on being in love, and was never in the least disturbed in his passion; and if he was not successful, at least the little wretch could have the pleasure of HINTING that he was, and looking particularly roguish when the Ravenswing was named, and assuring his friends at the club, that "upon his vort dere vas no trut IN DAT REBORT."

At last one day it happened that Mrs. Crump did not arrive in time for her daughter's lesson (perhaps it rained and the omnibus was full—a smaller circumstance than that has changed a whole life ere now)— Mrs. Crump did not arrive, and Baroski did, and Morgiana, seeing no great harm, sat down to her lesson as usual, and in the midst of it down went the music-master on his knees, and made a declaration in the most eloquent terms he could muster.

"Don't be a fool, Baroski!" said the lady—(I can't help it if her language was not more choice, and if she did not rise with cold dignity, exclaiming, "Unhand me, sir!")—"Don't be a fool!" said Mrs. Walker, "but get up and let's finish the lesson."

"You hard-hearted adorable little greature, vill you not listen to me?"

"No, I vill not listen to you, Benjamin!" concluded the lady. "Get up and take a chair, and don't go on in that ridiklous way, don't!"

But Baroski, having a speech by heart, determined to deliver himself of it in that posture, and begged Morgiana not to turn away her divine hice, and to listen to de voice of his despair, and so forth; he seized the lady's hand, and was going to press it to his lips, when she said, with more spirit, perhaps, than grace,—

"Leave go my hand, sir; I'll box your ears if you don't!"

But Baroski wouldn't release her hand, and was proceeding to imprint a kiss upon it; and Mrs. Crump, who had taken the omnibus at a quarter-past twelve instead of that at twelve, had just opened the drawing-room door and was walking in, when Morgiana, turning as red as a peony, and unable to disengage her left hand, which the musician held, raised up her right hand, and, with all her might and main, gave her lover such a tremendous slap in the face as caused him abruptly to release the hand which he held, and would have laid him prostrate on the carpet but for Mrs. Crump, who rushed forward and prevented him from falling by administering right and left a whole shower of slaps, such as he had never endured since the day he was at school.

"What imperence!" said that worthy lady; "you'll lay hands on my daughter, will you? (one, two). You'll insult a woman in distress, will you, you little coward? (one, two). Take that, and mind your manners, you filthy monster!"

Baroski bounced up in a fury. "By Chofe, you shall hear of dis!" shouted he; "you shall pay me dis!"

"As many more as you please, little Benjamin," cried the widow. "Augustus" (to the page), "was that the Captain's knock?" At this Baroski made for his hat. "Augustus, show this imperence to the door; and if he tries to come in again, call a policeman: do you hear?"

The music-master vanished very rapidly, and the two ladies, instead of being frightened or falling into hysterics, as their betters would have done, laughed at the odious monster's discomfiture, as they called him. "Such a man as that set himself up against my Howard!" said Morgiana, with becoming pride; but it was agreed between them that Howard should know nothing of what had occurred, for fear of quarrels, or lest he should be annoyed. So when he came home not a word was said; and only that his wife met him with more warmth than usual, you could not have guessed that anything extraordinary had occurred. It is not my fault that my heroine's sensibilities were not more keen, that she had not the least occasion for sal-volatile or symptom of a fainting fit; but so it was, and Mr. Howard Walker knew nothing of the quarrel between his wife and her instructor until—

Until he was arrested next day at the suit of Benjamin Baroski for two hundred and twenty guineas, and, in default of payment, was conducted by Mr. Tobias Larkins to his principal's lock-up house in Chancery Lane.

V

IN WHICH MR. WALKER FALLS INTO DIFFICULTIES, AND MRS. WALKER MAKES MANY FOOLISH ATTEMPTS TO RESCUE HIM

I hope the beloved reader is not silly enough to imagine that Mr. Walker, on finding himself inspunged for debt in Chancery Lane, was so foolish as to think of applying to any of his friends (those great personages who have appeared every now and then in the course of this little history, and have served to give it a fashionable air). No, no; he knew the world too well; and that, though Billingsgate would give him as many dozen of claret as he could carry away under his belt, as the phrase is (I can't help it, madam, if the phrase is not more genteel), and though Vauxhall would lend him his carriage, slap him on the back, and dine at his house,—their lordships would have seen Mr. Walker depending from a beam in front of the Old Bailey rather than have helped him to a hundred pounds.

And why, forsooth, should we expect otherwise in the world? I observe that men who complain of its selfishness are quite as selfish as the world is, and no more liberal of money than their neighbours; and I am quite sure with regard to Captain Walker that he would have treated a friend in want exactly as he when in want was treated. There was only his lady who was in the least afflicted by his captivity; and as for the club, that went on, we are bound to say, exactly as it did on the day previous to his disappearance.

By the way, about clubs—could we not, but for fear of detaining the fair reader too long, enter into a wholesome dissertation here on the manner of friendship established in those institutions, and the noble feeling of selfishness which they are likely to encourage in the male race? I put out of the question the stale topics of complaint, such as leaving home, encouraging gormandising and luxurious habits, etc.; but look also at the dealings of club-men with one another. Look at the rush for the evening paper! See how Shiverton orders a fire in the dog-days, and Swettenham opens the windows in February. See how Cramley takes the whole breast of the turkey on his plate, and how many times Jenkins sends away his beggarly half-pint of sherry! Clubbery is organised egotism. Club intimacy is carefully and wonderfully removed from friendship. You meet Smith for twenty years, exchange the day's news with him, laugh with him over the last joke, grow as well acquainted as two men may be together—and one day, at the end of the list of members of the club, you read in a little paragraph by itself, with all the honours,

MEMBER DECEASED.
Smith, John, Esq.;

or he, on the other hand, has the advantage of reading your own name selected for a similar typographical distinction. There it is, that abominable little exclusive list at the end of every club-catalogue—you can't avoid it. I belong to eight clubs myself, and know that one year Fitz-Boodle, George Savage, Esq. (unless it should please fate to remove my brother and his six sons, when of course it would be Fitz-Boodle, Sir George Savage, Bart.), will appear in the dismal category. There is that list; down I must go in it:—the day will come, and I shan't be seen in the bow-window, someone else will be sitting in the vacant armchair: the rubber will begin as usual, and yet somehow Fitz will not be there. "Where's Fitz?" says Trumpington, just arrived from the Rhine. "Don't you know?" says Punter, turning down his thumb to the carpet. "You led the club, I think?" says Ruff to his partner (the OTHER partner!), and the waiter snuffs the candles.

I HOPE IN THE COURSE of the above little pause, every single member of a club who reads this has profited by the perusal. He may belong, I say, to eight clubs; he will die, and not be missed by any of the five thousand members. Peace be to him; the waiters will forget him, and his name will pass away, and another great-coat will hang on the hook whence his own used to be dependent.

And this, I need not say, is the beauty of the club-institutions. If it were otherwise—if, forsooth, we were to be sorry when our friends died, or to draw out our purses when our friends were in want, we should be insolvent, and life would be miserable. Be it ours to button up our pockets and our hearts; and to make merry—it is enough to swim down this life-stream for ourselves; if Poverty is clutching hold of our heels, or Friendship would catch an arm, kick them both off. Every man for himself, is the word, and plenty to do too.

My friend Captain Walker had practised the above maxims so long and resolutely as to be quite aware when he came himself to be in distress, that not a single soul in the whole universe would help him, and he took his measures accordingly.

When carried to Mr. Bendigo's lock-up house, he summoned that gentleman in a very haughty way, took a blank banker's cheque out of his pocket-book, and filling it up for the exact sum of the writ, orders Mr. Bendigo forthwith to open the door and let him go forth.

Mr. Bendigo, smiling with exceeding archness, and putting a finger covered all over with diamond rings to his extremely aquiline nose, inquired of Mr. Walker whether he saw anything green about his face? intimating by this gay and good-humoured interrogatory his suspicion of the unsatisfactory nature of the document handed over to him by Mr. Walker.

"Hang it, sir!" says Mr. Walker, "go and get the cheque cashed, and be quick about it. Send your man in a cab, and here's a half-crown to pay for it." The confident air somewhat staggers the bailiff, who asked him whether he would like any refreshment while his man was absent getting the amount of the cheque, and treated his prisoner with great civility during the time of the messenger's journey.

But as Captain Walker had but a balance of two pounds five and twopence (this sum was afterwards divided among his creditors, the law expenses being previously deducted from it), the bankers of course declined to cash the Captain's draft for two hundred and odd pounds, simply writing the words "No effects" on the paper; on receiving which reply Walker, far from being cast down, burst out laughing very gaily, produced a real five-pound note, and called upon his host for a bottle of champagne, which the two worthies drank in perfect friendship and good-humour. The bottle was scarcely finished, and the young Israelitish gentleman who acts as waiter in Cursitor Street had only time to remove the flask and the glasses, when poor Morgiana with a flood of tears rushed into her husband's arms, and flung herself on his neck, and calling him her "dearest, blessed Howard," would have fainted at his feet; but that he, breaking out in a fury of oaths, asked her how, after getting him into that scrape through her infernal extravagance, she dared to show her face before him? This address speedily frightened the poor thing out of her fainting fit—there is nothing so good for female hysterics as a little conjugal sternness, nay, brutality, as many husbands can aver who are in the habit of employing the remedy.

"My extravagance, Howard?" said she, in a faint way; and quite put off her purpose of swooning by the sudden attack made upon her— "Surely, my love, you have nothing to complain of—"

"To complain of, ma'am?" roared the excellent Walker. "Is two hundred guineas to a music-master nothing to complain of? Did you bring me such a fortune as to authorise your taking guinea lessons? Haven't I raised you out of your sphere of life and introduced you to the best of the land? Haven't I dressed you like a duchess? Haven't I been for you such a husband as very few women in the world ever had, madam?—answer me that."

"Indeed, Howard, you were always very kind," sobbed the lady.

"Haven't I toiled and slaved for you—been out all day working for you? Haven't I allowed your vulgar old mother to come to your house— to my house, I say? Haven't I done all this?"

She could not deny it, and Walker, who was in a rage (and when a man is in a rage, for what on earth is a wife made but that he should vent his rage on her?), continued for some time in this strain, and so abused, frightened, and overcame poor Morgiana that she left her husband fully convinced that she was the most guilty of beings, and bemoaning his double bad fortune, that her Howard was ruined and she the cause of his misfortunes.

When she was gone, Mr. Walker resumed his equanimity (for he was not one of those men whom a few months of the King's Bench were likely to terrify), and drank several glasses of punch in company with his host; with whom in perfect calmness he talked over his affairs. That he intended to pay his debt and quit the spunging-house next day is a matter of course; no one ever was yet put in a spunging-house that did not pledge his veracity he intended to quit it to-morrow. Mr. Bendigo said he should be heartily glad to open the door to him, and in the meantime sent out diligently to see among his friends if there were any more detainers against the Captain, and to inform the Captain's creditors to come forward against him.

Morgiana went home in profound grief, it may be imagined, and could hardly refrain from bursting into tears when the sugar-loaf page asked whether master was coming home early, or whether he had taken his key; she lay awake tossing and wretched the whole night, and very early in the morning rose up, and dressed, and went out.

Before nine o'clock she was in Cursitor Street, and once more joyfully bounced into her husband's arms; who woke up yawning and swearing somewhat, with a severe headache, occasioned by the jollification of the previous night: for, strange though it may seem, there are perhaps no places in Europe where jollity is more practised than in prisons for debt; and I declare for my own part (I mean, of course, that I went to visit a friend) I have dined at Mr. Aminadab's as sumptuously as at Long's.

But it is necessary to account for Morgiana's joyfulness; which was strange in her husband's perplexity, and after her sorrow of the previous night. Well, then, when Mrs. Walker went out in the morning, she did so with a very large basket under her arm. "Shall I carry the basket, ma'am?" said the page, seizing it with much alacrity.

"No, thank you," cried his mistress, with equal eagerness: "it's only—"

"Of course, ma'am," replied the boy, sneering, "I knew it was that."

"Glass," continued Mrs. Walker, turning extremely red. "Have the goodness to call a coach, sir, and not to speak till you are questioned."

The young gentleman disappeared upon his errand: the coach was called and came. Mrs. Walker slipped into it with her basket, and the page went downstairs to his companions in the kitchen, and said, "It's a-comin'! master's in quod, and missus has gone out to pawn the plate." When the cook went out that day, she somehow had by mistake placed in her basket a dozen of table-knives and a plated egg-stand. When the lady's-maid took a walk in the course of the afternoon, she found she had occasion for eight cambric pocket-handkerchiefs, (marked with her mistress's cipher), half-a-dozen pair of shoes, gloves, long and short, some silk stockings, and a gold-headed scent-bottle. "Both the new cashmeres is gone," said she, "and there's nothing left in Mrs. Walker's trinket-box but a paper of pins and an old coral bracelet." As for the page, he rushed incontinently to his master's dressing-room and examined every one of the pockets of his clothes; made a parcel of some of them, and opened all the drawers which Walker had not locked before his departure. He only found three-halfpence and a bill stamp, and about forty-five tradesmen's accounts, neatly labelled and tied up with red tape. These three worthies, a groom who was a great admirer of Trimmer the lady's-maid, and a policeman a friend of the cook's, sat down to a comfortable dinner at the usual hour, and it was agreed among them all that Walker's ruin was certain. The cook made the policeman a present of a china punch-bowl which Mrs. Walker had given her; and the lady's-maid gave her friend the "Book of Beauty" for last year, and the third volume of Byron's poems from the drawing-room table.

"I'm dash'd if she ain't taken the little French clock, too," said the page, and so indeed Mrs. Walker had; it slipped in the basket where it lay enveloped in one of her shawls, and then struck madly and unnaturally a great number of times, as Morgiana was lifting her store of treasures out of the hackney-coach. The coachman wagged his head sadly as he saw her walking as quick as she could under her heavy load, and disappearing round the corner of the street at which Mr. Balls's celebrated jewellery establishment is situated. It is a grand shop, with magnificent silver cups and salvers, rare gold-headed canes, flutes, watches, diamond brooches, and a few fine specimens of the old masters in the window, and under the words—

BALLS, JEWELLER,

you read

Money Lent.

in the very smallest type, on the door.

The interview with Mr. Balls need not be described; but it must have been a satisfactory one, for at the end of half an hour Morgiana returned and bounded into the coach with sparkling eyes, and told the driver to GALLOP to Cursitor Street; which, smiling, he promised to do, and accordingly set off in that direction at the rate of four miles an hour. "I thought so," said the philosophic charioteer. "When a man's in quod, a woman don't mind her silver spoons;" and he was so delighted with her action, that he forgot to grumble when she came to settle accounts with him, even though she gave him only double his fare.

"Take me to him," said she to the young Hebrew who opened the door.

"To whom?" says the sarcastic youth; "there's twenty HIM's here. You're precious early."

"To Captain Walker, young man," replied Morgiana haughtily; whereupon the youth opening the second door, and seeing Mr. Bendigo in a flowered dressing-gown descending the stairs, exclaimed, "Papa, here's a lady for the Captain." "I'm come to free him," said she, trembling, and holding out a bundle of bank-notes. "Here's the amount of your claim, sir—two hundred and twenty guineas, as you told me last night." The Jew took the notes, and grinned as he looked at her, and grinned double as he looked at his son, and begged Mrs. Walker to step into his study and take a receipt. When the door of that apartment closed upon the lady and his father, Mr. Bendigo the younger fell back in an agony of laughter, which it is impossible to describe in words, and presently ran out into a court where some of the luckless inmates of the house were already taking the air, and communicated something to them which made those individuals also laugh as uproariously as he had previously done.

Well, after joyfully taking the receipt from Mr. Bendigo (how her cheeks flushed and her heart fluttered as she dried it on the blotting-book!), and after turning very pale again on hearing that the Captain had had a very bad night: "And well he might, poor dear!" said she (at which Mr. Bendigo, having no person to grin at, grinned at a marble bust of Mr. Pitt, which ornamented his sideboard)—Morgiana, I say, these preliminaries being concluded, was conducted to her husband's apartment, and once more flinging her arms round her dearest Howard's neck, told him with one of the sweetest smiles in the world, to make haste and get up and come home, for breakfast was waiting and the carriage at the door.

"What do you mean, love?" said the Captain, starting up and looking exceedingly surprised.

"I mean that my dearest is free; that the odious little creature is paid—at least the horrid bailiff is."

"Have you been to Baroski?" said Walker, turning very red.

"Howard!" said his wife, quite indignant.

"Did—did your mother give you the money?" asked the Captain.

"No; I had it by me" replies Mrs. Walker, with a very knowing look.

Walker was more surprised than ever. "Have you any more by you?" said he.

Mrs. Walker showed him her purse with two guineas. "That is all, love," she said. "And I wish," continued she, "you would give me a draft to pay a whole list of little bills that have somehow all come in within the last few days."

"Well, well, you shall have the cheque," continued Mr. Walker, and began forthwith to make his toilet, which completed, he rang for Mr. Bendigo, and his bill, and intimated his wish to go home directly.

The honoured bailiff brought the bill, but with regard to his being free, said it was impossible.

"How impossible?" said Mrs. Walker, turning very red: and then very pale. "Did I not pay just now?"

"So you did, and you've got the reshipt; but there's another detainer against the Captain for a hundred and fifty. Eglantine and Mossrose, of Bond Street;—perfumery for five years, you know."

"You don't mean to say you were such a fool as to pay without asking if there were any more detainers?" roared Walker to his wife.

"Yes, she was though," chuckled Mr. Bendigo; "but she'll know better the next time: and, besides, Captain, what's a hundred and fifty pounds to you?"

Though Walker desired nothing so much in the world at that moment as the liberty to knock down his wife, his sense of prudence overcame his desire for justice: if that feeling may be called prudence on his part, which consisted in a strong wish to cheat the bailiff into the idea that he (Walker) was an exceedingly respectable and wealthy man. Many worthy persons indulge in this fond notion, that they are imposing upon the world; strive to fancy, for instance, that their bankers consider them men of property because they keep a tolerable balance, pay little tradesmen's bills with ostentatious punctuality, and so forth— but the world, let us be pretty sure, is as wise as need be, and guesses our real condition with a marvellous instinct, or learns it with curious skill. The London tradesman is one of the keenest judges of human nature extant; and if a tradesman, how much more a bailiff? In reply to the ironic question, "What's a hundred and fifty pounds to you?" Walker, collecting himself, answers, "It is an infamous imposition, and I owe the money no more than you do; but, nevertheless, I shall instruct my lawyers to pay it in the course of the morning: under protest, of course."

"Oh, of course," said Mr. Bendigo, bowing and quitting the room, and leaving Mrs. Walker to the pleasure of a tete-a-tete with her husband.

And now being alone with the partner of his bosom, the worthy gentleman began an address to her which cannot be put down on paper here; because the world is exceedingly squeamish, and does not care to hear the whole truth about rascals, and because the fact is that almost every other word of the Captain's speech was a curse, such as would shock the beloved reader were it put in print.

Fancy, then, in lieu of the conversation, a scoundrel, disappointed and in a fury, wreaking his brutal revenge upon an amiable woman, who sits trembling and pale, and wondering at this sudden exhibition of wrath. Fancy how he clenches his fists and stands over her, and stamps and screams out curses with a livid face, growing wilder and wilder in his rage; wrenching her hand when she wants to turn away, and only stopping at last when she has fallen off the chair in a fainting fit, with a heart-breaking sob that made the Jew-boy who was listening at the key-hole turn quite pale and walk away. Well, it is best, perhaps, that such a conversation should not be told at length:—at the end of it, when Mr. Walker had his wife lifeless on the floor, he seized a water-jug and poured it over her; which operation pretty soon brought her to herself, and shaking her black ringlets, she looked up once more again timidly into his face, and took his hand, and began to cry.

He spoke now in a somewhat softer voice, and let her keep paddling on with his hand as before; he COULDN'T speak very fiercely to the poor girl in her attitude of defeat, and tenderness, and supplication. "Morgiana," said he, "your extravagance and carelessness have brought me to ruin, I'm afraid. If you had chosen to have gone to Baroski, a word from you would have made him withdraw the writ, and my property wouldn't have been sacrificed, as it has now been, for nothing. It mayn't be yet too late, however, to retrieve ourselves. This bill of Eglantine's is a regular conspiracy, I am sure, between Mossrose and Bendigo here: you must go to Eglantine—he's an old—an old flame of yours, you know."

She dropped his hand: "I can't go to Eglantine after what has passed between us," she said; but Walker's face instantly began to wear a certain look, and she said with a shudder, "Well, well, dear, I WILL go." "You will go to Eglantine, and ask him to take a bill for the amount of this shameful demand—at any date, never mind what. Mind, however, to see him alone, and I'm sure if you choose you can settle the business. Make haste; set off directly, and come back, as there may be more detainers in."

Trembling, and in a great flutter, Morgiana put on her bonnet and gloves, and went towards the door. "It's a fine morning," said Mr. Walker, looking out: "a walk will do you good; and—Morgiana—didn't you say you had a couple of guineas in your pocket?"

"Here it is," said she, smiling all at once, and holding up her face to be kissed. She paid the two guineas for the kiss. Was it not a mean act? "Is it possible that people can love where they do not respect?" says Miss Prim: "*I* never would." Nobody asked you, Miss Prim: but recollect Morgiana was not born with your advantages of education and breeding; and was, in fact, a poor vulgar creature, who loved Mr. Walker, not because her mamma told her, nor because he was an exceedingly eligible and well-brought-up young man, but because she could not help it, and knew no better. Nor is Mrs. Walker set up as a model of virtue: ah, no! when I want a model of virtue I will call in Baker Street, and ask for a sitting of my dear (if I may be permitted to say so) Miss Prim.

We have Mr. Howard Walker safely housed in Mr. Bendigo's establishment in Cursitor Street, Chancery Lane; and it looks like mockery and want of feeling towards the excellent hero of this story (or, as should rather be said, towards the husband of the heroine) to say what he might have been but for the unlucky little circumstance of Baroski's passion for Morgiana.

If Baroski had not fallen in love with Morgiana, he would not have given her two hundred guineas' worth of lessons; he would not have so far presumed as to seize her hand, and attempt to kiss it; if he had not attempted to kiss her, she would not have boxed his ears; he would not have taken out the writ against Walker; Walker would have been free, very possibly rich, and therefore certainly respected: he always said that a month's more liberty would have set him beyond the reach of misfortune.

The assertion is very likely a correct one; for Walker had a flashy enterprising genius, which ends in wealth sometimes; in the King's Bench not seldom; occasionally, alas! in Van Diemen's Land. He might have been rich, could he have kept his credit, and had not his personal expenses and extravagances pulled him down. He had gallantly availed himself of his wife's fortune; nor could any man in London, as he proudly said, have made five hundred pounds go so far. He had, as we have seen, furnished a house, sideboard, and cellar with it: he had a carriage, and horses in his stable, and with the remainder he had purchased shares in four companies—of three of which he was founder and director, had conducted innumerable bargains in the foreign stocks, had lived and entertained sumptuously, and made himself a very considerable income. He had set up THE CAPITOL Loan and Life Assurance Company, had discovered the Chimborazo gold mines, and the Society for Recovering and Draining the Pontine Marshes; capital ten millions; patron HIS HOLINESS THE POPE. It certainly was stated in an evening paper that His Holiness had made him a Knight of the Spur, and had offered to him the rank of Count; and he was raising a loan for His Highness, the Cacique of Panama, who had sent him (by way of dividend) the grand cordon of His Highness's order of the Castle and Falcon, which might be seen any day at his office in Bond Street, with the parchments signed and sealed by the Grand Master and Falcon King-at-arms of His Highness. In a week more Walker would have raised a hundred thousand pounds on His Highness's twenty per cent. loan; he would have had fifteen thousand pounds commission for himself; his companies would have risen to par, he would have realised his shares; he would have gone into Parliament; he would have been made a baronet, who knows? a peer, probably! "And I appeal to you, sir," Walker would say to his friends, "could any man have shown better proof of his affection for his wife than by laying out her little miserable money as I did? They call me heartless, sir, because I didn't succeed; sir, my life has been a series of sacrifices for that woman, such as no man ever performed before."

A proof of Walker's dexterity and capability for business may be seen in the fact that he had actually appeased and reconciled one of his bitterest enemies—our honest friend Eglantine. After Walker's marriage Eglantine, who had now no mercantile dealings with his former agent, became so enraged with him, that, as the only means of revenge in his power, he sent him in his bill for goods supplied to the amount of one hundred and fifty guineas, and sued him for the amount. But Walker stepped boldly over to his enemy, and in the course of half an hour they were friends.

Eglantine promised to forego his claim; and accepted in lieu of it three hundred-pound shares of the ex-Panama stock, bearing twenty-five per cent., payable half-yearly at the house of Hocus Brothers, St. Swithin's Lane; three hundred-pound shares, and the SECOND class of the order of the Castle and Falcon, with the riband and badge. "In four years, Eglantine, my boy, I hope to get you the Grand Cordon of the order," said Walker: "I hope to see you a KNIGHT GRAND CROSS, with a grant of a hundred thousand acres reclaimed from the Isthmus."

To do my poor Eglantine justice, he did not care for the hundred thousand acres—it was the star that delighted him—ah! how his fat chest heaved with delight as he sewed on the cross and riband to his dress-coat, and lighted up four wax candles and looked at himself in the glass. He was known to wear a great-coat after that—it was that he might wear the cross under it. That year he went on a trip to Boulogne. He was dreadfully ill during the voyage, but as the vessel entered the port he was seen to emerge from the cabin, his coat open, the star blazing on his chest; the soldiers saluted him as he walked the streets, he was called Monsieur le Chevalier, and when he went home he entered into negotiations with Walker to purchase a commission in His Highness's service. Walker said he would get him the nominal rank of Captain, the fees at the Panama War Office were five-and-twenty pounds, which sum honest Eglantine produced, and had his commission, and a pack of visiting cards printed as Captain Archibald Eglantine, K.C.F. Many a time he looked at them as they lay in his desk, and he kept the cross in his dressing-table, and wore it as he shaved every morning.

His Highness the Cacique, it is well known, came to England, and had lodgings in Regent Street, where he held a levee, at which Eglantine appeared in the Panama uniform, and was most graciously received by his Sovereign. His Highness proposed to make Captain Eglantine his aide-de-camp with the rank of Colonel, but the Captain's exchequer was rather low at that moment, and the fees at the "War Office" were peremptory. Meanwhile His Highness left Regent Street, was said by some to have returned to Panama, by others to be in his native city of Cork, by others to be leading a life of retirement in the New Cut, Lambeth; at any rate was not visible for some time, so that Captain Eglantine's advancement did not take place. Eglantine was somehow ashamed to mention his military and chivalric rank to Mr. Mossrose, when that gentleman came into partnership with him; and kept these facts secret, until they were detected by a very painful circumstance. On the very day when Walker was arrested at the suit of Benjamin Baroski, there appeared in the newspapers an account of the imprisonment of His Highness the Prince of Panama for a bill owing to a licensed victualler in Ratcliff Highway. The magistrate to whom the victualler subsequently came to complain passed many pleasantries on the occasion. He asked whether His Highness did not drink like a swan with two necks; whether he had brought any Belles savages with him from Panama, and so forth; and the whole court, said the report, "was convulsed with laughter when Boniface produced a green and yellow riband with a large star of the order of the Castle and Falcon, with which His Highness proposed to gratify him, in lieu of paying his little bill."

It was as he was reading the above document with a bleeding heart that Mr. Mossrose came in from his daily walk to the City. "Vell, Eglantine," says he, "have you heard the newsh?"

"About His Highness?"

"About your friend Valker; he's arrested for two hundred poundsh!"

Eglantine at this could contain no more; but told his story of how he had been induced to accept three hundred pounds of Panama stock for his account against Walker, and cursed his stars for his folly. "Vell, you've only to bring in another bill," said the younger perfumer; "swear he owes you a hundred and fifty pounds, and we'll have a writ out against him this afternoon."

And so a second writ was taken out against Captain Walker.

"You'll have his wife here very likely in a day or two," said Mr. Mossrose to his partner; "them chaps always sends their wives, and I hope you know how to deal with her."

"I don't value her a fig's hend," said Eglantine. "I'll treat her like the dust of the hearth. After that woman's conduct to me, I should like to see her have the haudacity to come here; and if she does, you'll see how I'll serve her."

The worthy perfumer was, in fact, resolved to be exceedingly hard-hearted in his behaviour towards his old love, and acted over at night in bed the scene which was to occur when the meeting should take place. Oh, thought he, but it will be a grand thing to see the proud Morgiana on her knees to me; and me a-pointing to the door, and saying, "Madam, you've steeled this 'eart against you, you have;—bury the recollection of old times, of those old times when I thought my 'eart would have broke, but it didn't—no: 'earts are made of sterner stuff. I didn't die, as I thought I should; I stood it, and live to see the woman I despised at my feet—ha, ha, at my feet!"

In the midst of these thoughts Mr. Eglantine fell asleep; but it was evident that the idea of seeing Morgiana once more agitated him considerably, else why should he have been at the pains of preparing so much heroism? His sleep was exceedingly fitful and troubled; he saw Morgiana in a hundred shapes; he dreamed that he was dressing her hair; that he was riding with her to Richmond; that the horse turned into a dragon, and Morgiana into Woolsey, who took him by the throat and choked him, while the dragon played the key-bugle. And in the morning when Mossrose was gone to his business in the City, and he sat reading the Morning Post in his study, ah! what a thump his heart gave as the lady of his dreams actually stood before him!

Many a lady who purchased brushes at Eglantine's shop would have given ten guineas for such a colour as his when he saw her. His heart beat violently, he was almost choking in his stays: he had been prepared for the visit, but his courage failed him now it had come. They were both silent for some minutes.

"You know what I am come for," at last said Morgiana from under her veil, but she put it aside as she spoke.

"I—that is—yes—it's a painful affair, mem," he said, giving one look at her pale face, and then turning away in a flurry. "I beg to refer you to Blunt, Hone, and Sharpus, my lawyers, mem," he added, collecting himself.

"I didn't expect this from You, Mr. Eglantine," said the lady, and began to sob.

"And after what's 'appened, I didn't expect a visit from You, mem. I thought Mrs. Capting Walker was too great a dame to visit poor Harchibald Eglantine (though some of the first men in the country Do visit him). Is there anything in which I can oblige you, mem?"

"O heavens!" cried the poor woman; "have I no friend left? I never thought that you, too, would have deserted me, Mr. Archibald."

The "Archibald," pronounced in the old way, had evidently an effect on the perfumer; he winced and looked at her very eagerly for a moment. "What can I do for you, mem?" at last said he.

"What is this bill against Mr. Walker, for which he is now in prison?"

"Perfumery supplied for five years; that man used more 'air-brushes than any duke in the land, and as for eau-de-Cologne, he must have bathed himself in it. He hordered me about like a lord. He never paid me one shilling—he stabbed me in my most vital part—but ah! ah! never mind THAT: and I said I would be revenged, and I AM."

The perfumer was quite in a rage again by this time, and wiped his fat face with his pocket-handkerchief, and glared upon Mrs. Walker with a most determined air.

"Revenged on whom? Archibald—Mr. Eglantine, revenged on me—on a poor woman whom you made miserable! You would not have done so once."

"Ha! and a precious way you treated me ONCE," said Eglantine: "don't talk to me, mem, of ONCE. Bury the recollection of once for hever! I thought my 'eart would have broke once, but no: 'earts are made of sterner stuff. I didn't die, as I thought I should; I stood it—and I live to see the woman who despised me at my feet."

"Oh, Archibald!" was all the lady could say, and she fell to sobbing again: it was perhaps her best argument with the perfumer.

"Oh, Harchibald, indeed!" continued he, beginning to swell; "don't call me Harchibald, Morgiana. Think what a position you might have held if you'd chose: when, when—you MIGHT have called me Harchibald. Now it's no use," added he, with harrowing pathos; "but, though I've been wronged, I can't bear to see women in tears—tell me what I can do."

"Dear good Mr. Eglantine, send to your lawyers and stop this horrid prosecution—take Mr. Walker's acknowledgment for the debt. If he is free, he is sure to have a very large sum of money in a few days, and will pay you all. Do not ruin him—do not ruin me by persisting now. Be the old kind Eglantine you were."

Eglantine took a hand, which Morgiana did not refuse; he thought about old times. He had known her since childhood almost; as a girl he dandled her on his knee at the "Kidneys;" as a woman he had adored her—his heart was melted.

"He did pay me in a sort of way," reasoned the perfumer with himself—"these bonds, though they are not worth much, I took 'em for better or for worse, and I can't bear to see her crying, and to trample on a woman in distress. Morgiana," he added, in a loud cheerful voice, "cheer up; I'll give you a release for your husband: I WILL be the old kind Eglantine I was."

"Be the old kind jackass you vash!" here roared a voice that made Mr. Eglantine start. "Vy, vat an old fat fool you are, Eglantine, to give up our just debts because a voman comes snivelling and crying to you—and such a voman, too!" exclaimed Mr. Mossrose, for his was the voice.

"Such a woman, sir?" cried the senior partner.

"Yes; such a woman—vy, didn't she jilt you herself?—hasn't she been trying the same game with Baroski; and are you so green as to give up a hundred and fifty pounds because she takes a fancy to come vimpering here? I won't, I can tell you. The money's as much mine as it is yours, and I'll have it or keep Walker's body, that's what I will."

At the presence of his partner, the timid good genius of Eglantine, which had prompted him to mercy and kindness, at once outspread its frightened wings and flew away.

"You see how it is, Mrs. W.," said he, looking down; "it's an affair of business—in all these here affairs of business Mr. Mossrose is the managing man; ain't you, Mr. Mossrose?"

"A pretty business it would be if I wasn't," replied Mossrose, doggedly. "Come, ma'am," says he, "I'll tell you vat I do: I take fifty per shent; not a farthing less—give me that, and out your husband goes."

"Oh, sir, Howard will pay you in a week."

"Vell, den, let him stop at my uncle Bendigo's for a week, and come out den—he's very comfortable there," said Shylock with a grin. "Hadn't you better go to the shop, Mr. Eglantine," continued he, "and look after your business? Mrs. Walker can't want you to listen to her all day."

Eglantine was glad of the excuse, and slunk out of the studio; not into the shop, but into his parlour; where he drank off a great glass of maraschino, and sat blushing and exceedingly agitated, until Mossrose came to tell him that Mrs. W. was gone, and wouldn't trouble him any more. But although he drank several more glasses of maraschino, and went to the play that night, and to the Cider-cellars afterwards, neither the liquor, nor the play, nor the delightful comic songs at the cellars, could drive Mrs. Walker out of his head, and the memory of old times, and the image of her pale weeping face.

Morgiana tottered out of the shop, scarcely heeding the voice of Mr. Mossrose, who said, "I'll take forty per shent" (and went back to his duty cursing himself for a soft-hearted fool for giving up so much of his rights to a puling woman). Morgiana, I say, tottered out of the shop, and went up Conduit Street, weeping, weeping with all her eyes. She was quite faint, for she had taken nothing that morning but the glass of water which the pastry-cook in the Strand had given her, and was forced to take hold of the railings of a house for support just as a little gentleman with a yellow handkerchief under his arm was issuing from the door.

"Good heavens, Mrs. Walker!" said the gentleman. It was no other than Mr. Woolsey, who was going forth to try a body-coat for a customer. "Are you ill?—what's the matter?—for God's sake come in!" and he took her arm under his, and led her into his back-parlour, and seated her, and had some wine and water before her in one minute, before she had said one single word regarding herself.

As soon as she was somewhat recovered, and with the interruption of a thousand sobs, the poor thing told as well as she could her little story. Mr. Eglantine had arrested Mr. Walker: she had been trying to gain time for him; Eglantine had refused.

"The hard-hearted cowardly brute to refuse HER anything!" said loyal Mr. Woolsey. "My dear," says he, "I've no reason to love your husband, and I know too much about him to respect him; but I love and respect YOU, and will spend my last shilling to serve you." At which Morgiana could only take his hand and cry a great deal more than ever. She said Mr. Walker would have a great deal of money in a week, that he was the best of husbands, and she was sure Mr. Woolsey would think better of him when he knew him; that Mr. Eglantine's bill was one hundred and fifty pounds, but that Mr. Mossrose would take forty per cent. if Mr. Woolsey could say how much that was.

"I'll pay a thousand pound to do you good," said Mr. Woolsey, bouncing up; "stay here for ten minutes, my dear, until my return, and all shall be right, as you will see." He was back in ten minutes, and had called a cab from the stand opposite (all the coachmen there had seen and commented on Mrs. Walker's woebegone looks), and they were off for Cursitor Street in a moment. "They'll settle the whole debt for twenty pounds," said he, and showed an order to that effect from Mr. Mossrose to Mr. Bendigo, empowering the latter to release Walker on receiving Mr. Woolsey's acknowledgment for the above sum.

"There's no use paying it," said Mr. Walker, doggedly; "it would only be robbing you, Mr. Woolsey—seven more detainers have come in while my wife has been away. I must go through the court now; but," he added in a whisper to the tailor, "my good sir, my debts of HONOUR are sacred, and if you will have the goodness to lend ME the twenty pounds, I pledge you my word as a gentleman to return it when I come out of quod."

It is probable that Mr. Woolsey declined this; for, as soon as he was gone, Walker, in a tremendous fury, began cursing his wife for dawdling three hours on the road. "Why the deuce, ma'am, didn't you take a cab?" roared he, when he heard she had walked to Bond Street. "Those writs have only been in half an hour, and I might have been off but for you."

"Oh, Howard," said she, "didn't you take—didn't I give you my—my last shilling?" and fell back and wept again more bitterly than ever.

"Well, love," said her amiable husband, turning rather red, "never mind, it wasn't your fault. It is but going through the court. It is no great odds. I forgive you."

VI

In which Mr. Walker still remains in difficulties, but shows great resignation under his misfortunes

The exemplary Walker, seeing that escape from his enemies was hopeless, and that it was his duty as a man to turn on them and face them, now determined to quit the splendid though narrow lodgings which Mr. Bendigo had provided for him, and undergo the martyrdom of the Fleet. Accordingly, in company with that gentleman, he came over to Her Majesty's prison, and gave himself into the custody of the officers there; and did not apply for the accommodation of the Rules (by which in those days the captivity of some debtors was considerably lightened), because he knew perfectly well that there was no person in the wide world who would give a security for the heavy sums for which Walker was answerable. What these sums were is no matter, and on this head we do not think it at all necessary to satisfy the curiosity of the reader. He may have owed hundreds—thousands, his creditors only can tell; he paid the dividend which has been formerly mentioned, and showed thereby his desire to satisfy all claims upon him to the uttermost farthing.

As for the little house in Connaught Square, when, after quitting her husband, Morgiana drove back thither, the door was opened by the page, who instantly thanked her to pay his wages; and in the drawing-room, on a yellow satin sofa, sat a seedy man (with a pot of porter beside him placed on an album for fear of staining the rosewood table), and the seedy man signified that he had taken possession of the furniture in execution for a judgment debt. Another seedy man was in the dining-room, reading a newspaper, and drinking gin; he informed Mrs. Walker that he was the representative of another judgment debt and of another execution:—"There's another on 'em in the kitchen," said the page, "taking an inwentory of the furniture; and he swears he'll have you took up for swindling, for pawning the plate."

"Sir," said Mr. Woolsey, for that worthy man had conducted Morgiana home—"sir," said he, shaking his stick at the young page, "if you give any more of your impudence, I'll beat every button off your jacket:" and as there were some four hundred of these ornaments, the page was silent. It was a great mercy for Morgiana that the honest and faithful tailor had accompanied her. The good fellow had waited very patiently for her for an hour in the parlour or coffee-room of the lock-up house, knowing full well that she would want a protector on her way homewards; and his kindness will be more appreciated when it is stated that, during the time of his delay in the coffee-room, he had been subject to the entreaties, nay, to the insults, of Cornet Fipkin of the Blues, who was in prison at the suit of Linsey, Woolsey and Co., and who happened to be taking his breakfast in the apartment when his obdurate creditor entered it. The Cornet (a hero of eighteen, who stood at least five feet three in his boots, and owed fifteen thousand pounds) was so enraged at the obduracy of his creditor that he said he would have thrown him out of the window but for the bars which guarded it; and entertained serious thoughts of knocking the tailor's head off, but that the latter, putting his right leg forward and his fists in a proper attitude, told the young officer to "come on;" on which the Cornet cursed the tailor for a "snob," and went back to his breakfast.

The execution people having taken charge of Mr. Walker's house, Mrs. Walker was driven to take refuge with her mamma near "Sadler's Wells," and the Captain remained comfortably lodged in the Fleet. He had some ready money, and with it managed to make his existence exceedingly comfortable. He lived with the best society of the place, consisting of several distinguished young noblemen and gentlemen. He spent the morning playing at fives and smoking cigars; the evening smoking cigars and dining comfortably. Cards came after dinner; and, as the Captain was an experienced player, and near a score of years older than most of his friends, he was generally pretty successful: indeed, if he had received all the money that was owed to him, he might have come out of prison and paid his creditors twenty shillings in the pound—that is, if he had been minded to do so. But there is no use in examining into that point too closely, for the fact is, young Fipkin only paid him forty pounds out of seven hundred, for which he gave him I.O.U.'s; Algernon Deuceace not only did not pay him three hundred and twenty which he lost at blind hookey, but actually borrowed seven and sixpence in money from Walker, which has never been repaid to this day; and Lord Doublequits actually lost nineteen thousand pounds to him at heads and tails, which he never paid, pleading drunkenness and his minority. The reader may recollect a paragraph which went the round of the papers entitled—

"Affair of honour in the Fleet Prison.—Yesterday morning (behind the pump in the second court) Lord D-bl-qu-ts and Captain H-w-rd W-lk-r (a near relative, we understand, of his Grace the Duke of N-rf-lk) had a hostile meeting and exchanged two shots. These two young sprigs of nobility were attended to the ground by Major Flush, who, by the way, is FLUSH no longer, and Captain Pam, late of the— Dragoons. Play is said to have been the cause of the quarrel, and the gallant Captain is reported to have handled the noble lord's nose rather roughly at one stage of the transactions."

When Morgiana at "Sadler's Wells" heard these news, she was ready to faint with terror; and rushed to the Fleet Prison, and embraced her lord and master with her usual expansion and fits of tears: very much to that gentleman's annoyance, who happened to be in company with Pain and Flush at the time, and did not care that his handsome wife should be seen too much in the dubious precincts of the Fleet. He had at least so much shame about him, and had always rejected her entreaties to be allowed to inhabit the prison with him.

"It is enough," would he say, casting his eyes heavenward, and with a most lugubrious countenance—"it is enough, Morgiana, that *I* should suffer, even though your thoughtlessness has been the cause of my ruin. But enough of THAT! I will not rebuke you for faults for which I know you are now repentant; and I never could bear to see you in the midst of the miseries of this horrible place. Remain at home with your mother, and let me drag on the weary days here alone. If you can get me any more of that pale sherry, my love, do. I require something to cheer me in solitude, and have found my chest very much relieved by that wine. Put more pepper and eggs, my dear, into the next veal-pie you make me. I can't eat the horrible messes in the coffee-room here."

It was Walker's wish, I can't tell why, except that it is the wish of a great number of other persons in this strange world, to make his wife believe that he was wretched in mind and ill in health; and all assertions to this effect the simple creature received with numberless tears of credulity: she would go home to Mrs. Crump, and say how her darling Howard was pining away, how he was ruined for HER, and with what angelic sweetness he bore his captivity. The fact is, he bore it with so much resignation that no other person in the world could see that he was unhappy. His life was undisturbed by duns; his day was his own from morning till night; his diet was good, his acquaintances jovial, his purse tolerably well supplied, and he had not one single care to annoy him.

Mrs. Crump and Woolsey, perhaps, received Morgiana's account of her husband's miseries with some incredulity. The latter was now a daily visitor to "Sadler's Wells." His love for Morgiana had become a warm fatherly generous regard for her; it was out of the honest fellow's cellar that the wine used to come which did so much good to Mr. Walker's chest; and he tried a thousand ways to make Morgiana happy.

A very happy day, indeed, it was when, returning from her visit to the Fleet, she found in her mother's sitting-room her dear grand rosewood piano, and every one of her music-books, which the kind-hearted tailor had purchased at the sale of Walker's effects. And I am not ashamed to say that Morgiana herself was so charmed, that when, as usual, Mr. Woolsey came to drink tea in the evening, she actually gave him a kiss; which frightened Mr. Woolsey, and made him blush exceedingly. She sat down, and played him that evening every one of the songs which he liked—the OLD songs—none of your Italian stuff. Podmore, the old music-master, was there too, and was delighted and astonished at the progress in singing which Morgiana had made; and when the little party separated, he took Mr. Woolsey by the hand, and said, "Give me leave to tell you, sir, that you're a TRUMP."

"That he is," said Canterfield, the first tragic; "an honour to human nature. A man whose hand is open as day to melting charity, and whose heart ever melts at the tale of woman's distress."

"Pooh, pooh, stuff and nonsense, sir," said the tailor; but, upon my word, Mr. Canterfield's words were perfectly correct. I wish as much could be said in favour of Woolsey's old rival, Mr. Eglantine, who attended the sale too, but it was with a horrid kind of satisfaction at the thought that Walker was ruined. He bought the yellow satin sofa before mentioned, and transferred it to what he calls his "sitting-room," where it is to this day, bearing many marks of the best bear's grease. Woolsey bid against Baroski for the piano, very nearly up to the actual value of the instrument, when the artist withdrew from competition; and when he was sneering at the ruin of Mr. Walker, the tailor sternly interrupted him by saying, "What the deuce are You sneering at? You did it, sir; and you're paid every shilling of your claim, ain't you?" On which Baroski turned round to Miss Larkins, and said, Mr. Woolsey was a "snop;" the very word, though pronounced somewhat differently, which the gallant Cornet Fipkin had applied to him.

Well; so he WAS a snob. But, vulgar as he was, I declare, for my part, that I have a greater respect for Mr. Woolsey than for any single nobleman or gentleman mentioned in this true history.

It will be seen from the names of Messrs. Canterfield and Podmore that Morgiana was again in the midst of the widow Crump's favourite theatrical society; and this, indeed, was the case. The widow's little room was hung round with the pictures which were mentioned at the commencement of the story as decorating the bar of the "Bootjack;" and several times in a week she received her friends from "The Wells," and entertained them with such humble refreshments of tea and crumpets as her modest means permitted her to purchase. Among these persons Morgiana lived and sang quite as contentedly as she had ever done among the demireps of her husband's society; and, only she did not dare to own it to herself, was a great deal happier than she had been for many a day. Mrs. Captain Walker was still a great lady amongst them. Even in his ruin, Walker, the director of three companies, and the owner of the splendid pony-chaise, was to these simple persons an awful character; and when mentioned they talked with a great deal of gravity of his being in the country, and hoped Mrs. Captain W. had good news of him. They all knew he was in the Fleet; but had he not in prison fought a duel with a viscount? Montmorency (of the Norfolk Circuit) was in the Fleet too; and when Canterfield went to see poor Montey, the latter had pointed out Walker to his friend, who actually hit Lord George Tennison across the shoulders in play with a racket-bat; which event was soon made known to the whole green-room.

"They had me up one day," said Montmorency, "to sing a comic song, and give my recitations; and we had champagne and lobster-salad: Such nobs!" added the player. "Billingsgate and Vauxhall were there too, and left college at eight o'clock."

When Morgiana was told of the circumstance by her mother, she hoped her dear Howard had enjoyed the evening, and was thankful that for once he could forget his sorrows. Nor, somehow, was she ashamed of herself for being happy afterwards, but gave way to her natural good-humour without repentance or self-rebuke. I believe, indeed (alas! why are we made acquainted with the same fact regarding ourselves long after it is past and gone?)—I believe these were the happiest days of Morgiana's whole life. She had no cares except the pleasant one of attending on her husband, an easy smiling temperament which made her regardless of to-morrow; and, add to this, a delightful hope relative to a certain interesting event which was about to occur, and which I shall not particularise further than by saying, that she was cautioned against too much singing by Mr. Squills, her medical attendant; and that widow Crump was busy making up a vast number of little caps and diminutive cambric shirts, such as delighted GRANDMOTHERS are in the habit of fashioning. I hope this is as genteel a way of signifying the circumstance which was about to take place in the Walker family as Miss Prim herself could desire. Mrs. Walker's mother was about to become a grandmother. There's a phrase! The Morning Post, which says this story is vulgar, I'm sure cannot quarrel with that. I don't believe the whole Court Guide would convey an intimation more delicately.

Well, Mrs. Crump's little grandchild was born, entirely to the dissatisfaction, I must say, of his father; who, when the infant was brought to him in the Fleet, had him abruptly covered up in his cloak again, from which he had been removed by the jealous prison doorkeepers: why, do you think? Walker had a quarrel with one of them, and the wretch persisted in believing that the bundle Mrs. Crump was bringing to her son-in-law was a bundle of disguised brandy!

"The brutes!" said the lady; "and the father's a brute, too," said she. "He takes no more notice of me than if I was a kitchen-maid, and of Woolsey than if he was a leg of mutton—the dear blessed little cherub!"

Mrs. Crump was a mother-in-law; let us pardon her hatred of her daughter's husband.

The Woolsey compared in the above sentence both to a leg of mutton and a cherub, was not the eminent member of the firm of Linsey, Woolsey, and Co., but the little baby, who was christened Howard Woolsey Walker, with the full consent of the father; who said the tailor was a deuced good fellow, and felt really obliged to him for the sherry, for a frock-coat which he let him have in prison, and for his kindness to Morgiana. The tailor loved the little boy with all his soul; he attended his mother to her churching, and the child to the font; and, as a present to his little godson on his christening, he sent two yards of the finest white kerseymere in his shop, to make him a cloak. The Duke had had a pair of inexpressibles off that very piece.

House-furniture is bought and sold, music-lessons are given, children are born and christened, ladies are confined and churched—time, in other words, passes—and yet Captain Walker still remains in prison! Does it not seem strange that he should still languish there between palisaded walls near Fleet Market, and that he should not be restored to that active and fashionable world of which he was an ornament? The fact is, the Captain had been before the court for the examination of his debts; and the Commissioner, with a cruelty quite shameful towards a fallen man, had qualified his ways of getting money in most severe language, and had sent him back to prison again for the space of nine calendar months, an indefinite period, and until his accounts could be made up. This delay Walker bore like a philosopher, and, far from repining, was still the gayest fellow of the tennis-court, and the soul of the midnight carouse.

There is no use in raking up old stories, and hunting through files of dead newspapers, to know what were the specific acts which made the Commissioner so angry with Captain Walker. Many a rogue has come before the Court, and passed through it since then: and I would lay a wager that Howard Walker was not a bit worse than his neighbours. But as he was not a lord, and as he had no friends on coming out of prison, and had settled no money on his wife, and had, as it must be confessed, an exceedingly bad character, it is not likely that the latter would be forgiven him when once more free in the world. For instance, when Doublequits left the Fleet, he was received with open arms by his family, and had two-and-thirty horses in his stables before a week was over. Pam, of the Dragoons, came out, and instantly got a place as government courier—a place found so good of late years (and no wonder, it is better pay than that of a colonel), that our noblemen and gentry eagerly press for it. Frank Hurricane was sent out as registrar of Tobago, or Sago, or Ticonderago; in fact, for a younger son of good family it is rather advantageous to get into debt twenty or thirty thousand pounds: you are sure of a good place afterwards in the colonies. Your friends are so anxious to get rid of you, that they will move heaven and earth to serve you. And so all the above companions of misfortune with Walker were speedily made comfortable; but HE had no rich parents; his old father was dead in York jail. How was he to start in the world again? What friendly hand was there to fill his pocket with gold, and his cup with sparkling champagne? He was, in fact, an object of the greatest pity—for I know of no greater than a gentleman of his habits without the means of gratifying them. He must live well, and he has not the means. Is there a more pathetic case? As for a mere low beggar—some labourless labourer, or some weaver out of place—don't let us throw away our compassion upon THEM. Psha! they're accustomed to starve. They CAN sleep upon boards, or dine off a crust; whereas a gentleman would die in the same situation. I think this was poor Morgiana's way of reasoning. For Walker's cash in prison beginning presently to run low, and knowing quite well that the dear fellow could not exist there without the luxuries to which he had been accustomed, she borrowed money from her mother, until the poor old lady was a sec. She even confessed, with tears, to Woolsey, that she was in particular want of twenty pounds, to pay a poor milliner, whose debt she could not bear to put in her husband's schedule. And I need not say she carried the money to her husband, who might have been greatly benefited by it—only he had a bad run of luck at the cards; and how the deuce can a man help THAT?

Woolsey had repurchased for her one of the Cashmere shawls. She left it behind her one day at the Fleet prison, and some rascal stole it there; having the grace, however, to send Woolsey the ticket, signifying the place where it had been pawned. Who could the scoundrel have been? Woolsey swore a great oath, and fancied he knew; but if it was Walker himself (as Woolsey fancied, and probably as was the case) who made away with the shawl, being pressed thereto by necessity, was it fair to call him a scoundrel for so doing, and should we not rather laud the delicacy of his proceeding? He was poor: who can command the cards? But he did not wish his wife should know How poor: he could not bear that she should suppose him arrived at the necessity of pawning a shawl.

She who had such beautiful ringlets, of a sudden pleaded cold in the head, and took to wearing caps. One summer evening, as she and the baby and Mrs. Crump and Woolsey (let us say all four babies together) were laughing and playing in Mrs. Crump's drawing-room—playing the most absurd gambols, fat Mrs. Crump, for instance, hiding behind the sofa, Woolsey chuck-chucking, cock-a-doodle-dooing, and performing those indescribable freaks which gentlemen with philoprogenitive organs will execute in the company of children—in the midst of their play the baby gave a tug at his mother's cap; off it came—her hair was cut close to her head!

Morgiana turned as red as sealing-wax, and trembled very much; Mrs. Crump screamed, "My child, where is your hair?" and Woolsey, bursting out with a most tremendous oath against Walker that would send Miss Prim into convulsions, put his handkerchief to his face, and actually wept. "The infernal bubble-ubble-ackguard!" said he, roaring and clenching his fists.

As he had passed the Bower of Bloom a few days before, he saw Mossrose, who was combing out a jet-black ringlet, and held it up, as if for Woolsey's examination, with a peculiar grin. The tailor did not understand the joke, but he saw now what had happened. Morgiana had sold her hair for five guineas; she would have sold her arm had her husband bidden her. On looking in her drawers it was found she had sold almost all her wearing apparel; the child's clothes were all there, however. It was because her husband talked of disposing of a gilt coral that the child had, that she had parted with the locks which had formed her pride.

"I'll give you twenty guineas for that hair, you infamous fat coward," roared the little tailor to Eglantine that evening. "Give it up, or I'll kill you-"

"Mr. Mossrose! Mr. Mossrose!" shouted the perfumer.

"Vell, vatsh de matter, vatsh de row, fight avay, my boys; two to one on the tailor," said Mr. Mossrose, much enjoying the sport (for Woolsey, striding through the shop without speaking to him, had rushed into the studio, where he plumped upon Eglantine).

"Tell him about that hair, sir."

"That hair! Now keep yourself quiet, Mister Timble, and don't tink for to bully ME. You mean Mrs. Valker's 'air? Vy, she sold it me."

"And the more blackguard you for buying it! Will you take twenty guineas for it?"

"No," said Mossrose.

"Twenty-five?"

"Can't," said Mossrose.

"Hang it! will you take forty? There!"

"I vish I'd kep it," said the Hebrew gentleman, with unfeigned regret. "Eglantine dressed it this very night."

"For Countess Baldenstiern, the Swedish Hambassador's lady," says Eglantine (his Hebrew partner was by no means a favourite with the ladies, and only superintended the accounts of the concern). "It's this very night at Devonshire 'Ouse, with four hostrich plumes, lappets, and trimmings. And now, Mr. Woolsey, I'll trouble you to apologise."

Mr. Woolsey did not answer, but walked up to Mr. Eglantine, and snapped his fingers so close under the perfumer's nose that the latter started back and seized the bell-rope. Mossrose burst out laughing, and the tailor walked majestically from the shop, with both hands stuck between the lappets of his coat.

"My dear," said he to Morgiana a short time afterwards, "you must not encourage that husband of yours in his extravagance, and sell the clothes off your poor back that he may feast and act the fine gentleman in prison."

"It is his health, poor dear soul!" interposed Mrs. Walker: "his chest. Every farthing of the money goes to the doctors, poor fellow!"

"Well, now listen: I am a rich man" (it was a great fib, for Woolsey's income, as a junior partner of the firm, was but a small one); "I can very well afford to make him an allowance while he is in the Fleet, and have written to him to say so. But if you ever give him a penny, or sell a trinket belonging to you, upon my word and honour I will withdraw the allowance, and, though it would go to my heart, I'll never see you again. You wouldn't make me unhappy, would you?"

"I'd go on my knees to serve you, and Heaven bless you," said the wife.

"Well, then, you must give me this promise." And she did. "And now," said he, "your mother, and Podmore, and I have been talking over matters, and we've agreed that you may make a very good income for yourself; though, to be sure, I wish it could have been managed any other way; but needs must, you know. You're the finest singer in the universe."

"La!" said Morgiana, highly delighted.

"*I* never heard anything like you, though I'm no judge. Podmore says he is sure you will do very well, and has no doubt you might get very good engagements at concerts or on the stage; and as that husband will never do any good, and you have a child to support, sing you must."

"Oh! how glad I should be to pay his debts and repay all he has done for me," cried Mrs. Walker. "Think of his giving two hundred guineas to Mr. Baroski to have me taught. Was not that kind of him? Do you REALLY think I should succeed?

"There's Miss Larkins has succeeded."

"The little high-shouldered vulgar thing!" says Morgiana. "I'm sure I ought to succeed if SHE did."

"She sing against Morgiana?" said Mrs. Crump. "I'd like to see her, indeed! She ain't fit to snuff a candle to her."

"I dare say not," said the tailor, "though I don't understand the thing myself: but if Morgiana can make a fortune, why shouldn't she?"

"Heaven knows we want it, Woolsey," cried Mrs. Crump. "And to see her on the stage was always the wish of my heart:" and so it had formerly been the wish of Morgiana; and now, with the hope of helping her husband and child, the wish became a duty, and she fell to practising once more from morning till night.

One of the most generous of men and tailors who ever lived now promised, if further instruction should be considered necessary (though that he could hardly believe possible), that he would lend Morgiana any sum required for the payment of lessons; and accordingly she once more betook herself, under Podmore's advice, to the singing school. Baroski's academy was, after the passages between them, out of the question, and she placed herself under the instruction of the excellent English composer Sir George Thrum, whose large and awful wife, Lady Thrum, dragon of virtue and propriety, kept watch over the master and the pupils, and was the sternest guardian of female virtue on or off any stage.

Morgiana came at a propitious moment. Baroski had launched Miss Larkins under the name of Ligonier. The Ligonier was enjoying considerable success, and was singing classical music to tolerable audiences; whereas Miss Butts, Sir George's last pupil, had turned out a complete failure, and the rival house was only able to make a faint opposition to the new star with Miss M'Whirter, who, though an old favourite, had lost her upper notes and her front teeth, and, the fact was, drew no longer.

Directly Sir George heard Mrs. Walker, he tapped Podmore, who accompanied her, on the waistcoat, and said, "Poddy, thank you; we'll cut the orange boy's throat with that voice." It was by the familiar title of orange boy that the great Baroski was known among his opponents.

"We'll crush him, Podmore," said Lady Thrum, in her deep hollow voice. "You may stop and dine." And Podmore stayed to dinner, and ate cold mutton, and drank Marsala with the greatest reverence for the great English composer. The very next day Lady Thrum hired a pair of horses, and paid a visit to Mrs. Crump and her daughter at "Sadler's Wells."

All these things were kept profoundly secret from Walker, who received very magnanimously the allowance of two guineas a week which Woolsey made him, and with the aid of the few shillings his wife could bring him, managed to exist as best he might. He did not dislike gin when he could get no claret, and the former liquor, under the name of "tape," used to be measured out pretty liberally in what was formerly Her Majesty's prison of the Fleet.

Morgiana pursued her studies under Thrum, and we shall hear in the next chapter how it was she changed her name to RAVENSWING.

VII

In which Morgiana advances towards fame and honour, and in which several great literary characters make their appearance

"We must begin, my dear madam," said Sir George Thrum, "by unlearning all that Mr. Baroski (of whom I do not wish to speak with the slightest disrespect) has taught you!"

Morgiana knew that every professor says as much, and submitted to undergo the study requisite for Sir George's system with perfect good grace. Au fond, as I was given to understand, the methods of the two artists were pretty similar; but as there was rivalry between them, and continual desertion of scholars from one school to another, it was fair for each to take all the credit he could get in the success of any pupil. If a pupil failed, for instance, Thrum would say Baroski had spoiled her irretrievably; while the German would regret "Dat dat yong voman, who had a good organ, should have trown away her dime wid dat old Drum." When one of these deserters succeeded, "Yes, yes," would either professor cry, "I formed her; she owes her fortune to me." Both of them thus, in future days, claimed the education of the famous Ravenswing; and even Sir George Thrum, though he wished to ecraser the Ligonier, pretended that her present success was his work because once she had been brought by her mother, Mrs. Larkins, to sing for Sir George's approval.

When the two professors met it was with the most delighted cordiality on the part of both. "Mein lieber Herr," Thrum would say (with some malice), "your sonata in x flat is divine." "Chevalier," Baroski would reply, "dat andante movement in w is worthy of Beethoven. I gif you my sacred honour," and so forth. In fact, they loved each other as gentlemen in their profession always do.

The two famous professors conduct their academies on very opposite principles. Baroski writes ballet music; Thrum, on the contrary, says "he cannot but deplore the dangerous fascinations of the dance," and writes more for Exeter Hall and Birmingham. While Baroski drives a cab in the Park with a very suspicious Mademoiselle Leocadie, or Amenaide, by his side, you may see Thrum walking to evening church with his lady, and hymns are sung there of his own composition. He belongs to the "Athenaeum Club," he goes to the Levee once a year, he does everything that a respectable man should; and if, by the means of this respectability, he manages to make his little trade far more profitable than it otherwise would be, are we to quarrel with him for it?

Sir George, in fact, had every reason to be respectable. He had been a choir-boy at Windsor, had played to the old King's violoncello, had been intimate with him, and had received knighthood at the hand of his revered sovereign. He had a snuff-box which His Majesty gave him, and portraits of him and the young princes all over the house. He had also a foreign order (no other, indeed, than the Elephant and Castle of Kalbsbraten-Pumpernickel), conferred upon him by the Grand Duke when here with the allied sovereigns in 1814. With this ribbon round his neck, on gala days, and in a white waistcoat, the old gentleman looked splendid as he moved along in a blue coat with the Windsor button, and neat black small-clothes, and silk stockings. He lived in an old tall dingy house, furnished in the reign of George III, his beloved master, and not much more cheerful now than a family vault. They are awfully funereal, those ornaments of the close of the last century— tall gloomy horse-hair chairs, mouldy Turkey carpets with wretched druggets to guard them, little cracked sticking-plaster miniatures of people in tours and pigtails over high-shouldered mantelpieces, two dismal urns on each side of a lanky sideboard, and in the midst a queer twisted receptacle for worn-out knives with green handles. Under the sideboard stands a cellaret that looks as if it held half a bottle of currant wine, and a shivering plate-warmer that never could get any comfort out of the wretched old cramped grate yonder. Don't you know in such houses the grey gloom that hangs over the stairs, the dull-coloured old carpet that winds its way up the same, growing thinner, duller, and more threadbare as it mounts to the bedroom floors? There is something awful in the bedroom of a respectable old couple of sixty-five. Think of the old feathers, turbans, bugles, petticoats, pomatum-pots, spencers, white satin shoes, false fronts, the old flaccid boneless stays tied up in faded riband, the dusky fans, the old forty-years-old baby linen, the letters of Sir George when he was young, the doll of poor Maria who died in 1803, Frederick's first corduroy breeches, and the newspaper which contains the account of his distinguishing himself at the siege of Seringapatam. All these lie somewhere, damp and squeezed down into glum old presses and wardrobes. At that glass the wife has sat many times these fifty years; in that old morocco bed her children were born. Where are they now? Fred the brave captain, and Charles the saucy colleger: there hangs a drawing of him done by Mr. Beechey, and that sketch by Cosway was the very likeness of Louisa before—

"Mr. Fitz-Boodle! for Heaven's sake come down. What are you doing in a lady's bedroom?"

"The fact is, madam, I had no business there in life; but, having had quite enough wine with Sir George, my thoughts had wandered upstairs into the sanctuary of female excellence, where your Ladyship nightly reposes. You do not sleep so well now as in old days, though there is no patter of little steps to wake you overhead."

They call that room the nursery still, and the little wicket still hangs at the upper stairs: it has been there for forty years—bon Dieu! Can't you see the ghosts of little faces peering over it? I wonder whether they get up in the night as the moonlight shines into the blank vacant old room, and play there solemnly with little ghostly horses, and the spirits of dolls, and tops that turn and turn but don't hum.

Once more, sir, come down to the lower storey—that is to the Morgiana story—with which the above sentences have no more to do than this morning's leading article in The Times; only it was at this house of Sir George Thrum's that I met Morgiana. Sir George, in old days, had instructed some of the female members of our family, and I recollect cutting my fingers as a child with one of those attenuated green-handled knives in the queer box yonder.

In those days Sir George Thrum was the first great musical teacher of London, and the royal patronage brought him a great number of fashionable pupils, of whom Lady Fitz-Boodle was one. It was a long long time ago: in fact, Sir George Thrum was old enough to remember persons who had been present at Mr. Braham's first appearance, and the old gentleman's days of triumph had been those of Billington and Incledon, Catalani and Madame Storace.

He was the author of several operas ("The Camel Driver," "Britons Alarmed; or, the Siege of Bergen-op-Zoom," etc. etc.), and, of course, of songs which had considerable success in their day, but are forgotten now, and are as much faded and out of fashion as those old carpets which we have described in the professor's house, and which were, doubtless, very brilliant once. But such is the fate of carpets, of flowers, of music, of men, and of the most admirable novels—even this story will not be alive for many centuries. Well, well, why struggle against Fate?

But, though his heyday of fashion was gone, Sir George still held his place among the musicians of the old school, conducted occasionally at the Ancient Concerts and the Philharmonic, and his glees are still favourites after public dinners, and are sung by those old bacchanalians, in chestnut wigs, who attend for the purpose of amusing the guests on such occasions of festivity. The great old people at the gloomy old concerts before mentioned always pay Sir George marked respect; and, indeed, from the old gentleman's peculiar behaviour to his superiors, it is impossible they should not be delighted with him, so he leads at almost every one of the concerts in the old-fashioned houses in town.

Becomingly obsequious to his superiors, he is with the rest of the world properly majestic, and has obtained no small success by his admirable and undeviating respectability. Respectability has been his great card through life; ladies can trust their daughters at Sir George Thrum's academy. "A good musician, madam," says he to the mother of a new pupil, "should not only have a fine ear, a good voice, and an indomitable industry, but, above all, a faultless character—faultless, that is, as far as our poor nature will permit. And you will remark that those young persons with whom your lovely daughter, Miss Smith, will pursue her musical studies, are all, in a moral point of view, as spotless as that charming young lady. How should it be otherwise? I have been myself the father of a family; I have been honoured with the intimacy of the wisest and best of kings, my late sovereign George III, and I can proudly show an example of decorum to my pupils in my Sophia. Mrs. Smith, I have the honour of introducing to you my Lady Thrum."

The old lady would rise at this, and make a gigantic curtsey, such a one as had begun the minuet at Ranelagh fifty years ago; and, the introduction ended, Mrs. Smith would retire, after having seen the portraits of the princes, his late Majesty's snuff-box, and a piece of music which he used to play, noted by himself—Mrs. Smith, I say, would drive back to Baker Street, delighted to think that her Frederica had secured so eligible and respectable a master. I forgot to say that, during the interview between Mrs. Smith and Sir George, the latter would be called out of his study by his black servant, and my Lady Thrum would take that opportunity of mentioning when he was knighted, and how he got his foreign order, and deploring the sad condition of OTHER musical professors, and the dreadful immorality which sometimes arose in consequence of their laxness. Sir George was a good deal engaged to dinners in the season, and if invited to dine with a nobleman, as he might possibly be on the day when Mrs. Smith requested the honour of his company, he would write back "that he should have had the sincerest happiness in waiting upon Mrs. Smith in Baker Street, if, previously, my Lord Tweedledale had not been so kind as to engage him." This letter, of course, shown by Mrs. Smith to her friends, was received by them with proper respect; and thus, in spite of age and new fashions, Sir George still reigned pre-eminent for a mile round Cavendish Square. By the young pupils of the academy he was called Sir Charles Grandison; and, indeed, fully deserved this title on account of the indomitable respectability of his whole actions.

It was under this gentleman that Morgiana made her debut in public life. I do not know what arrangements may have been made between Sir George Thrum and his pupil regarding the profits which were to accrue to the former from engagements procured by him for the latter; but there was, no doubt, an understanding between them. For Sir George, respectable as he was, had the reputation of being extremely clever at a bargain; and Lady Thrum herself, in her great high-tragedy way, could purchase a pair of soles or select a leg of mutton with the best housekeeper in London.

When, however, Morgiana had been for some six months under his tuition, he began, for some reason or other, to be exceedingly hospitable, and invited his friends to numerous entertainments: at one of which, as I have said, I had the pleasure of meeting Mrs. Walker.

Although the worthy musician's dinners were not good, the old knight had some excellent wine in his cellar, and his arrangement of his party deserves to be commended.

For instance, he meets me and Bob Fitz-Urse in Pall Mall, at whose paternal house he was also a visitor. "My dear young gentlemen," says he, "will you come and dine with a poor musical composer? I have some Comet hock, and, what is more curious to you, perhaps, as men of wit, one or two of the great literary characters of London whom you would like to see—quite curiosities, my dear young friends." And we agreed to go.

To the literary men he says: "I have a little quiet party at home: Lord Roundtowers, the Honourable Mr. Fitz-Urse of the Life Guards, and a few more. Can you tear yourself away from the war of wits, and take a quiet dinner with a few mere men about town?"

The literary men instantly purchase new satin stocks and white gloves, and are delighted to fancy themselves members of the world of fashion. Instead of inviting twelve Royal Academicians, or a dozen authors, or a dozen men of science to dinner, as his Grace the Duke of—and the Right Honourable Sir Robert—are in the habit of doing once a year, this plan of fusion is the one they should adopt. Not invite all artists, as they would invite all farmers to a rent dinner; but they should have a proper commingling of artists and men of the world. There is one of the latter whose name is George Savage Fitz-Boodle, who—But let us return to Sir George Thrum.

Fitz-Urse and I arrive at the dismal old house, and are conducted up the staircase by a black servant, who shouts out, "Missa Fiss-Boodle—the HONOURABLE Missa Fiss-Urse!" It was evident that Lady Thrum had instructed the swarthy groom of the chambers (for there is nothing particularly honourable in my friend Fitz's face that I know of, unless an abominable squint may be said to be so). Lady Thrum, whose figure is something like that of the shot-tower opposite Waterloo Bridge, makes a majestic inclination and a speech to signify her pleasure at receiving under her roof two of the children of Sir George's best pupils. A lady in black velvet is seated by the old fireplace, with whom a stout gentleman in an exceedingly light coat and ornamental waistcoat is talking very busily. "The great star of the night," whispers our host. "Mrs. Walker, gentlemen—the RAVENSWING! She is talking to the famous Mr. Slang, of the—Theatre."

"Is she a fine singer?" says Fitz-Urse. "She's a very fine woman."

"My dear young friends, you shall hear to-night! I, who have heard every fine voice in Europe, confidently pledge my respectability that the Ravenswing is equal to them all. She has the graces, sir, of a Venus with the mind of a Muse. She is a siren, sir, without the dangerous qualities of one. She is hallowed, sir, by her misfortunes as by her genius; and I am proud to think that my instructions have been the means of developing the wondrous qualities that were latent within her until now."

"You don't say so!" says gobemouche Fitz-Urse.

Having thus indoctrinated Mr. Fitz-Urse, Sir George takes another of his guests, and proceeds to work upon him. "My dear Mr. Bludyer, how do you do? Mr. Fitz-Boodle, Mr. Bludyer, the brilliant and accomplished wit, whose sallies in the Tomahawk delight us every Saturday. Nay, no blushes, my dear sir; you are very wicked, but oh! So pleasant. Well, Mr. Bludyer, I am glad to see you, sir, and hope you will have a favourable opinion of our genius, sir. As I was saying to Mr. Fitz-Boodle, she has the graces of a Venus with the mind of a Muse. She is a siren, without the dangerous qualities of one," etc. This little speech was made to half-a-dozen persons in the course of the evening—persons, for the most part, connected with the public journals or the theatrical world. There was Mr. Squinny, the editor of the Flowers of Fashion; Mr. Desmond Mulligan, the poet, and reporter for a morning paper; and other worthies of their calling. For though Sir George is a respectable man, and as high-minded and moral an old gentleman as ever wore knee-buckles, he does not neglect the little arts of popularity, and can condescend to receive very queer company if need be.

For instance, at the dinner-party at which I had the honour of assisting, and at which, on the right hand of Lady Thrum, sat the oblige nobleman, whom the Thrums were a great deal too wise to omit (the sight of a lord does good to us commoners, or why else should we be so anxious to have one?). In the second place of honour, and on her ladyship's left hand, sat Mr. Slang, the manager of one of the theatres; a gentleman whom my Lady Thrum would scarcely, but for a great necessity's sake, have been induced to invite to her table. He had the honour of leading Mrs. Walker to dinner, who looked splendid in black velvet and turban, full of health and smiles.

Lord Roundtowers is an old gentleman who has been at the theatres five times a week for these fifty years, a living dictionary of the stage, recollecting every actor and actress who has appeared upon it for half a century. He perfectly well remembered Miss Delancy in Morgiana; he knew what had become of Ali Baba, and how Cassim had left the stage, and was now the keeper of a public-house. All this store of knowledge he kept quietly to himself, or only delivered in confidence to his next neighbour in the intervals of the banquet, which he enjoys prodigiously. He lives at an hotel: if not invited to dine, eats a mutton-chop very humbly at his club, and finishes his evening after the play at Crockford's, whither he goes not for the sake of the play, but of the supper there. He is described in the Court Guide as of "Simmer's Hotel," and of Roundtowers, county Cork. It is said that the round towers really exist. But he has not been in Ireland since the rebellion; and his property is so hampered with ancestral mortgages, and rent-charges, and annuities, that his income is barely sufficient to provide the modest mutton-chop before alluded to. He has, any time these fifty years, lived in the wickedest company in London, and is, withal, as harmless, mild, good-natured, innocent an old gentleman as can readily be seen.

"Roundy," shouts the elegant Mr. Slang, across the table, with a voice which makes Lady Thrum shudder, "Tuff, a glass of wine."

My Lord replies meekly, "Mr. Slang, I shall have very much pleasure. What shall it be?"

"There is Madeira near you, my Lord," says my Lady, pointing to a tall thin decanter of the fashion of the year.

"Madeira! Marsala, by Jove, your Ladyship means!" shouts Mr. Slang. "No, no, old birds are not caught with chaff. Thrum, old boy, let's have some of your Comet hock."

"My Lady Thrum, I believe that Is Marsala," says the knight, blushing a little, in reply to a question from his Sophia. "Ajax, the hock to Mr. Slang."

"I'm in that," yells Bludyer from the end of the table. "My Lord, I'll join you."

"Mr.—, I beg your pardon—I shall be very happy to take wine with you, sir."

"It is Mr. Bludyer, the celebrated newspaper writer," whispers Lady Thrum.

"Bludyer, Bludyer? A very clever man, I dare say. He has a very loud voice, and reminds me of Brett. Does your Ladyship remember Brett, who played the 'Fathers' at the Haymarket in 1802?"

"What an old stupid Roundtowers is!" says Slang, archly, nudging Mrs. Walker in the side. "How's Walker, eh?"

"My husband is in the country," replied Mrs. Walker, hesitatingly.

"Gammon! I know where he is! Law bless you!—don't blush. I've been there myself a dozen times. We were talking about quod, Lady Thrum. Were you ever in college?"

"I was at the Commemoration at Oxford in 1814, when the sovereigns were there, and at Cambridge when Sir George received his degree of Doctor of Music."

"Laud, Laud, THAT's not the college WE mean."

"There is also the college in Gower Street, where my grandson—"

"This is the college in QUEER STREET, ma'am, haw, haw! Mulligan, you divvle (in an Irish accent), a glass of wine with you. Wine, here, you waiter! What's your name, you black nigger? 'Possum up a gum-tree, eh? Fill him up. Dere he go" (imitating the Mandingo manner of speaking English)

In this agreeable way would Mr. Slang rattle on, speedily making himself the centre of the conversation, and addressing graceful familiarities to all the gentlemen and ladies round him.

It was good to see how the little knight, the most moral and calm of men, was compelled to receive Mr. Slang's stories and the frightened air with which, at the conclusion of one of them, he would venture upon a commendatory grin. His lady, on her part too, had been laboriously civil; and, on the occasion on which I had the honour of meeting this gentleman and Mrs. Walker, it was the latter who gave the signal for withdrawing to the lady of the house, by saying, "I think, Lady Thrum, it is quite time for us to retire." Some exquisite joke of Mr. Slang's was the cause of this abrupt disappearance. But, as they went upstairs to the drawing-room, Lady Thrum took occasion to say, "My dear, in the course of your profession you will have to submit to many such familiarities on the part of persons of low breeding, such as I fear Mr. Slang is. But let me caution you against giving way to your temper as you did. Did you not perceive that *I* never allowed him to see my inward dissatisfaction? And I make it a particular point that you should be very civil to him to-night. Your interests—our interests depend upon it."

"And are my interests to make me civil to a wretch like that?"

"Mrs. Walker, would you wish to give lessons in morality and behaviour to Lady Thrum?" said the old lady, drawing herself up with great dignity. It was evident that she had a very strong desire indeed to conciliate Mr. Slang; and hence I have no doubt that Sir George was to have a considerable share of Morgiana's earnings.

Mr. Bludyer, the famous editor of the Tomahawk, whose jokes Sir George pretended to admire so much (Sir George who never made a joke in his life), was a press bravo of considerable talent and no principle, and who, to use his own words, would "back himself for a slashing article against any man in England!" He would not only write, but fight on a pinch; was a good scholar, and as savage in his manner as with his pen. Mr. Squinny is of exactly the opposite school, as delicate as milk-and-water, harmless in his habits, fond of the flute when the state of his chest will allow him, a great practiser of waltzing and dancing in general, and in his journal mildly malicious. He never goes beyond the bounds of politeness, but manages to insinuate a great deal that is disagreeable to an author in the course of twenty lines of criticism. Personally he is quite respectable, and lives with two maiden aunts at Brompton. Nobody, on the contrary, knows where Mr. Bludyer lives. He has houses of call, mysterious taverns, where he may be found at particular hours by those who need him, and where panting publishers are in the habit of hunting him up. For a bottle of wine and a guinea he will write a page of praise or abuse of any man living, or on any subject, or on any line of politics. "Hang it, sir!" says he, "pay me enough and I will write down my own father!" According to the state of his credit, he is dressed either almost in rags or else in the extremest flush of the fashion. With the latter attire he puts on a haughty and aristocratic air, and would slap a duke on the shoulder. If there is one thing more dangerous than to refuse to lend him a sum of money when he asks for it, it is to lend it to him; for he never pays, and never pardons a man to whom he owes. "Walker refused to cash a bill for me," he had been heard to say, "and I'll do for his wife when she comes out on the stage!" Mrs. Walker and Sir George Thrum were in an agony about the Tomahawk; hence the latter's invitation to Mr. Bludyer. Sir George was in a great tremor about the Flowers of Fashion, hence his invitation to Mr. Squinny. Mr. Squinny was introduced to Lord Roundtowers and Mr. Fitz-Urse as one of the most delightful and talented of our young men of genius; and Fitz, who believes everything anyone tells him, was quite pleased to have the honour of sitting near the live editor of a paper. I have reason to think that Mr. Squinny himself was no less delighted: I saw him giving his card to Fitz-Urse at the end of the second course.

No particular attention was paid to Mr. Desmond Mulligan. Political enthusiasm is his forte. He lives and writes in a rapture. He is, of course, a member of an inn of court, and greatly addicted to after-dinner speaking as a preparation for the bar, where as a young man of genius he hopes one day to shine. He is almost the only man to whom Bludyer is civil; for, if the latter will fight doggedly when there is a necessity for so doing, the former fights like an Irishman, and has a pleasure in it. He has been "on the ground" I don't know how many times, and quitted his country on account of a quarrel with Government regarding certain articles published by him in the Phoenix newspaper. With the third bottle, he becomes overpoweringly great on the wrongs of Ireland, and at that period generally volunteers a couple or more of Irish melodies, selecting the most melancholy in the collection. At five in the afternoon, you are sure to see him about the House of Commons, and he knows the "Reform Club" (he calls it the Refawrum) as well as if he were a member. It is curious for the contemplative mind to mark those mysterious hangers-on of Irish members of Parliament—strange runners and aides-de-camp which all the honourable gentlemen appear to possess. Desmond, in his political capacity, is one of these, and besides his calling as reporter to a newspaper, is "our well-informed correspondent" of that famous Munster paper, the Green Flag of Skibbereen.

With Mr. Mulligan's qualities and history I only became subsequently acquainted. On the present evening he made but a brief stay at the dinner-table, being compelled by his professional duties to attend the House of Commons.

The above formed the party with whom I had the honour to dine. What other repasts Sir George Thrum may have given, what assemblies of men of mere science he may have invited to give their opinion regarding his prodigy, what other editors of papers he may have pacified or rendered favourable, who knows? On the present occasion, we did not quit the dinner-table until Mr. Slang the manager was considerably excited by wine, and music had been heard for some time in the drawing-room overhead during our absence. An addition had been made to the Thrum party by the arrival of several persons to spend the evening,—a man to play on the violin between the singing, a youth to play on the piano, Miss Horsman to sing with Mrs. Walker, and other scientific characters. In a corner sat a red-faced old lady, of whom the mistress of the mansion took little notice; and a gentleman with a royal button, who blushed and looked exceedingly modest.

"Hang me!" says Mr. Bludyer, who had perfectly good reasons for recognising Mr. Woolsey, and who on this day chose to assume his aristocratic air; "there's a tailor in the room! What do they mean by asking ME to meet tradesmen?"

"Delancy, my dear," cries Slang, entering the room with a reel, "how's your precious health? Give us your hand! When ARE we to be married? Make room for me on the sofa, that's a duck!"

"Get along, Slang," says Mrs. Crump, addressed by the manager by her maiden name (artists generally drop the title of honour which people adopt in the world, and call each other by their simple surnames)—"get along, Slang, or I'll tell Mrs. S.!" The enterprising manager replies by sportively striking Mrs. Crump on the side a blow which causes a great giggle from the lady insulted, and a most good-humoured threat to box Slang's ears. I fear very much that Morgiana's mother thought Mr. Slang an exceedingly gentlemanlike and agreeable person; besides, she was eager to have his good opinion of Mrs. Walker's singing.

WILLIAM MAKEPEACE THACKERAY

The manager stretched himself out with much gracefulness on the sofa, supporting two little dumpy legs encased in varnished boots on a chair.

"Ajax, some tea to Mr. Slang," said my Lady, looking towards that gentleman with a countenance expressive of some alarm, I thought.

"That's right, Ajax, my black prince!" exclaimed Slang when the negro brought the required refreshment; "and now I suppose you'll be wanted in the orchestra yonder. Don't Ajax play the cymbals, Sir George?"

"Ha, ha, ha! very good—capital!" answered the knight, exceedingly frightened; "but ours is not a MILITARY band. Miss Horsman, Mr. Craw, my dear Mrs. Ravenswing, shall we begin the trio? Silence, gentlemen, if you please; it is a little piece from my opera of the 'Brigand's Bride.' Miss Horsman takes the Page's part, Mr. Craw is Stiletto the Brigand, my accomplished pupil is the Bride;" and the music began.

The Bride

"My heart with joy is beating,
My eyes with tears are dim;

The Page

"Her heart with joy is beating
Her eyes are fixed on him;

The Brigand

"My heart with rage is beating,
In blood my eye-balls swim!"

What may have been the merits of the music or the singing, I, of course, cannot guess. Lady Thrum sat opposite the tea-cups, nodding her head and beating time very gravely. Lord Roundtowers, by her side, nodded his head too, for awhile, and then fell asleep. I should have done the same but for the manager, whose actions were worth of remark. He sang with all the three singers, and a great deal louder than any of them; he shouted bravo! or hissed as he thought proper; he criticised all the points of Mrs. Walker's person. "She'll do, Crump, she'll do—a splendid arm—you'll see her eyes in the shilling gallery! What sort of a foot has she? She's five feet three, if she's an inch! Bravo—slap up—capital—hurrah!" And he concluded by saying, with the aid of the Ravenswing, he would put Ligonier's nose out of Joint!

The enthusiasm of Mr. Slang almost reconciled Lady Thrum to the abruptness of his manners, and even caused Sir George to forget that his chorus had been interrupted by the obstreperous familiarity of the manager.

"And what do You think, Mr. Bludyer," said the tailor, delighted that his protegee should be thus winning all hearts: "isn't Mrs. Walker a tip-top singer, eh, sir?"

"I think she's a very bad one, Mr. Woolsey," said the illustrious author, wishing to abbreviate all communications with a tailor to whom he owed forty pounds.

"Then, sir," says Mr. Woolsey, fiercely, "I'll—I'll thank you to pay me my little bill!"

It is true there was no connection between Mrs. Walker's singing and Woolsey's little bill; that the "Then, sir," was perfectly illogical on Woolsey's part; but it was a very happy hit for the future fortunes of Mrs. Walker. Who knows what would have come of her debut but for that "Then, sir," and whether a "smashing article" from the Tomahawk might not have ruined her for ever?

"Are you a relation of Mrs. Walker's?" said Mr. Bludyer, in reply to the angry tailor.

"What's that to you, whether I am or not?" replied Woolsey, fiercely. "But I'm the friend of Mrs. Walker, sir; proud am I to say so, sir; and, as the poet says, sir, 'a little learning's a dangerous thing,' sir; and I think a man who don't pay his bills may keep his tongue quiet at least, sir, and not abuse a lady, sir, whom everybody else praises, sir. You shan't humbug Me any more, sir; you shall hear from my attorney to-morrow, so mark that!"

"Hush, my dear Mr. Woolsey," cried the literary man, "don't make a noise; come into this window: is Mrs. Walker Really a friend of yours?"

"I've told you so, sir."

"Well, in that case, I shall do my utmost to serve her and, look you, Woolsey, any article you choose to send about her to the Tomahawk I promise you I'll put in."

"Will you, though? then we'll say nothing about the little bill."

"You may do on that point," answered Bludyer, haughtily, "exactly as you please. I am not to be frightened from my duty, mind that; and mind, too, that I can write a slashing article better than any man in England: I could crush her by ten lines."

The tables were now turned, and it was Woolsey's turn to be alarmed.

"Pooh! pooh! I Was angry," said he, "because you abuse Mrs. Walker, who's an angel on earth; but I'm very willing to apologise. I say—come—let me take your measure for some new clothes, eh! Mr. B.?"

"I'll come to your shop," answered the literary man, quite appeased. "Silence! they're beginning another song."

The songs, which I don't attempt to describe (and, upon my word and honour, as far as I can understand matters, I believe to this day that Mrs. Walker was only an ordinary singer)—the songs lasted a great deal longer than I liked; but I was nailed, as it were, to the spot, having agreed to sup at Knightsbridge barracks with Fitz-Urse, whose carriage was ordered at eleven o'clock.

"My dear Mr. Fitz-Boodle," said our old host to me, "you can do me the greatest service in the world."

"Speak, sir!" said I.

"Will you ask your honourable and gallant friend, the Captain, to drive home Mr. Squinny to Brompton?"

"Can't Mr. Squinny get a cab?"

Sir George looked particularly arch. "Generalship, my dear young friend—a little harmless generalship. Mr. Squinny will not give much for My opinion of my pupil, but he will value very highly the opinion of the Honourable Mr. FitzUrse."

For a moral man, was not the little knight a clever fellow? He had bought Mr. Squinny for a dinner worth ten shillings, and for a ride in a carriage with a lord's son. Squinny was carried to Brompton, and set down at his aunts' door, delighted with his new friends, and exceedingly sick with a cigar they had made him smoke.

VIII

IN WHICH MR. WALKER SHOWS GREAT
PRUDENCE AND FORBEARANCE

The describing of all these persons does not advance Morgiana's story much. But, perhaps, some country readers are not acquainted with the class of persons by whose printed opinions they are guided, and are simple enough to imagine that mere merit will make a reputation on the stage or elsewhere. The making of a theatrical success is a much more complicated and curious thing than such persons fancy it to be. Immense are the pains taken to get a good word from Mr. This of the Star, or Mr. That of the Courier, to propitiate the favour of the critic of the day, and get the editors of the metropolis into a good humour,—above all, to have the name of the person to be puffed perpetually before the public. Artists cannot be advertised like Macassar oil or blacking, and they want it to the full as much; hence endless ingenuity must be practised in order to keep the popular attention awake. Suppose a great actor moves from London to Windsor, the Brentford Champion must state that "Yesterday Mr. Blazes and suite passed rapidly through our city; the celebrated comedian is engaged, we hear, at Windsor, to give some of his inimitable readings of our great national bard to the MOST ILLUSTRIOUS AUDIENCE in the realm." This piece of intelligence the Hammersmith Observer will question the next week, as thus:—"A contemporary, the Brentford Champion, says that Blazes is engaged to give Shakspearian readings at Windsor to "the most illustrious audience in the realm." We question this fact very much. We would, indeed, that it were true; but the MOST ILLUSTRIOUS AUDIENCE in the realm prefer FOREIGN melodies to THE NATIVE WOOD-NOTES WILD of the sweet song-bird of Avon. Mr. Blazes is simply gone to Eton, where his son, Master Massinger Blazes, is suffering, we regret to hear, under a severe attack of the chicken-pox. This complaint (incident to youth) has raged, we understand, with frightful virulence in Eton School."

And if, after the above paragraphs, some London paper chooses to attack the folly of the provincial press, which talks of Mr. Blazes, and chronicles his movements, as if he were a crowned head, what harm is done? Blazes can write in his own name to the London journal, and say that it is not His fault if provincial journals choose to chronicle his movements, and that he was far from wishing that the afflictions of those who are dear to him should form the subject of public comment, and be held up to public ridicule. "We had no intention of hurting the feelings of an estimable public servant," writes the editor; "and our remarks on the chicken-pox were general, not personal. We sincerely trust that Master Massinger Blazes has recovered from that complaint, and that he may pass through the measles, the whooping-cough, the fourth form, and all other diseases to which youth is subject, with comfort to himself, and credit to his parents and teachers." At his next appearance on the stage after this controversy, a British public calls for Blazes three times after the play; and somehow there is sure to be someone with a laurel-wreath in a stage-box, who flings that chaplet at the inspired artist's feet.

I don't know how it was, but before the debut of Morgiana, the English press began to heave and throb in a convulsive manner, as if indicative of the near birth of some great thing. For instance, you read in one paper,—

"Anecdote of Karl Maria Von Weber.—When the author of 'Oberon' was in England, he was invited by a noble duke to dinner, and some of the most celebrated of our artists were assembled to meet him. The signal being given to descend to the salle-a-manger, the German composer was invited by his noble host (a bachelor) to lead the way. 'Is it not the fashion in your country,' said he, simply, 'for the man of the first eminence to take the first place? Here is one whose genius entitles him to be first Anywhere.' And, so saying, he pointed to our admirable English composer, Sir George Thrum. The two musicians were friends to the last, and Sir George has still the identical piece of rosin which the author of the 'Freischutz' gave him."—The Moon (morning paper), June 2.

"George III. a composer.—Sir George Thrum has in his possession the score of an air, the words from 'Samson Agonistes,' an autograph of the late revered monarch. We hear that that excellent composer has in store for us not only an opera, but a pupil, with whose transcendent merits the elite of our aristocracy are already familiar."—Ibid., June 5.

"Music with a Vengeance.—The march to the sound of which the 49th and 75th regiments rushed up the breach of Badajoz was the celebrated air from 'Britons Alarmed; or, The Siege of Bergen-op-Zoom,' by our famous English composer, Sir George Thrum. Marshal Davoust said that the French line never stood when that air was performed to the charge of the bayonet. We hear the veteran musician has an opera now about to appear, and have no doubt that Old England will now, as then, show its superiority over ALL foreign opponents."—Albion.

"We have been accused of preferring the produit of the etranger to the talent of our own native shores; but those who speak so, little know us. We are fanatici per la musica wherever it be, and welcome merit dans chaque pays du monde. What do we say? Le merite n'a point de pays, as Napoleon said; and Sir George Thrum (Chevalier de l'Ordre de l'Elephant et Chateau de Kalbsbraten-Pumpernickel,) is a maestro whose fame appartient a l'Europe.

"We have just heard the lovely eleve, whose rare qualities the Cavaliere has brought to perfection,—we have heard THE RAVENSWING (pourquoi cacher un nom que demain un monde va saluer?), and a creature more beautiful and gifted never bloomed before dans nos climats. She sang the delicious duet of the 'Nabucodonosore,' with Count Pizzicato, with a bellezza, a grandezza, a raggio, that excited in the bosom of the audience a corresponding furore: her scherzando was exquisite, though we confess we thought the concluding fioritura in the passage in Y flat a leetle, a very leetle sforzata. Surely the words,

> *'Giorno d'orrore,*
> *Delire, dolore,*
> *Nabucodonosore,'*

should be given andante, and not con strepito: but this is a faute bien legere in the midst of such unrivalled excellence, and only mentioned here that we may have SOMETHING to criticise.

"We hear that the enterprising impresario of one of the royal theatres has made an engagement with the Diva; and, if we have a regret, it is that she should be compelled to sing in the unfortunate language of our rude northern clime, which does not preter itself near so well to the bocca of the cantatrice as do the mellifluous accents of the Lingua Toscana, the langue par excellence of song.

"The Ravenswing's voice is a magnificent contra-basso of nine octaves," etc.—Flowers of Fashion, June 10.

"Old Thrum, the composer, is bringing out an opera and a pupil. The opera is good, the pupil first-rate. The opera will do much more than compete with the infernal twaddle and disgusting slip-slop of Donizetti, and the milk-and-water fools who imitate him: it will (and we ask the readers of the Tomahawk, were we EVER mistaken?) surpass all these; it is GOOD, of downright English stuff. The airs are fresh and pleasing, the choruses large and noble, the instrumentation solid and rich, the music is carefully written. We wish old Thrum and his opera well.

"His pupil is a SURE CARD, a splendid woman, and a splendid singer. She is so handsome that she might sing as much out of tune as Miss Ligonier, and the public would forgive her; and sings so well, that were she as ugly as the aforesaid Ligonier, the audience would listen to her. The Ravenswing, that is her fantastical theatrical name (her real name is the same with that of a notorious scoundrel in the Fleet, who invented the Panama swindle, the Pontine Marshes' swindle, the Soap swindle— How ARE YOU OFF FOR SOAP Now, Mr. W-lk-r?)—the Ravenswing, we say, will do. Slang has engaged her at thirty guineas per week, and she appears next month in Thrum's opera, of which the words are written by a great ass with some talent—we mean Mr. Mulligan.

"There is a foreign fool in the Flowers of Fashion who is doing his best to disgust the public by his filthy flattery. It is enough to make one sick. Why is the foreign beast not kicked out of the paper?"—The Tomahawk, June 17.

The first three "anecdotes" were supplied by Mulligan to his paper, with many others which need not here be repeated: he kept them up with amazing energy and variety. Anecdotes of Sir George Thrum met you unexpectedly in queer corners of country papers: puffs of the English school of music appeared perpetually in "Notices to Correspondents" in the Sunday prints, some of which Mr. Slang commanded, and in others over which the indefatigable Mulligan had a control. This youth was the soul of the little conspiracy for raising Morgiana into fame: and humble as he is, and great and respectable as is Sir George Thrum, it is my belief that the Ravenswing would never have been the Ravenswing she is but for the ingenuity and energy of the honest Hibernian reporter.

It is only the business of the great man who writes the leading articles which appear in the large type of the daily papers to compose those astonishing pieces of eloquence; the other parts of the paper are left to the ingenuity of the sub-editor, whose duty it is to select paragraphs, reject or receive horrid accidents, police reports, etc.; with which, occupied as he is in the exercise of his tremendous functions, the editor himself cannot be expected to meddle. The fate of Europe is his province; the rise and fall of empires, and the great questions of State demand the editor's attention: the humble puff, the paragraph about the last murder, or the state of the crops, or the sewers in Chancery Lane, is confided to the care of the sub; and it is curious to see what a prodigious number of Irishmen exist among the sub-editors of London. When the Liberator enumerates the services of his countrymen, how the battle of Fontenoy was won by the Irish Brigade, how the battle of Waterloo would have been lost but for the Irish regiments, and enumerates other acts for which we are indebted to Milesian heroism and genius—he ought at least to mention the Irish brigade of the press, and the amazing services they do to this country.

The truth is, the Irish reporters and soldiers appear to do their duty right well; and my friend Mr. Mulligan is one of the former. Having the interests of his opera and the Ravenswing strongly at heart, and being amongst his brethren an exceedingly popular fellow, he managed matters so that never a day passed but some paragraph appeared somewhere regarding the new singer, in whom, for their countryman's sake, all his brothers and sub-editors felt an interest.

These puffs, destined to make known to all the world the merits of the Ravenswing, of course had an effect upon a gentleman very closely connected with that lady, the respectable prisoner in the Fleet, Captain Walker. As long as he received his weekly two guineas from Mr. Woolsey, and the occasional half-crowns which his wife could spare in her almost daily visits to him, he had never troubled himself to inquire what her pursuits were, and had allowed her (though the worthy woman longed with all her might to betray herself) to keep her secret. He was far from thinking, indeed, that his wife would prove such a treasure to him.

But when the voice of fame and the columns of the public journals brought him each day some new story regarding the merits, genius, and beauty of the Ravenswing; when rumours reached him that she was the favourite pupil of Sir George Thrum; when she brought him five guineas after singing at the "Philharmonic" (other five the good soul had spent in purchasing some smart new cockades, hats, cloaks, and laces, for her little son); when, finally, it was said that Slang, the great manager, offered her an engagement at thirty guineas per week, Mr. Walker became exceedingly interested in his wife's proceedings, of which he demanded from her the fullest explanation.

Using his marital authority, he absolutely forbade Mrs. Walker's appearance on the public stage; he wrote to Sir George Thrum a letter expressive of his highest indignation that negotiations so important should ever have been commenced without his authorisation; and he wrote to his dear Slang (for these gentlemen were very intimate, and in the course of his transactions as an agent Mr. W. had had many dealings with Mr. S.) asking his dear Slang whether the latter thought his friend Walker would be so green as to allow his wife to appear on the stage, and he remain in prison with all his debts on his head?

And it was a curious thing now to behold how eager those very creditors who but yesterday (and with perfect correctness) had denounced Mr. Walker as a swindler; who had refused to come to any composition with him, and had sworn never to release him; how they on a sudden became quite eager to come to an arrangement with him, and offered, nay, begged and prayed him to go free,—only giving them his own and Mrs. Walker's acknowledgment of their debt, with a promise that a part of the lady's salary should be devoted to the payment of the claim.

"The lady's salary!" said Mr. Walker, indignantly, to these gentlemen and their attorneys. "Do you suppose I will allow Mrs. Walker to go on the stage?—do you suppose I am such a fool as to sign bills to the full amount of these claims against me, when in a few months more I can walk out of prison without paying a shilling? Gentlemen, you take Howard Walker for an idiot. I like the Fleet, and rather than pay I'll stay here for these ten years."

In other words, it was the Captain's determination to make some advantageous bargain for himself with his creditors and the gentlemen who were interested in bringing forward Mrs. Walker on the stage. And who can say that in so determining he did not act with laudable prudence and justice?

"You do not, surely, consider, my very dear sir, that half the amount of Mrs. Walker's salaries is too much for my immense trouble and pains in teaching her?" cried Sir George Thrum (who, in reply to Walker's note, thought it most prudent to wait personally on that gentleman). "Remember that I am the first master in England; that I have the best interest in England; that I can bring her out at the Palace, and at every concert and musical festival in England; that I am obliged to teach her every single note that she utters; and that without me she could no more sing a song than her little baby could walk without its nurse."

"I believe about half what you say," said Mr. Walker.

"My dear Captain Walker! would you question my integrity? Who was it that made Mrs. Millington's fortune,—the celebrated Mrs. Millington, who has now got a hundred thousand pounds? Who was it that brought out the finest tenor in Europe, Poppleton? Ask the musical world, ask those great artists themselves, and they will tell you they owe their reputation, their fortune, to Sir George Thrum."

"It is very likely," replied the Captain, coolly. "You ARE a good master, I dare say, Sir George; but I am not going to article Mrs. Walker to you for three years, and sign her articles in the Fleet. Mrs. Walker shan't sing till I'm a free man, that's flat: if I stay here till you're dead she shan't."

"Gracious powers, sir!" exclaimed Sir George, "do you expect me to pay your debts?"

"Yes, old boy," answered the Captain, "and to give me something handsome in hand, too; and that's my ultimatum: and so I wish you good morning, for I'm engaged to play a match at tennis below."

This little interview exceedingly frightened the worthy knight, who went home to his lady in a delirious state of alarm occasioned by the audacity of Captain Walker.

Mr. Slang's interview with him was scarcely more satisfactory. He owed, he said, four thousand pounds. His creditors might be brought to compound for five shillings in the pound. He would not consent to allow his wife to make a single engagement until the creditors were satisfied, and until he had a handsome sum in hand to begin the world with. "Unless my wife comes out, you'll be in the Gazette yourself, you know you will. So you may take her or leave her, as you think fit."

"Let her sing one night as a trial," said Mr. Slang.

"If she sings one night, the creditors will want their money in full," replied the Captain. "I shan't let her labour, poor thing, for the profit of those scoundrels!" added the prisoner, with much feeling. And Slang left him with a much greater respect for Walker than he had ever before possessed. He was struck with the gallantry of the man who could triumph over misfortunes, nay, make misfortune itself an engine of good luck.

Mrs. Walker was instructed instantly to have a severe sore throat. The journals in Mr. Slang's interest deplored this illness pathetically; while the papers in the interest of the opposition theatre magnified it with great malice. "The new singer," said one, "the great wonder which Slang promised us, is as hoarse as a RAVEN!" "Doctor Thorax pronounces," wrote another paper, "that the quinsy, which has suddenly prostrated Mrs. Ravenswing, whose singing at the Philharmonic, previous to her appearance at the 'T.R—,' excited so much applause, has destroyed the lady's voice for ever. We luckily need no other prima donna, when that place, as nightly thousands acknowledge, is held by Miss Ligonier." The

Looker-on said, "That although some well-informed contemporaries had declared Mrs. W. Ravenswing's complaint to be a quinsy, others, on whose authority they could equally rely, had pronounced it to be a consumption. At all events, she was in an exceedingly dangerous state; from which, though we do not expect, we heartily trust she may recover. Opinions differ as to the merits of this lady, some saying that she was altogether inferior to Miss Ligonier, while other connoisseurs declare the latter lady to be by no means so accomplished a person. This point, we fear," continued the Looker-on, "can never now be settled; unless, which we fear is improbable, Mrs. Ravenswing should ever so far recover as to be able to make her debut; and even then, the new singer will not have a fair chance unless her voice and strength shall be fully restored. This information, which we have from exclusive resources, may be relied on," concluded the Looker-on, "as authentic."

It was Mr. Walker himself, that artful and audacious Fleet prisoner, who concocted those very paragraphs against his wife's health which appeared in the journals of the Ligonier party. The partisans of that lady were delighted, the creditors of Mr. Walker astounded, at reading them. Even Sir George Thrum was taken in, and came to the Fleet prison in considerable alarm.

"Mum's the word, my good sir!" said Mr. Walker. "Now is the time to make arrangements with the creditors."

Well, these arrangements were finally made. It does not matter how many shillings in the pound satisfied the rapacious creditors of Morgiana's husband. But it is certain that her voice returned to her all of a sudden upon the Captain's release. The papers of the Mulligan faction again trumpeted her perfections; the agreement with Mr. Slang was concluded; that with Sir George Thrum the great composer satisfactorily arranged; and the new opera underlined in immense capitals in the bills, and put in rehearsal with immense expenditure on the part of the scene-painter and costumier.

Need we tell with what triumphant success the "Brigand's Bride" was received? All the Irish sub-editors the next morning took care to have such an account of it as made Miss Ligonier and Baroski die with envy. All the reporters who could spare time were in the boxes to support their friend's work. All the journeymen tailors of the establishment of Linsey, Woolsey, and Co. had pit tickets given to them, and applauded with all their might. All Mr. Walker's friends of the "Regent Club" lined the side-boxes with white kid gloves; and in a little box by themselves sat Mrs. Crump and Mr. Woolsey, a great deal too much agitated to applaud—so agitated, that Woolsey even forgot to fling down the bouquet he had brought for the Ravenswing.

But there was no lack of those horticultural ornaments. The theatre servants wheeled away a wheelbarrow-full (which were flung on the stage the next night over again); and Morgiana, blushing, panting, weeping, was led off by Mr. Poppleton, the eminent tenor, who had crowned her with one of the most conspicuous of the chaplets.

Here she flew to her husband, and flung her arms round his neck. He was flirting behind the side-scenes with Mademoiselle Flicflac, who had been dancing in the divertissement; and was probably the only man in the theatre of those who witnessed the embrace that did not care for it. Even Slang was affected, and said with perfect sincerity that he wished he had been in Walker's place. The manager's fortune was made, at least for the season. He acknowledged so much to Walker, who took a week's salary for his wife in advance that very night.

There was, as usual, a grand supper in the green-room. The terrible Mr. Bludyer appeared in a new coat of the well-known Woolsey cut, and the little tailor himself and Mrs. Crump were not the least happy of the party. But when the Ravenswing took Woolsey's hand, and said she never would have been there but for him, Mr. Walker looked very grave, and hinted to her that she must not, in her position, encourage the attentions of persons in that rank of life. "I shall pay," said he, proudly, "every farthing that is owing to Mr. Woolsey, and shall employ him for the future. But you understand, my love, that one cannot at one's own table receive one's own tailor."

Slang proposed Morgiana's health in a tremendous speech, which elicited cheers, and laughter, and sobs, such as only managers have the art of drawing from the theatrical gentlemen and ladies in their employ. It was observed, especially among the chorus-singers at the bottom of the table, that their emotion was intense. They had a meeting the next day and voted a piece of plate to Adolphus Slang, Esquire, for his eminent services in the cause of the drama.

Walker returned thanks for his lady. That was, he said, the proudest moment of his life. He was proud to think that he had educated her for the stage, happy to think that his sufferings had not been in vain, and that his exertions in her behalf were crowned with full success. In her name and his own he thanked the company, and sat down, and was once more particularly attentive to Mademoiselle Flicflac.

WILLIAM MAKEPEACE THACKERAY

Then came an oration from Sir George Thrum, in reply to Slang's toast to HIM. It was very much to the same effect as the speech by Walker, the two gentlemen attributing to themselves individually the merit of bringing out Mrs. Walker. He concluded by stating that he should always hold Mrs. Walker as the daughter of his heart, and to the last moment of his life should love and cherish her. It is certain that Sir George was exceedingly elated that night, and would have been scolded by his lady on his return home, but for the triumph of the evening.

Mulligan's speech of thanks, as author of the "Brigand's Bride," was, it must be confessed, extremely tedious. It seemed there would be no end to it; when he got upon the subject of Ireland especially, which somehow was found to be intimately connected with the interests of music and the theatre. Even the choristers pooh-poohed this speech, coming though it did from the successful author, whose songs of wine, love, and battle, they had been repeating that night.

The "Brigand's Bride" ran for many nights. Its choruses were tuned on the organs of the day. Morgiana's airs, "The Rose upon my Balcony" and the "Lightning on the Cataract" (recitative and scena) were on everybody's lips, and brought so many guineas to Sir George Thrum that he was encouraged to have his portrait engraved, which still may be seen in the music-shops. Not many persons, I believe, bought proof impressions of the plate, price two guineas; whereas, on the contrary, all the young clerks in banks, and all the FAST young men of the universities, had pictures of the Ravenswing in their apartments—as Biondetta (the brigand's bride), as Zelyma (in the "Nuptials of Benares"), as Barbareska (in the "Mine of Tobolsk"), and in all her famous characters. In the latter she disguises herself as a Uhlan, in order to save her father, who is in prison; and the Ravenswing looked so fascinating in this costume in pantaloons and yellow boots, that Slang was for having her instantly in Captain Macheath, whence arose their quarrel.

She was replaced at Slang's theatre by Snooks, the rhinoceros-tamer, with his breed of wild buffaloes. Their success was immense. Slang gave a supper, at which all the company burst into tears; and assembling in the green-room next day, they, as usual, voted a piece of plate to Adolphus Slang, Esquire, for his eminent services to the drama.

In the Captain Macheath dispute Mr. Walker would have had his wife yield; but on this point, and for once, she disobeyed her husband and left the theatre. And when Walker cursed her (according to his wont) for her abominable selfishness and disregard of his property, she burst into tears and said she had spent but twenty guineas on herself and baby during the year, that her theatrical dressmaker's bills were yet unpaid, and that she had never asked him how much he spent on that odious French figurante.

All this was true, except about the French figurante. Walker, as the lord and master, received all Morgiana's earnings, and spent them as a gentleman should. He gave very neat dinners at a cottage in Regent's Park (Mr. and Mrs. Walker lived at Green Street, Grosvenor Square), he played a good deal at the "Regent;" but as to the French figurante, it must be confessed, that Mrs. Walker was in a sad error: THAT lady and the Captain had parted long ago; it was Madame Dolores de Tras-os-Montes who inhabited the cottage in St. John's Wood now.

But if some little errors of this kind might be attributable to the Captain, on the other hand, when his wife was in the provinces, he was the most attentive of husbands; made all her bargains, and received every shilling before he would permit her to sing a note. Thus he prevented her from being cheated, as a person of her easy temper doubtless would have been, by designing managers and needy concert-givers. They always travelled with four horses; and Walker was adored in every one of the principal hotels in England. The waiters flew at his bell. The chambermaids were afraid he was a sad naughty man, and thought his wife no such great beauty; the landlords preferred him to any duke. HE never looked at their bills, not he! In fact his income was at least four thousand a year for some years of his life.

Master Woolsey Walker was put to Doctor Wapshot's seminary, whence, after many disputes on the Doctor's part as to getting his half-year's accounts paid, and after much complaint of ill-treatment on the little boy's side, he was withdrawn, and placed under the care of the Reverend Mr. Swishtail, at Turnham Green; where all his bills are paid by his godfather, now the head of the firm of Woolsey and Co.

As a gentleman, Mr. Walker still declines to see him; but he has not, as far as I have heard, paid the sums of money which he threatened to refund; and, as he is seldom at home the worthy tailor can come to Green Street at his leisure. He and Mrs. Crump, and Mrs. Walker often take the omnibus to Brentford, and a cake with them to little Woolsey at school; to whom the tailor says he will leave every shilling of his property.

The Walkers have no other children; but when she takes her airing in the Park she always turns away at the sight of a low phaeton, in which sits a woman with rouged cheeks, and a great number of overdressed children and a French bonne, whose name, I am given to understand, is Madame Dolores de Tras-os-Montes. Madame de Tras-os-Montes always puts a great gold glass to her eye as the Ravenswing's carriage passes, and looks into it with a sneer. The two coachmen used always to exchange queer winks at each other in the ring, until Madame de Tras-os-Montes lately adopted a tremendous chasseur, with huge whiskers and a green and gold livery; since which time the formerly named gentlemen do not recognise each other.

The Ravenswing's life is one of perpetual triumph on the stage; and, as every one of the fashionable men about town have been in love with her, you may fancy what a pretty character she has. Lady Thrum would die sooner than speak to that unhappy young woman; and, in fact, the Thrums have a new pupil, who is a siren without the dangerous qualities of one, who has the person of Venus, and the mind of a Muse, and who is coming out at one of the theatres immediately. Baroski says, "De liddle Rafenschwing is just as font of me as effer!" People are very shy about receiving her in society; and when she goes to sing at a concert, Miss Prim starts up and skurries off in a state of the greatest alarm, lest "that person" should speak to her.

Walker is voted a good, easy, rattling, gentlemanly fellow, and nobody's enemy but his own. His wife, they say, is dreadfully extravagant: and, indeed, since his marriage, and in spite of his wife's large income, he has been in the Bench several times; but she signs some bills and he comes out again, and is as gay and genial as ever. All mercantile speculations he has wisely long since given up; he likes to throw a main of an evening, as I have said, and to take his couple of bottles at dinner. On Friday he attends at the theatre for his wife's salary, and transacts no other business during the week. He grows exceedingly stout, dyes his hair, and has a bloated purple look about the nose and cheeks, very different from that which first charmed the heart of Morgiana.

By the way, Eglantine has been turned out of the Bower of Bloom, and now keeps a shop at Tunbridge Wells. Going down thither last year without a razor, I asked a fat seedy man lolling in a faded nankeen jacket at the door of a tawdry little shop in the Pantiles, to shave me. He said in reply, "Sir, I do not practise in that branch of the profession!" and turned back into the little shop. It was Archibald Eglantine. But in the wreck of his fortunes he still has his captain's uniform, and his grand cross of the order of the Castle and Falcon of Panama.

G. Fitz-Boodle, Esq., to O. Yorke, Esq.

ZUM TRIERISCHEN HOP, COBLENZ: July 10, 1843

MY DEAR YORKE,

The story of the Ravenswing was written a long time since, and I never could account for the bad taste of the publishers of the metropolis who refused it an insertion in their various magazines. This fact would never have been alluded to but for the following circumstance:—

Only yesterday, as I was dining at this excellent hotel, I remarked a bald-headed gentleman in a blue coat and brass buttons, who looked like a colonel on half-pay, and by his side a lady and a little boy of twelve, whom the gentleman was cramming with an amazing quantity of cherries and cakes. A stout old dame in a wonderful cap and ribands was seated by the lady's side, and it was easy to see they were English, and I thought I had already made their acquaintance elsewhere.

The younger of the ladies at last made a bow with an accompanying blush.

"Surely," said I, "I have the honour of speaking to Mrs. Ravenswing?"

"Mrs. Woolsey, sir," said the gentleman; "my wife has long since left the stage:" and at this the old lady in the wonderful cap trod on my toes very severely, and nodded her head and all her ribands in a most mysterious way. Presently the two ladies rose and left the table, the elder declaring that she heard the baby crying.

"Woolsey, my dear, go with your mamma," said Mr. Woolsey, patting the boy on the head. The young gentleman obeyed the command, carrying off a plate of macaroons with him.

"Your son is a fine boy, sir," said I.

"My step-son, sir," answered Mr. Woolsey; and added, in a louder voice, "I knew you, Mr. Fitz-Boodle, at once, but did not mention your name for fear of agitating my wife. She don't like to have the memory of old times renewed, sir; her former husband, whom you know, Captain Walker, made her very unhappy. He died in America, sir, of this, I fear" (pointing to the bottle), "and Mrs. W. quitted the stage a year before I quitted business. Are you going on to Wiesbaden?"

They went off in their carriage that evening, the boy on the box making great efforts to blow out of the postilion's tasselled horn.

I am glad that poor Morgiana is happy at last, and hasten to inform you of the fact. I am going to visit the old haunts of my youth at Pumpernickel. Adieu.

Yours,
G. F.-B.

MR. AND MRS. FRANK BERRY

I

THE FIGHT AT SLAUGHTER HOUSE

I am very fond of reading about battles, and have most of Marlborough's and Wellington's at my fingers' ends; but the most tremendous combat I ever saw, and one that interests me to think of more than Malplaquet or Waterloo (which, by the way, has grown to be a downright nuisance, so much do men talk of it after dinner, prating most disgustingly about "the Prussians coming up," and what not)—I say the most tremendous combat ever known was that between Berry and Biggs the gown-boy, which commenced in a certain place called Middle Briars, situated in the midst of the cloisters that run along the side of the playground of Slaughter House School, near Smithfield, London. It was there, madam, that your humble servant had the honour of acquiring, after six years' labour, that immense fund of classical knowledge which in after life has been so exceedingly useful to him.

The circumstances of the quarrel were these:—Biggs, the gown-boy (a man who, in those days, I thought was at least seven feet high, and was quite thunderstruck to find in after life that he measured no more than five feet four), was what we called "second cock" of the school; the first cock was a great big, good-humoured, lazy, fair-haired fellow, Old Hawkins by name, who, because he was large and good-humoured, hurt nobody. Biggs, on the contrary, was a sad bully; he had half-a-dozen fags, and beat them all unmercifully. Moreover, he had a little brother, a boarder in Potky's house, whom, as a matter of course, he hated and maltreated worse than anyone else.

Well, one day, because young Biggs had not brought his brother his hoops, or had not caught a ball at cricket, or for some other equally good reason, Biggs the elder so belaboured the poor little fellow, that Berry, who was sauntering by, and saw the dreadful blows which the elder brother was dealing to the younger with his hockey-stick, felt a compassion for the little fellow (perhaps he had a jealousy against Biggs, and wanted to try a few rounds with him, but that I can't vouch for); however, Berry passing by, stopped and said, "Don't you think you have thrashed the boy enough, Biggs?" He spoke this in a very civil tone, for he never would have thought of interfering rudely with the sacred privilege that an upper boy at a public school always has of beating a junior, especially when they happen to be brothers.

The reply of Biggs, as might be expected, was to hit young Biggs with the hockey-stick twice as hard as before, until the little wretch howled with pain. "I suppose it's no business of yours, Berry," said Biggs, thumping away all the while, and laid on worse and worse.

Until Berry (and, indeed, little Biggs) could bear it no longer, and the former, bouncing forward, wrenched the stick out of old Biggs's hands, and sent it whirling out of the cloister window, to the great wonder of a crowd of us small boys, who were looking on. Little boys always like to see a little companion of their own soundly beaten.

"There!" said Berry, looking into Biggs's face, as much as to say, "I've gone and done it;" and he added to the brother, "Scud away, you little thief; I've saved you this time."

"Stop, young Biggs!" roared out his brother after a pause; "or I'll break every bone in your infernal scoundrelly skin!"

Young Biggs looked at Berry, then at his brother, then came at his brother's order, as if back to be beaten again; but lost heart, and ran away as fast as his little legs could carry him.

"I'll do for him another time," said Biggs. "Here, under-boy, take my coat;" and we all began to gather round and formed a ring.

"We had better wait till after school, Biggs," cried Berry, quite cool, but looking a little pale. "There are only five minutes now, and it will take you more than that to thrash me."

Biggs upon this committed a great error; for he struck Berry slightly across the face with the back of his hand, saying, "You are in a funk." But this was a feeling which Frank Berry did not in the least entertain; for, in reply to Biggs's back-hander, and as quick as thought, and with all his might and main—pong! he delivered a blow upon old Biggs's nose that made the claret spirt, and sent the second cock down to the ground as if he had been shot.

He was up again, however, in a minute, his face white and gashed with blood, his eyes glaring, a ghastly spectacle; and Berry, meanwhile, had taken his coat off, and by this time there were gathered in the cloisters, on all the windows, and upon each other's shoulders, one hundred and twenty young gentlemen at the very least, for the news had gone out through the playground of "a fight between Berry and Biggs."

But Berry was quite right in his remark about the propriety of deferring the business, for at this minute Mr. Chip, the second master, came down the cloisters going into school, and grinned in his queer way as he saw the state of Biggs's face. "Holloa, Mr. Biggs," said he, "I suppose you have run against a finger-post." That was the regular joke with us at school, and you may be sure we all laughed heartily: as we always did when Mr. Chip made a joke, or anything like a joke. "You had better go to the pump, sir, and get yourself washed, and not let Doctor Buckle see you in that condition." So saying, Mr. Chip disappeared to his duties in the under-school, whither all we little boys followed him.

It was Wednesday, a half-holiday, as everybody knows, and boiled-beef day at Slaughter House. I was in the same boarding-house with Berry, and we all looked to see whether he ate a good dinner, just as one would examine a man who was going to be hanged. I recollected, in after-life, in Germany, seeing a friend who was going to fight a duel eat five larks for his breakfast, and thought I had seldom witnessed greater courage. Berry ate moderately of the boiled beef—BOILED CHILD we used to call it at school, in our elegant jocular way; he knew a great deal better than to load his stomach upon the eve of such a contest as was going to take place.

Dinner was very soon over, and Mr. Chip, who had been all the while joking Berry, and pressing him to eat, called him up into his study, to the great disappointment of us all, for we thought he was going to prevent the fight; but no such thing. The Reverend Edward Chip took Berry into his study, and poured him out two glasses of port-wine, which he made him take with a biscuit, and patted him on the back, and went off. I have no doubt he was longing, like all of us, to see the battle; but etiquette, you know, forbade.

When we went out into the green, Old Hawkins was there—the great Hawkins, the cock of the school. I have never seen the man since, but still think of him as of something awful, gigantic, mysterious: he who could thrash everybody, who could beat all the masters; how we longed for him to put in his hand and lick Buckle! He was a dull boy, not very high in the school, and had all his exercises written for him. Buckle knew this, but respected him; never called him up to read Greek plays; passed over all his blunders, which were many; let him go out of half-holidays into the town as he pleased: how should any man dare to stop him—the great calm magnanimous silent Strength! They say he licked a Life-Guardsman: I wonder whether it was Shaw, who killed all those Frenchmen? No, it could not be Shaw, for he was dead au champ d'honneur; but he WOULD have licked Shaw if he had been alive. A bargeman I know he licked, at Jack Randall's in Slaughter House Lane. Old Hawkins was too lazy to play at cricket; he sauntered all day in the sunshine about the green, accompanied by little Tippins, who was in the sixth form, laughed and joked at Hawkins eternally, and was the person who wrote all his exercises.

Instead of going into town this afternoon, Hawkins remained at Slaughter House, to see the great fight between the second and third cocks.

The different masters of the school kept boarding-houses (such as Potky's, Chip's, Wickens's, Pinney's, and so on), and the playground, or "green" as it was called, although the only thing green about the place was the broken glass on the walls that separate Slaughter House from Wilderness Row and Goswell Street—(many a time have I seen Mr. Pickwick look out of his window in that street, though we did not know him then)—the playground, or green, was common to all. But if any stray boy from Potky's was found, for instance, in, or entering into, Chip's house, the most dreadful tortures were practised upon him: as I can answer in my own case.

Fancy, then, our astonishment at seeing a little three-foot wretch, of the name of Wills, one of Hawkins's fags (they were both in Potky's), walk undismayed amongst us lions at Chip's house, as the "rich and rare" young lady did in Ireland. We were going to set upon him and devour or otherwise maltreat him, when he cried out in a little shrill impertinent voice, "TELL BERRY I WANT HIM!"

We all roared with laughter. Berry was in the sixth form, and Wills or any under-boy would as soon have thought of "wanting" him, as I should of wanting the Duke of Wellington.

Little Wills looked round in an imperious kind of way. "Well," says he, stamping his foot, "do you hear? TELL BERRY THAT HAWKINS WANTS HIM!"

As for resisting the law of Hawkins, you might as soon think of resisting immortal Jove. Berry and Tolmash, who was to be his bottle-holder, made their appearance immediately, and walked out into the green where Hawkins was waiting, and, with an irresistible audacity that only belonged to himself, in the face of nature and all the regulations of the place, was smoking a cigar. When Berry and Tolmash found him, the three began slowly pacing up and down in the sunshine, and we little boys watched them.

Hawkins moved his arms and hands every now and then, and was evidently laying down the law about boxing. We saw his fists darting out every now and then with mysterious swiftness, hitting one, two, quick as thought, as if in the face of an adversary; now his left hand went up, as if guarding his own head, now his immense right fist dreadfully flapped the air, as if punishing his imaginary opponent's miserable ribs. The conversation lasted for some ten minutes, about which time gown-boys' dinner was over, and we saw these youths, in their black horned-button jackets and knee-breeches, issuing from their door in the cloisters. There were no hoops, no cricket-bats, as usual on a half-holiday. Who would have thought of play in expectation of such tremendous sport as was in store for us?

Towering among the gown-boys, of whom he was the head and the tyrant, leaning upon Bushby's arm, and followed at a little distance by many curious pale awe-stricken boys, dressed in his black silk stockings, which he always sported, and with a crimson bandanna tied round his waist, came Biggs. His nose was swollen with the blow given before school, but his eyes flashed fire. He was laughing and sneering with Bushby, and evidently intended to make minced meat of Berry.

The betting began pretty freely: the bets were against poor Berry. Five to three were offered—in ginger-beer. I took six to four in raspberry open tarts. The upper boys carried the thing farther still: and I know for a fact, that Swang's book amounted to four pound three (but he hedged a good deal), and Tittery lost seventeen shillings in a single bet to Pitts, who took the odds.

As Biggs and his party arrived, I heard Hawkins say to Berry, "For heaven's sake, my boy, fib with your right, and MIND HIS LEFT HAND!"

Middle Briars was voted to be too confined a space for the combat, and it was agreed that it should take place behind the under-school in the shade, whither we all went. Hawkins, with his immense silver hunting-watch, kept the time; and water was brought from the pump close to Notley's the pastrycook's, who did not admire fisticuffs at all on half-holidays, for the fights kept the boys away from his shop. Gutley was the only fellow in the school who remained faithful to him, and he sat on the counter—the great gormandising brute!—eating tarts the whole day.

This famous fight, as every Slaughter House man knows, lasted for two hours and twenty-nine minutes, by Hawkins's immense watch. All this time the air resounded with cries of "Go it, Berry!" "Go it, Biggs!" "Pitch into him!" "Give it him!" and so on. Shall I describe the hundred and two rounds of the combat?—No!—It would occupy too much space, and the taste for such descriptions has passed away.

1st round. Both the combatants fresh, and in prime order. The weight and inches somewhat on the gown-boy's side. Berry goes gallantly in, and delivers a clinker on the gown-boy's jaw. Biggs makes play with his left. Berry down.

4th round. Claret drawn in profusion from the gown-boy's grogshop. (He went down, and had his front tooth knocked out, but the blow cut Berry's knuckles a great deal.)

15th round. Chancery. Fibbing. Biggs makes dreadful work with his left. Break away. Rally. Biggs down. Betting still six to four on the gown-boy.

20th round. The men both dreadfully punished. Berry somewhat shy of his adversary's left hand.

29th to 42nd round. The Chipsite all this while breaks away from the gown-boy's left, and goes down on a knee. Six to four on the gown-boy, until the fortieth round, when the bets became equal.

102nd and last round. For half-an-hour the men had stood up to each other, but were almost too weary to strike. The gown-boy's face hardly to be recognised, swollen and streaming with blood. The Chipsite in a similar condition, and still more punished about his side from his enemy's left hand. Berry gives a blow at his adversary's face, and falls over him as he falls.

The gown-boy can't come up to time. And thus ended the great fight of Berry and Biggs.

And what, pray, has this horrid description of a battle and parcel of schoolboys to do with Men's Wives?

What has it to do with Men's Wives?—A great deal more, madam, than you think for. Only read Chapter II, and you shall hear.

II

The combat at Versailles

I afterwards came to be Berry's fag, and, though beaten by him daily, he allowed, of course, no one else to lay a hand upon me, and I got no more thrashing than was good for me. Thus an intimacy grew up between us, and after he left Slaughter House and went into the dragoons, the honest fellow did not forget his old friend, but actually made his appearance one day in the playground in moustaches and a braided coat, and gave me a gold pencil-case and a couple of sovereigns. I blushed when I took them, but take them I did; and I think the thing I almost best recollect in my life, is the sight of Berry getting behind an immense bay cab-horse, which was held by a correct little groom, and was waiting near the school in Slaughter House Square. He proposed, too, to have me to "Long's," where he was lodging for the time; but this invitation was refused on my behalf by Doctor Buckle, who said, and possibly with correctness, that I should get little good by spending my holiday with such a scapegrace.

Once afterwards he came to see me at Christ Church, and we made a show of writing to one another, and didn't, and always had a hearty mutual goodwill; and though we did not quite burst into tears on parting, were yet quite happy when occasion threw us together, and so almost lost sight of each other. I heard lately that Berry was married, and am rather ashamed to say, that I was not so curious as even to ask the maiden name of his lady.

Last summer I was at Paris, and had gone over to Versailles to meet a party, one of which was a young lady to whom I was tenderly— But, never mind. The day was rainy, and the party did not keep its appointment; and after yawning through the interminable Palace picture-galleries, and then making an attempt to smoke a cigar in the Palace garden—for which crime I was nearly run through the body by a rascally sentinel—I was driven, perforce, into the great bleak lonely place before the Palace, with its roads branching off to all the towns in the world, which Louis and Napoleon once intended to conquer, and there enjoyed my favourite pursuit at leisure, and was meditating whether I should go back to "Vefour's" for dinner, or patronise my friend

M. Duboux of the "Hotel des Reservoirs" who gives not only a good dinner, but as dear a one as heart can desire. I was, I say, meditating these things, when a carriage passed by. It was a smart low calash, with a pair of bay horses and a postilion in a drab jacket that twinkled with innumerable buttons, and I was too much occupied in admiring the build of the machine, and the extreme tightness of the fellow's inexpressibles, to look at the personages within the carriage, when the gentleman roared out "Fitz!" and the postilion pulled up, and the lady gave a shrill scream, and a little black-muzzled spaniel began barking and yelling with all his might, and a man with moustaches jumped out of the vehicle, and began shaking me by the hand.

"Drive home, John," said the gentleman: "I'll be with you, my love, in an instant—it's an old friend. Fitz, let me present you to Mrs. Berry."

The lady made an exceedingly gentle inclination of her black-velvet bonnet, and said, "Pray, my love, remember that it is just dinner-time. However, never mind ME." And with another slight toss and a nod to the postilion, that individual's white leather breeches began to jump up and down again in the saddle, and the carriage disappeared, leaving me shaking my old friend Berry by the hand.

He had long quitted the army, but still wore his military beard, which gave to his fair pink face a fierce and lion-like look. He was extraordinarily glad to see me, as only men are glad who live in a small town, or in dull company. There is no destroyer of friendships like London, where a man has no time to think of his neighbour, and has far too many friends to care for them. He told me in a breath of his marriage, and how happy he was, and straight insisted that I must come home to dinner, and see more of Angelica, who had invited me herself—didn't I hear her?

"Mrs. Berry asked YOU, Frank; but I certainly did not hear her ask ME!"

"She would not have mentioned the dinner but that she meant me to ask you. I know she did," cried Frank Berry. "And, besides—hang it—I'm master of the house. So come you shall. No ceremony, old boy— one or two friends—snug family party—and we'll talk of old times over a bottle of claret."

There did not seem to me to be the slightest objection to this arrangement, except that my boots were muddy, and my coat of the morning sort. But as it was quite impossible to go to Paris and back again in a quarter of an hour, and as a man may dine with perfect comfort to

WILLIAM MAKEPEACE THACKERAY

himself in a frock-coat, it did not occur to me to be particularly squeamish, or to decline an old friend's invitation upon a pretext so trivial.

Accordingly we walked to a small house in the Avenue de Paris, and were admitted first into a small garden ornamented by a grotto, a fountain, and several nymphs in plaster-of-Paris, then up a mouldy old steep stair into a hall, where a statue of Cupid and another of Venus welcomed us with their eternal simper; then through a salle-a-manger where covers were laid for six; and finally to a little saloon, where Fido the dog began to howl furiously according to his wont.

It was one of the old pavilions that had been built for a pleasure-house in the gay days of Versailles, ornamented with abundance of damp Cupids and cracked gilt cornices, and old mirrors let into the walls, and gilded once, but now painted a dingy French white. The long low windows looked into the court, where the fountain played its ceaseless dribble, surrounded by numerous rank creepers and weedy flowers, but in the midst of which the statues stood with their bases quite moist and green.

I hate fountains and statues in dark confined places: that cheerless, endless plashing of water is the most inhospitable sound ever heard. The stiff grin of those French statues, or ogling Canova Graces, is by no means more happy, I think, than the smile of a skeleton, and not so natural. Those little pavilions in which the old roues sported were never meant to be seen by daylight, depend on't. They were lighted up with a hundred wax-candles, and the little fountain yonder was meant only to cool their claret. And so, my first impression of Berry's place of abode was rather a dismal one. However, I heard him in the salle-a-manger drawing the corks, which went off with a CLOOP, and that consoled me.

As for the furniture of the rooms appertaining to the Berrys, there was a harp in a leather case, and a piano, and a flute-box, and a huge tambour with a Saracen's nose just begun, and likewise on the table a multiplicity of those little gilt books, half sentimental and half religious, which the wants of the age and of our young ladies have produced in such numbers of late. I quarrel with no lady's taste in that way; but heigho! I had rather that Mrs. Fitz-Boodle should read "Humphry Clinker!"

Besides these works, there was a "Peerage," of course. What genteel family was ever without one?

I was making for the door to see Frank drawing the corks, and was bounced at by the amiable little black-muzzled spaniel, who fastened his teeth in my pantaloons, and received a polite kick in consequence, which sent him howling to the other end of the room, and the animal was just in the act of performing that feat of agility, when the door opened and madame made her appearance. Frank came behind her, peering over her shoulder with rather an anxious look.

Mrs. Berry is an exceedingly white and lean person. She has thick eyebrows, which meet rather dangerously over her nose, which is Grecian, and a small mouth with no lips—a sort of feeble pucker in the face as it were. Under her eyebrows are a pair of enormous eyes, which she is in the habit of turning constantly ceiling-wards. Her hair is rather scarce, and worn in bandeaux, and she commonly mounts a sprig of laurel, or a dark flower or two, which with the sham tour—I believe that is the name of the knob of artificial hair that many ladies sport—gives her a rigid and classical look. She is dressed in black, and has invariably the neatest of silk stockings and shoes: for forsooth her foot is a fine one, and she always sits with it before her, looking at it, stamping it, and admiring it a great deal. "Fido," she says to her spaniel, "you have almost crushed my poor foot;" or, "Frank," to her husband, "bring me a footstool:" or, "I suffer so from cold in the feet," and so forth; but be the conversation what it will, she is always sure to put HER FOOT into it.

She invariably wears on her neck the miniature of her late father, Sir George Catacomb, apothecary to George III.; and she thinks those two men the greatest the world ever saw. She was born in Baker Street, Portman Square, and that is saying almost enough of her. She is as long, as genteel, and as dreary, as that deadly-lively place, and sports, by way of ornament, her papa's hatchment, as it were, as every tenth Baker Street house has taught her.

What induced such a jolly fellow as Frank Berry to marry Miss Angelica Catacomb no one can tell. He met her, he says, at a ball at Hampton Court, where his regiment was quartered, and where, to this day, lives "her aunt Lady Pash." She alludes perpetually in conversation to that celebrated lady; and if you look in the "Baronetage" to the pedigree of the Pash family, you may see manuscript notes by Mrs. Frank Berry, relative to them and herself. Thus, when you see in print that Sir John Pash married Angelica, daughter of Graves Catacomb, Esquire, in a neat hand you find written, AND SISTER OF THE LATE SIR GEORGE CATACOMB, OF BAKER STREET, PORTMAN SQUARE: "A.B." follows of course. It is a wonder how fond ladies are of writing in books, and signing their charming initials! Mrs. Berry's before-mentioned little gilt books are scored with pencil-marks, or occasionally at the margin with a!—note of interjection, or the words "Too True, A.B." and so on. Much may be learned with regard to lovely woman by a look at the books she reads in; and I had gained no inconsiderable knowledge of Mrs. Berry by the ten minutes spent in the drawing-room, while she was at her toilet in the adjoining bedchamber.

"You have often heard me talk of George Fitz," says Berry, with an appealing look to madame.

"Very often," answered his lady, in a tone which clearly meant "a great deal too much." "Pray, sir," continued she, looking at my boots with all her might, "are we to have your company at dinner?"

"Of course you are, my dear; what else do you think he came for? You would not have the man go back to Paris to get his evening coat, would you?"

"At least, my love, I hope you will go and put on Yours, and change those muddy boots. Lady Pash will be here in five minutes, and you know Dobus is as punctual as clockwork." Then turning to me with a sort of apology that was as consoling as a box on the ear, "We have some friends at dinner, sir, who are rather particular persons; but I am sure when they hear that you only came on a sudden invitation, they will excuse your morning dress.—Bah! what a smell of smoke!"

With this speech madame placed herself majestically on a sofa, put out her foot, called Fido, and relapsed into an icy silence. Frank had long since evacuated the premises, with a rueful look at his wife, but never daring to cast a glance at me. I saw the whole business at once: here was this lion of a fellow tamed down by a she Van Amburgh, and fetching and carrying at her orders a great deal more obediently than her little yowling black-muzzled darling of a Fido.

I am not, however, to be tamed so easily, and was determined in this instance not to be in the least disconcerted, or to show the smallest sign of ill-humour: so to renouer the conversation, I began about Lady Pash.

"I heard you mention the name of Pash, I think?" said I. "I know a lady of that name, and a very ugly one it is too."

"It is most probably not the same person," answered Mrs. Berry, with a look which intimated that a fellow like me could never have had the honour to know so exalted a person.

"I mean old Lady Pash of Hampton Court. Fat woman—fair, ain't she?—and wears an amethyst in her forehead, has one eye, a blond wig, and dresses in light green?"

"Lady Pash, sir, is MY AUNT," answered Mrs. Berry (not altogether displeased, although she expected money from the old lady; but you know we love to hear our friends abused when it can be safely done).

"Oh, indeed! she was a daughter of old Catacomb's of Windsor, I remember, the undertaker. They called her husband Callipash, and her ladyship Pishpash. So you see, madam, that I know the whole family!"

"Mr. Fitz-Simons!" exclaimed Mrs. Berry, rising, "I am not accustomed to hear nicknames applied to myself and my family; and must beg you, when you honour us with your company, to spare our feelings as much as possible. Mr. Catacomb had the confidence of his SOVEREIGN, sir, and Sir John Pash was of Charles II.'s creation. The one was my uncle, sir; the other my grandfather!"

"My dear madam, I am extremely sorry, and most sincerely apologise for my inadvertence. But you owe me an apology too: my name is not Fitz-Simons, but Fitz-Boodle."

"What! of Boodle Hall—my husband's old friend; of Charles I.'s creation? My dear sir, I beg you a thousand pardons, and am delighted to welcome a person of whom I have heard Frank say so much. Frank!" (to Berry, who soon entered in very glossy boots and a white waistcoat), "do you know, darling, I mistook Mr. Fitz-Boodle for Mr. Fitz-Simons—that horrid Irish horse-dealing person; and I never, never, never can pardon myself for being so rude to him."

The big eyes here assumed an expression that was intended to kill me outright with kindness: from being calm, still, reserved, Angelica suddenly became gay, smiling, confidential, and folatre. She told me she had heard I was a sad creature, and that she intended to reform me, and that I must come and see Frank a great deal.

Now, although Mr. Fitz-Simons, for whom I was mistaken, is as low a fellow as ever came out of Dublin, and having been a captain in somebody's army, is now a blackleg and horse-dealer by profession; yet, if I had brought him home to Mrs. Fitz-Boodle to dinner, I should have liked far better that that imaginary lady should have received him with decent civility, and not insulted the stranger within her husband's gates. And, although it was delightful to be received so cordially when the mistake was discovered, yet I found that ALL Berry's old acquaintances were by no means so warmly welcomed; for another old school-chum presently made his appearance, who was treated in a very different manner.

This was no other than poor Jack Butts, who is a sort of small artist and picture-dealer by profession, and was a dayboy at Slaughter House when we were there, and very serviceable in bringing in sausages, pots of pickles, and other articles of merchandise, which we could not otherwise procure. The poor fellow has been employed, seemingly, in the same office of fetcher and carrier ever since; and occupied that post for Mrs. Berry. It was, "Mr. Butts, have you finished that drawing for Lady Pash's album?" and Butts produced it; and, "Did you match the silk for me at Delille's?" and there was the silk, bought, no doubt, with the poor fellow's last five francs; and, "Did you go to the furniture-man in the Rue St. Jacques; and bring the canary-seed, and call about my shawl at that odious dawdling Madame Fichet's; and have you brought the guitar-strings?"

Butts hadn't brought the guitar-strings; and thereupon Mrs. Berry's countenance assumed the same terrible expression which I had formerly remarked in it, and which made me tremble for Berry.

"My dear Angelica," though said he with some spirit, "Jack Butts isn't a baggage-waggon, nor a Jack-of-all-trades; you make him paint pictures for your women's albums, and look after your upholsterer, and your canary-bird, and your milliners, and turn rusty because he forgets your last message."

"I did not turn RUSTY, Frank, as you call it elegantly. I'm very much obliged to Mr. Butts for performing my commissions—very much obliged. And as for not paying for the pictures to which you so kindly allude, Frank, *I* should never have thought of offering payment for so paltry a service; but I'm sure I shall be happy to pay if Mr. Butts will send me in his bill."

"By Jove, Angelica, this is too much!" bounced out Berry; but the little matrimonial squabble was abruptly ended, by Berry's French man flinging open the door and announcing MILADI PASH and Doctor Dobus, which two personages made their appearance.

The person of old Pash has been already parenthetically described. But quite different from her dismal niece in temperament, she is as jolly an old widow as ever wore weeds. She was attached somehow to the Court, and has a multiplicity of stories about the princesses and the old King, to which Mrs. Berry never fails to call your attention in her grave, important way. Lady Pash has ridden many a time to the Windsor hounds; she made her husband become a member of the Four-in-hand Club, and has numberless stories about Sir Godfrey Webster, Sir John Lade, and the old heroes of those times. She has lent a rouleau to Dick Sheridan, and remembers Lord Byron when he was a sulky slim young lad. She says Charles Fox was the pleasantest fellow she ever met with, and has not the slightest objection to inform you that one of the princes was very much in love with her. Yet somehow she is only fifty-two years old, and I have never been able to understand her calculation. One day or other before her eye went out, and before those pearly teeth of hers were stuck to her gums by gold, she must have been a pretty-looking body enough. Yet, in spite of the latter inconvenience, she eats and drinks too much every day, and tosses off a glass of maraschino with a trembling pudgy hand, every finger of which twinkles with a dozen, at least, of old rings. She has a story about every one of those rings, and a stupid one too. But there is always something pleasant, I think, in stupid family stories: they are good-hearted people who tell them.

As for Mrs. Muchit, nothing need be said of her; she is Pash's companion; she has lived with Lady Pash since the peace. Nor does my Lady take any more notice of her than of the dust of the earth. She calls her "poor Muchit," and considers her a half-witted creature. Mrs. Berry hates her cordially, and thinks she is a designing toad-eater, who has formed a conspiracy to rob her of her aunt's fortune. She never spoke a word to poor Muchit during the whole of dinner, or offered to help her to anything on the table.

In respect to Dobus, he is an old Peninsular man, as you are made to know before you have been very long in his company; and, like most army surgeons, is a great deal more military in his looks and conversation, than the combatant part of the forces. He has adopted the sham-Duke-of-Wellington air, which is by no means uncommon in veterans; and, though one of the easiest and softest fellows in existence, speaks slowly and briefly, and raps out an oath or two occasionally, as it is said a certain great captain does. Besides the above, we sat down to table with Captain Goff, late of the—Highlanders; the Reverend Lemuel Whey, who preaches at St. Germains; little Cutler, and the Frenchman, who always WILL be at English parties on the Continent, and who, after making some frightful efforts to speak English, subsides and is heard no more. Young married ladies and heads of families generally have him for the purpose of waltzing, and in return he informs his friends of the club or the cafe that he has made the conquest of a charmante Anglaise. Listen to me, all family men who read this! and never LET AN UNMARRIED FRENCHMAN INTO YOUR DOORS. This lecture alone is worth the price of the book. It is not that they do any harm in one case out of a thousand, Heaven forbid! but they mean harm. They look on our Susannas with unholy dishonest eyes. Hearken to two of the grinning rogues chattering together as they clink over the asphalte of the Boulevard with lacquered boots, and plastered hair, and waxed moustaches, and turned-down shirt-collars, and stays and goggling eyes, and hear how they talk of a good simple giddy vain dull Baker Street creature, and canvass her points, and show her letters, and insinuate—never mind, but I tell you my soul grows angry when I think of the same; and I can't hear of an Englishwoman marrying a Frenchman without feeling a sort of shame and pity for her.

To return to the guests. The Reverend Lemuel Whey is a tea-party man, with a curl on his forehead and a scented pocket-handkerchief. He ties his white neckcloth to a wonder, and I believe sleeps in it. He brings his flute with him; and prefers Handel, of course; but has one or two pet profane songs of the sentimental kind, and will occasionally lift up his little pipe in a glee. He does not dance, but the honest fellow would give the world to do it; and he leaves his clogs in the passage, though it is a wonder he wears them, for in the muddiest weather he never has a speck on his foot. He was at St. John's College, Cambridge, and was rather gay for a term or two, he says. He is, in a word, full of the milk-and-water of human kindness, and his family lives near Hackney.

As for Goff, he has a huge shining bald forehead, and immense bristling Indian-red whiskers. He wears white wash-leather gloves, drinks fairly, likes a rubber, and has a story for after dinner, beginning, "Doctor, ye racklackt Sandy M'Lellan, who joined us in the West Indies. Wal, sir," etc. These and little Cutler made up the party.

Now it may not have struck all readers, but any sharp fellow conversant with writing must have found out long ago, that if there had been something exceedingly interesting to narrate with regard to this dinner at Frank Berry's, I should have come out with it a couple of pages since, nor have kept the public looking for so long a time at the dish-covers and ornaments of the table.

But the simple fact must now be told, that there was nothing of the slightest importance occurred at this repast, except that it gave me an opportunity of studying Mrs. Berry in many different ways; and, in spite of the extreme complaisance which she now showed me, of forming, I am sorry to say, a most unfavourable opinion of that fair lady. Truth to tell, I would much rather she should have been civil to Mrs. Muchit, than outrageously complimentary to your humble servant; and as she professed not to know what on earth there was for dinner, would it not have been much more natural for her not to frown, and bob, and wink, and point, and pinch her lips as often as Monsieur Anatole, her French domestic, not knowing the ways of English dinner-tables, placed anything out of its due order? The allusions to Boodle Hall were innumerable, and I don't know any greater bore than to be obliged to talk of a place which belongs to one's elder brother. Many questions were likewise asked about the dowager and her Scotch relatives, the Plumduffs, about whom Lady Pash knew a great deal, having seen them at Court and at Lord Melville's. Of course she had seen them at Court and at Lord Melville's, as she might have seen thousands of Scotchmen besides; but what mattered it to me, who care not a jot for old Lady Fitz-Boodle? "When you write, you'll say you met an old friend of her Ladyship's," says Mrs. Berry, and I faithfully promised I would when I wrote; but if the New Post Office paid us for writing letters (as very possibly it will soon), I could not be bribed to send a line to old Lady Fitz.

In a word, I found that Berry, like many simple fellows before him, had made choice of an imperious, ill-humoured, and underbred female for a wife, and could see with half an eye that he was a great deal too much her slave.

The struggle was not over yet, however. Witness that little encounter before dinner; and once or twice the honest fellow replied rather smartly during the repast, taking especial care to atone as much as possible for his wife's inattention to Jack and Mrs. Muchit, by particular attention to those personages, whom he helped to everything round about and pressed perpetually to champagne; he drank but little himself, for his amiable wife's eye was constantly fixed on him.

Just at the conclusion of the dessert, madame, who had bouded Berry during dinner-time, became particularly gracious to her lord and master, and tenderly asked me if I did not think the French custom was a good one, of men leaving table with the ladies.

"Upon my word, ma'am," says I, "I think it's a most abominable practice."

"And so do I," says Cutler.

"A most abominable practice! Do you hear THAT?" cries Berry, laughing, and filling his glass.

"I'm sure, Frank, when we are alone you always come to the drawing-room," replies the lady, sharply.

"Oh, yes! when we're alone, darling," says Berry, blushing; "but now we're NOT alone—ha, ha! Anatole, du Bordeaux!"

"I'm sure they sat after the ladies at Carlton House; didn't they, Lady Pash?" says Dobus, who likes his glass.

"THAT they did!" says my Lady, giving him a jolly nod.

"I racklackt," exclaims Captain Goff, "when I was in the Mauritius, that Mestress MacWhirter, who commanded the Saxty-Sackond, used to say, 'Mac, if ye want to get lively, ye'll not stop for more than two hours after the leddies have laft ye: if ye want to get drunk, ye'll just dine at the mass.' So ye see, Mestress Barry, what was Mac's allowance—haw, haw! Mester Whey, I'll trouble ye for the o-lives."

But although we were in a clear majority, that indomitable woman, Mrs. Berry, determined to make us all as uneasy as possible, and would take the votes all round. Poor Jack, of course, sided with her, and Whey said he loved a cup of tea and a little music better than all the wine of Bordeaux. As for the Frenchman, when Mrs. Berry said, "And what do you think, M. le Vicomte?"

"Vat you speak?" said M. de Blagueval, breaking silence for the first time during two hours. "Yase—eh? to me you speak?"

"Apry deeny, aimy-voo ally avec les dam?"

"Comment avec les dames?"

"Ally avec les dam com a Parry, ou resty avec les Messew com on Onglyterre?"

"Ah, madame! vous me le demandez?" cries the little wretch, starting up in a theatrical way, and putting out his hand, which Mrs. Berry took, and with this the ladies left the room. Old Lady Pash trotted after her niece with her hand in Whey's, very much wondering at such practices, which were not in the least in vogue in the reign of George III.

Mrs. Berry cast a glance of triumph at her husband, at the defection; and Berry was evidently annoyed that three-eighths of his male forces had left him.

But fancy our delight and astonishment, when in a minute they all three came back again; the Frenchman looking entirely astonished, and the parson and the painter both very queer. The fact is, old downright Lady Pash, who had never been in Paris in her life before, and had no notion of being deprived of her usual hour's respite and nap, said at once to Mrs. Berry, "My dear Angelica, you're surely not going to keep these three men here? Send them back to the dining-room, for I've a thousand things to say to you." And Angelica, who expects to inherit her aunt's property, of course did as she was bid; on which the old lady fell into an easy chair, and fell asleep immediately,—so soon, that is, as the shout caused by the reappearance of the three gentlemen in the dining-room had subsided.

I had meanwhile had some private conversation with little Cutler regarding the character of Mrs. Berry. "She's a regular screw," whispered he; "a regular Tartar. Berry shows fight, though, sometimes, and I've known him have his own way for a week together. After dinner he is his own master, and hers when he has had his share of wine; and that's why she will never allow him to drink any."

Was it a wicked, or was it a noble and honourable thought which came to us both at the same minute, to rescue Berry from his captivity? The ladies, of course, will give their verdict according to their gentle natures; but I know what men of courage will think, and by their jovial judgment will abide.

We received, then, the three lost sheep back into our innocent fold again with the most joyous shouting and cheering. We made Berry (who was, in truth, nothing loth) order up I don't know how much more claret. We obliged the Frenchman to drink malgre lui, and in the course of a short time we had poor Whey in such a state of excitement, that he actually volunteered to sing a song, which he said he had heard at some very gay supper-party at Cambridge, and which begins:

> "A pye sat on a pear-tree,
> A pye sat on a pear-tree,
> A pye sat on a pear-tree,
> Heigh-ho, heigh-ho, heigh-ho!"

Fancy Mrs. Berry's face as she looked in, in the midst of that Bacchanalian ditty, when she saw no less a person than the Reverend Lemuel Whey carolling it!

"Is it you, my dear?" cries Berry, as brave now as any Petruchio. "Come in, and sit down, and hear Whey's song."

"Lady Pash is asleep, Frank," said she.

"Well, darling! that's the very reason. Give Mrs. Berry a glass, Jack, will you?"

"Would you wake your aunt, sir?" hissed out madame.

"NEVER MIND ME, LOVE! I'M AWAKE, AND LIKE IT!" cried the venerable Lady Pash from the salon. "Sing away, gentlemen!"

At which we all set up an audacious cheer; and Mrs. Berry flounced back to the drawing-room, but did not leave the door open, that her aunt might hear our melodies.

Berry had by this time arrived at that confidential state to which a third bottle always brings the well-regulated mind; and he made a clean confession to Cutler and myself of his numerous matrimonial annoyances. He was not allowed to dine out, he said, and but seldom to ask his friends to meet him at home. He never dared smoke a cigar for the life of him, not even in the stables. He spent the mornings dawdling in eternal shops, the evenings at endless tea-parties, or in reading poems or missionary tracts to his wife. He was compelled to take physic whenever she thought he looked a little pale, to change his shoes and stockings whenever he came in from a walk. "Look here," said he, opening his chest, and shaking his fist at Dobus; "look what Angelica and that infernal Dobus have brought me to."

I thought it might be a flannel waistcoat into which madame had forced him; but it was worse: I give you my word of honour it was a PITCH-PLASTER!

We all roared at this, and the doctor as loud as anyone; but he vowed that he had no hand in the pitch-plaster. It was a favourite family remedy of the late apothecary Sir George Catacomb, and had been put on by Mrs. Berry's own fair hands.

When Anatole came in with coffee, Berry was in such high courage, that he told him to go to the deuce with it; and we never caught sight of Lady Pash more, except when, muffled up to the nose, she passed through the salle-a-manger to go to her carriage, in which Dobus and the parson were likewise to be transported to Paris. "Be a man, Frank," says she, "and hold your own"—for the good old lady had taken her nephew's part in the matrimonial business—"and you, Mr. Fitz-Boodle, come and see him often. You're a good fellow, take old one-eyed Callipash's word for it. Shall I take you to Paris?"

Dear kind Angelica, she had told her aunt all I said!

"Don't go, George," says Berry, squeezing me by the hand. So I said I was going to sleep at Versailles that night; but if she would give a convoy to Jack Butts, it would be conferring a great obligation on him; with which favour the old lady accordingly complied, saying to him, with great coolness, "Get up and sit with John in the rumble, Mr. What-d'ye-call-'im." The fact is, the good old soul despises an artist as much as she does a tailor.

Jack tripped to his place very meekly; and "Remember Saturday," cried the Doctor; and "Don't forget Thursday!" exclaimed the divine,—"a bachelor's party, you know." And so the cavalcade drove thundering down the gloomy old Avenue de Paris.

The Frenchman, I forgot to say, had gone away exceedingly ill long before; and the reminiscences of "Thursday" and "Saturday" evoked by Dobus and Whey, were, to tell the truth, parts of our conspiracy; for in the heat of Berry's courage, we had made him promise to dine with us all round en garcon; with all except Captain Goff, who "racklacted" that he was engaged every day for the next three weeks: as indeed he is, to a thirty-sous ordinary which the gallant officer frequents, when not invited elsewhere.

Cutler and I then were the last on the field; and though we were for moving away, Berry, whose vigour had, if possible, been excited by the bustle and colloquy in the night air, insisted upon dragging us back again, and actually proposed a grill for supper!

We found in the salle-a-manger a strong smell of an extinguished lamp, and Mrs. Berry was snuffing out the candles on the sideboard.

"Hullo, my dear!" shouts Berry: "easy, if you please; we've not done yet!"

"Not done yet, Mr. Berry!" groans the lady, in a hollow sepulchral tone.

"No, Mrs. B., not done yet. We are going to have some supper, ain't we, George?"

"I think it's quite time to go home," said Mr. Fitz-Boodle (who, to say the truth, began to tremble himself).

"I think it is, sir; you are quite right, sir; you will pardon me, gentlemen, I have a bad headache, and will retire."

"Good-night, my dear!" said that audacious Berry. "Anatole, tell the cook to broil a fowl and bring some wine."

If the loving couple had been alone, or if Cutler had not been an attache to the embassy, before whom she was afraid of making herself ridiculous, I am confident that Mrs. Berry would have fainted away on the spot; and that all Berry's courage would have tumbled down lifeless by the side of her. So she only gave a martyrised look, and left the room; and while we partook of the very unnecessary repast, was good enough to sing some hymn-tunes to an exceedingly slow movement in the next room, intimating that she was awake, and that, though suffering, she found her consolations in religion.

These melodies did not in the least add to our friend's courage. The devilled fowl had, somehow, no devil in it. The champagne in the glasses looked exceedingly flat and blue. The fact is, that Cutler and I were now both in a state of dire consternation, and soon made a move for our hats, and lighting each a cigar in the hall, made across the little green where the Cupids and nymphs were listening to the dribbling fountain in the dark.

"I'm hanged if I don't have a cigar too!" says Berry, rushing after us; and accordingly putting in his pocket a key about the size of a shovel, which hung by the little handle of the outer grille, forth he sallied, and joined us in our fumigation.

He stayed with us a couple of hours, and returned homewards in perfect good spirits, having given me his word of honour he would dine with us the next day. He put his immense key into the grille, and unlocked it; but the gate would not open: IT WAS BOLTED WITHIN.

He began to make a furious jangling and ringing at the bell; and in oaths, both French and English, called upon the recalcitrant Anatole.

After much tolling of the bell, a light came cutting across the crevices of the inner door; it was thrown open, and a figure appeared with a lamp,—a tall slim figure of a woman, clothed in white from head to foot.

It was Mrs. Berry, and when Cutler and I saw her, we both ran away as fast as our legs could carry us.

Berry, at this, shrieked with a wild laughter. "Remember to-morrow, old boys," shouted he,—"six o'clock;" and we were a quarter of a mile off when the gate closed, and the little mansion of the Avenue de Paris was once more quiet and dark.

The next afternoon, as we were playing at billiards, Cutler saw Mrs. Berry drive by in her carriage; and as soon as rather a long rubber was over, I thought I would go and look for our poor friend, and so went down to the Pavilion. Every door was open, as the wont is in France, and I walked in unannounced, and saw this:

He was playing a duet with her on the flute. She had been out but for half-an-hour, after not speaking all the morning; and having seen Cutler at the billiard-room window, and suspecting we might take advantage of her absence, she had suddenly returned home again, and had flung herself, weeping, into her Frank's arms, and said she could not bear to leave him in anger. And so, after sitting for a little while sobbing on his knee, she had forgotten and forgiven every thing!

The dear angel! I met poor Frank in Bond Street only yesterday; but he crossed over to the other side of the way. He had on goloshes, and is grown very fat and pale. He has shaved off his moustaches, and, instead, wears a respirator. He has taken his name off all his clubs, and lives very grimly in Baker Street. Well, ladies, no doubt you say he is right: and what are the odds, so long as You are happy?

Dennis Haggarty's wife

There was an odious Irishwoman who with her daughter used to frequent the "Royal Hotel" at Leamington some years ago, and who went by the name of Mrs. Major Gam. Gam had been a distinguished officer in His Majesty's service, whom nothing but death and his own amiable wife could overcome. The widow mourned her husband in the most becoming bombazeen she could muster, and had at least half an inch of lampblack round the immense visiting tickets which she left at the houses of the nobility and gentry her friends.

Some of us, I am sorry to say, used to call her Mrs. Major Gammon; for if the worthy widow had a propensity, it was to talk largely of herself and family (of her own family, for she held her husband's very cheap), and of the wonders of her paternal mansion, Molloyville, county of Mayo. She was of the Molloys of that county; and though I never heard of the family before, I have little doubt, from what Mrs. Major Gam stated, that they were the most ancient and illustrious family of that part of Ireland. I remember there came down to see his aunt a young fellow with huge red whiskers and tight nankeens, a green coat, and an awful breastpin, who, after two days' stay at the Spa, proposed marriage to Miss S—, or, in default, a duel with her father; and who drove a flash curricle with a bay and a grey, and who was presented with much pride by Mrs. Gam as Castlereagh Molloy of Molloyville. We all agreed that he was the most insufferable snob of the whole season, and were delighted when a bailiff came down in search of him.

Well, this is all I know personally of the Molloyville family; but at the house if you met the widow Gam, and talked on any subject in life, you were sure to hear of it. If you asked her to have peas at dinner, she would say, "Oh, sir, after the peas at Molloyville, I really don't care for any others,—do I, dearest Jemima? We always had a dish in the month of June, when my father gave his head gardener a guinea (we had three at Molloyville), and sent him with his compliments and a quart of peas to our neighbour, dear Lord Marrowfat. What a sweet place Marrowfat Park is! isn't it, Jemima?" If a carriage passed by the window, Mrs. Major Gammon would be sure to tell you that there were three carriages at Molloyville, "the barouche, the chawiot, and the covered cyar." In the same manner she would favour you with the number and names of the footmen of the establishment; and on a visit to Warwick Castle (for this bustling woman made one in every party of pleasure that was formed from the hotel), she gave us to understand that the great walk by the river was altogether inferior to the principal avenue of Molloyville Park. I should not have been able to tell so much about Mrs. Gam and her daughter, but that, between ourselves, I was particularly sweet upon a young lady at the time, whose papa lived at the "Royal," and was under the care of Doctor Jephson.

The Jemima appealed to by Mrs. Gam in the above sentence was, of course, her daughter, apostrophised by her mother, "Jemima, my soul's darling?" or, "Jemima, my blessed child!" or, "Jemima, my own love!" The sacrifices that Mrs. Gam had made for that daughter were, she said, astonishing. The money she had spent in masters upon her, the illnesses through which she had nursed her, the ineffable love the mother bore her, were only known to Heaven, Mrs. Gam said. They used to come into the room with their arms round each other's waists: at dinner between the courses the mother would sit with one hand locked in her daughter's; and if only two or three young men were present at the time, would be pretty sure to kiss her Jemima more than once during the time whilst the bohea was poured out.

As for Miss Gam, if she was not handsome, candour forbids me to say she was ugly. She was neither one nor t'other. She was a person who wore ringlets and a band round her forehead; she knew four songs, which became rather tedious at the end of a couple of months' acquaintance; she had excessively bare shoulders; she inclined to wear numbers of cheap ornaments, rings, brooches, ferronnieres, smelling-bottles, and was always, we thought, very smartly dressed: though old Mrs. Lynx hinted that her gowns and her mother's were turned over and over again, and that her eyes were almost put out by darning stockings.

These eyes Miss Gam had very large, though rather red and weak, and used to roll them about at every eligible unmarried man in the place. But though the widow subscribed to all the balls, though she hired a fly to go to the meet of the hounds, though she was constant at church, and Jemima sang louder than any person there except the clerk, and though, probably, any person who made her a happy husband would be invited down to enjoy the three footmen, gardeners, and carriages at Molloyville, yet no English gentleman was found sufficiently audacious to propose. Old Lynx used to say that the pair had been at Tunbridge, Harrogate, Brighton, Ramsgate, Cheltenham, for this eight years past; where they had met, it seemed, with no better fortune. Indeed, the widow looked rather high for her blessed child: and as she looked with the contempt which no small number of Irish people feel upon all persons who get their bread by labour or commerce; and as she was a person whose energetic manners, costume, and brogue were not much to the taste of quiet English country gentlemen, Jemima—sweet, spotless flower—still remained on her hands, a thought withered, perhaps, and seedy.

Now, at this time, the 120th Regiment was quartered at Weedon Barracks, and with the corps was a certain Assistant-Surgeon Haggarty, a large, lean, tough, raw-boned man, with big hands, knock-knees, and carroty whiskers, and, withal, as honest a creature as ever handled a lancet. Haggarty, as his name imports, was of the very same nation as Mrs. Gam, and, what is more, the honest fellow had some of the peculiarities which belonged to the widow, and bragged about his family almost as much as she did. I do not know of what particular part of Ireland they were kings; but monarchs they must have been, as have been the ancestors of so many thousand Hibernian families; but they had been men of no small consideration in Dublin, "where my father," Haggarty said, "is as well known as King William's statue, and where he 'rowls his carriage, too,' let me tell ye."

Hence, Haggarty was called by the wags "Rowl the carriage," and several of them made inquiries of Mrs. Gam regarding him: "Mrs. Gam, when you used to go up from Molloyville to the Lord Lieutenant's balls, and had your townhouse in Fitzwilliam Square, used you to meet the famous Doctor Haggarty in society?"

"Is it Surgeon Haggarty of Gloucester Street ye mean? The black Papist! D'ye suppose that the Molloys would sit down to table with a creature of that sort?"

"Why, isn't he the most famous physician in Dublin, and doesn't he rowl his carriage there?"

"The horrid wretch! He keeps a shop, I tell ye, and sends his sons out with the medicine. He's got four of them off into the army, Ulick and Phil, and Terence and Denny, and now it's Charles that takes out the physic. But how should I know about these odious creatures? Their mother was a Burke, of Burke's Town, county Cavan, and brought Surgeon Haggarty two thousand pounds. She was a Protestant; and I am surprised how she could have taken up with a horrid odious Popish apothecary!"

From the extent of the widow's information, I am led to suppose that the inhabitants of Dublin are not less anxious about their neighbours than are the natives of English cities; and I think it is very probable that Mrs. Gam's account of the young Haggartys who carried out the medicine is perfectly correct, for a lad in the 120th made a caricature of Haggarty coming out of a chemist's shop with an oilcloth basket under his arm, which set the worthy surgeon in such a fury that there would have been a duel between him and the ensign, could the fiery doctor have had his way.

Now, Dionysius Haggarty was of an exceedingly inflammable temperament, and it chanced that of all the invalids, the visitors, the young squires of Warwickshire, the young manufacturers from Birmingham, the young officers from the barracks—it chanced, unluckily for Miss Gam and himself, that he was the only individual who was in the least smitten by her personal charms. He was very tender and modest about his love, however, for it must be owned that he respected Mrs. Gam hugely, and fully admitted, like a good simple fellow as he was, the superiority of that lady's birth and breeding to his own. How could he hope that he, a humble assistant-surgeon, with a thousand pounds his Aunt Kitty left him for all his fortune—how could he hope that one of the race of Molloyville would ever condescend to marry him?

Inflamed, however, by love, and inspired by wine, one day at a picnic at Kenilworth, Haggarty, whose love and raptures were the talk of the whole regiment, was induced by his waggish comrades to make a proposal in form.

"Are you aware, Mr. Haggarty, that you are speaking to a Molloy?" was all the reply majestic Mrs. Gam made when, according to the usual formula, the fluttering Jemima referred her suitor to "Mamma." She left him with a look which was meant to crush the poor fellow to earth; she gathered up her cloak and bonnet, and precipitately called for her fly. She took care to tell every single soul in Leamington that the son of the odious Papist apothecary had had the audacity to propose for her daughter (indeed a proposal, coming from whatever quarter it may, does no harm), and left Haggarty in a state of extreme depression and despair.

His down-heartedness, indeed, surprised most of his acquaintances in and out of the regiment, for the young lady was no beauty, and a doubtful fortune, and Dennis was a man outwardly of an unromantic turn, who seemed to have a great deal more liking for beefsteak and whisky-punch than for women, however fascinating.

But there is no doubt this shy uncouth rough fellow had a warmer and more faithful heart hid within him than many a dandy who is as handsome as Apollo. I, for my part, never can understand why a man falls in love, and heartily give him credit for so doing, never mind with what or whom. THAT I take to be a point quite as much beyond an individual's own control as the catching of the small-pox or the colour of his hair. To the surprise of all, Assistant-Surgeon Dionysius Haggarty was deeply and seriously in love; and I am told that one day he very nearly killed the before-mentioned young ensign with a carving-knife, for venturing to make a second caricature, representing Lady Gammon and Jemima in a fantastical park, surrounded by three gardeners, three carriages, three footmen, and the covered cyar. He would have no joking concerning them. He became moody and quarrelsome of habit. He was for some time much more in the surgery and hospital than in the mess. He gave up the eating, for the most part, of those vast quantities of beef and pudding, for which his stomach used to afford such ample and swift accommodation; and when the cloth was drawn, instead of taking twelve tumblers, and singing Irish melodies, as he used to do, in a horrible cracked yelling voice, he would retire to his own apartment, or gloomily pace the barrack-yard, or madly whip and spur a grey mare he had on the road to Leamington, where his Jemima (although invisible for him) still dwelt.

The season at Leamington coming to a conclusion by the withdrawal of the young fellows who frequented that watering-place, the widow Gam retired to her usual quarters for the other months of the year. Where these quarters were, I think we have no right to ask, for I believe she had quarrelled with her brother at Molloyville, and besides, was a great deal too proud to be a burden on anybody.

Not only did the widow quit Leamington, but very soon afterwards the 120th received its marching orders, and left Weedon and Warwickshire. Haggarty's appetite was by this time partially restored, but his love was not altered, and his humour was still morose and gloomy. I am informed that at this period of his life he wrote some poems relative to his unhappy passion; a wild set of verses of several lengths, and in his handwriting, being discovered upon a sheet of paper in which a pitch-plaster was wrapped up, which Lieutenant and Adjutant Wheezer was compelled to put on for a cold.

Fancy then, three years afterwards, the surprise of all Haggarty's acquaintances on reading in the public papers the following announcement:

"Married, at Monkstown on the 12th instant, Dionysius Haggarty, Esq., of H.M. 120th Foot, to Jemima Amelia Wilhelmina Molloy, daughter of the late Major Lancelot Gam, R.M., and granddaughter of the late, and niece of the present Burke Bodkin Blake Molloy, Esq., Molloyville, county Mayo."

"Has the course of true love at last begun to run smooth?" thought I, as I laid down the paper; and the old times, and the old leering bragging widow, and the high shoulders of her daughter, and the jolly days with the 120th, and Doctor Jephson's one-horse chaise, and the Warwickshire hunt, and—and Louisa S—, but never mind HER,—came back to my mind. Has that good-natured simple fellow at last met with his reward? Well, if he has not to marry the mother-in-law too, he may get on well enough.

Another year announced the retirement of Assistant-Surgeon Haggarty from the 120th, where he was replaced by Assistant-Surgeon Angus Rothsay Leech, a Scotchman, probably; with whom I have not the least acquaintance, and who has nothing whatever to do with this little history.

Still more years passed on, during which time I will not say that I kept a constant watch upon the fortunes of Mr. Haggarty and his lady; for, perhaps, if the truth were known, I never thought for a moment about them; until one day, being at Kingstown, near Dublin, dawdling on the beach, and staring at the Hill of Howth, as most people at that watering-place do, I saw coming towards me a tall gaunt man, with a pair of bushy red whiskers, of which I thought I had seen the like in former years, and a face which could be no other than Haggarty's. It was Haggarty, ten years older than when we last met, and greatly more grim and thin. He had on one shoulder a young gentleman in a dirty tartan costume, and a face exceedingly like his own peeping from under a battered plume of black feathers, while with his other hand he was dragging a light green go-cart, in which reposed a female infant of some two years old. Both were roaring with great power of lungs.

As soon as Dennis saw me, his face lost the dull puzzled expression which had seemed to characterise it; he dropped the pole of the go-cart from one hand, and his son from the other, and came jumping forward to greet me with all his might, leaving his progeny roaring in the road.

"Bless my sowl," says he, "sure it's Fitz-Boodle? Fitz, don't you remember me? Dennis Haggarty of the 120th? Leamington, you know? Molloy, my boy, hould your tongue, and stop your screeching, and Jemima's too; d'ye hear? Well, it does good to sore eyes to see an old face. How fat you're grown, Fitz; and were ye ever in Ireland before? and a'n't ye delighted with it? Confess, now, isn't it beautiful?"

This question regarding the merits of their country, which I have remarked is put by most Irish persons, being answered in a satisfactory manner, and the shouts of the infants appeased from an apple-stall hard by, Dennis and I talked of old times; I congratulated him on his marriage with the lovely girl whom we all admired, and hoped he had a fortune with her, and so forth. His appearance, however, did not bespeak a great fortune: he had an old grey hat, short old trousers, an old waistcoat with regimental buttons, and patched Blucher boots, such as are not usually sported by persons in easy life.

"Ah!" says he, with a sigh, in reply to my queries, "times are changed since them days, Fitz-Boodle. My wife's not what she was—the beautiful creature you knew her. Molloy, my boy, run off in a hurry to your mamma, and tell her an English gentleman is coming home to dine; for you'll dine with me, Fitz, in course?" And I agreed to partake of that meal; though Master Molloy altogether declined to obey his papa's orders with respect to announcing the stranger.

"Well, I must announce you myself," said Haggarty, with a smile. "Come, it's just dinner-time, and my little cottage is not a hundred yards off." Accordingly, we all marched in procession to Dennis's little cottage, which was one of a row and a half of one-storied houses, with little courtyards before them, and mostly with very fine names on the doorposts of each. "Surgeon Haggarty" was emblazoned on Dennis's gate, on a stained green copper-plate; and, not content with this, on the door-post above the bell was an oval with the inscription of "New Molloyville." The bell was broken, of course; the court, or garden-path, was mouldy, weedy, seedy; there were some dirty rocks, by way of ornament, round a faded glass-plat in the centre, some clothes and rags hanging out of most part of the windows of New Molloyville, the immediate entrance to which was by a battered scraper, under a broken trellis-work, up which a withered creeper declined any longer to climb.

"Small, but snug," says Haggarty: "I'll lead the way, Fitz; put your hat on the flower-pot there, and turn to the left into the drawing-room." A fog of onions and turf-smoke filled the whole of the house, and gave signs that dinner was not far off. Far off? You could hear it frizzling in the kitchen, where the maid was also endeavouring to hush the crying of a third refractory child. But as we entered, all three of Haggarty's darlings were in full roar.

"Is it you, Dennis?" cried a sharp raw voice, from a dark corner in the drawing-room to which we were introduced, and in which a dirty tablecloth was laid for dinner, some bottles of porter and a cold mutton-bone being laid out on a rickety grand piano hard by. "Ye're always late, Mr. Haggarty. Have you brought the whisky from Nowlan's? I'll go bail ye've not, now."

"My dear, I've brought an old friend of yours and mine to take pot-luck with us to-day," said Dennis.

"When is he to come?" said the lady. At which speech I was rather surprised, for I stood before her.

"Here he is, Jemima my love," answered Dennis, looking at me. "Mr. Fitz-Boodle: don't you remember him in Warwickshire, darling?"

"Mr. Fitz-Boodle! I am very glad to see him," said the lady, rising and curtseying with much cordiality.

Mrs. Haggarty was blind.

Mrs. Haggarty was not only blind, but it was evident that smallpox had been the cause of her loss of vision. Her eyes were bound with a bandage, her features were entirely swollen, scarred and distorted by the horrible effects of the malady. She had been knitting in a corner when we entered, and was wrapped in a very dirty bedgown. Her voice to me was quite different to that in which she addressed her husband. She spoke to Haggarty in broad Irish: she addressed me in that most odious of all languages—Irish-English, endeavouring to the utmost to disguise her brogue, and to speak with the true dawdling distingue English air.

"Are you long in I-a-land?" said the poor creature in this accent. "You must faind it a sad ba'ba'ous place, Mr. Fitz-Boodle, I'm shu-ah! It was vary kaind of you to come upon us en famille, and accept a dinner sans ceremonie. Mr. Haggarty, I hope you'll put the waine into aice, Mr. Fitz-Boodle must be melted with this hot weathah."

For some time she conducted the conversation in this polite strain, and I was obliged to say, in reply to a query of hers, that I did not find her the least altered, though I should never have recognised her but for this rencontre. She told Haggarty with a significant air to get the wine from the cellah, and whispered to me that he was his own butlah; and the poor fellow, taking the hint, scudded away into the town for a pound of beefsteak and a couple of bottles of wine from the tavern.

"Will the childhren get their potatoes and butther here?" said a barefoot girl, with long black hair flowing over her face, which she thrust in at the door.

"Let them sup in the nursery, Elizabeth, and send—ah! Edwards to me."

"Is it cook you mane, ma'am?" said the girl.

"Send her at once!" shrieked the unfortunate woman; and the noise of frying presently ceasing, a hot woman made her appearance, wiping her brows with her apron, and asking, with an accent decidedly Hibernian, what the misthress wanted.

"Lead me up to my dressing-room, Edwards: I really am not fit to be seen in this dishabille by Mr. Fitz-Boodle."

"Fait' I can't!" says Edwards; "sure the masther's at the butcher's, and can't look to the kitchen-fire!"

"Nonsense, I must go!" cried Mrs. Haggarty; and Edwards, putting on a resigned air, and giving her arm and face a further rub with her apron, held out her arm to Mrs. Dennis, and the pair went upstairs.

She left me to indulge my reflections for half-an-hour, at the end of which period she came downstairs dressed in an old yellow satin, with the poor shoulders exposed just as much as ever. She had mounted a tawdry cap, which Haggarty himself must have selected for her. She had all sorts of necklaces, bracelets, and earrings in gold, in garnets, in mother-of-pearl, in ormolu. She brought in a furious savour of musk, which drove the odours of onions and turf-smoke before it; and she waved across her wretched angular mean scarred features an old cambric handkerchief with a yellow lace-border.

"And so you would have known me anywhere, Mr. Fitz-Boodle?" said she, with a grin that was meant to be most fascinating. "I was sure you would; for though my dreadful illness deprived me of my sight, it is a mercy that it did not change my features or complexion at all!"

This mortification had been spared the unhappy woman; but I don't know whether, with all her vanity, her infernal pride, folly, and selfishness, it was charitable to leave her in her error.

Yet why correct her? There is a quality in certain people which is above all advice, exposure, or correction. Only let a man or woman have DULNESS sufficient, and they need bow to no extant authority. A dullard recognises no betters; a dullard can't see that he is in the wrong; a dullard has no scruples of conscience, no doubts of pleasing, or succeeding, or doing right; no qualms for other people's feelings, no respect but for the fool himself. How can you make a fool perceive he is a fool? Such a personage can no more see his own folly than he can see his own ears. And the great quality of Dulness is to be unalterably contented with itself. What myriads of souls are there of this admirable sort,—selfish, stingy, ignorant, passionate, brutal; bad sons, mothers, fathers, never known to do kind actions!

To pause, however, in this disquisition, which was carrying us far off Kingstown, New Molloyville, Ireland—nay, into the wide world wherever Dulness inhabits—let it be stated that Mrs. Haggarty, from my brief acquaintance with her and her mother, was of the order of persons just mentioned. There was an air of conscious merit about her, very hard to swallow along with the infamous dinner poor Dennis managed, after much delay, to get on the table. She did not fail to invite me to Molloyville, where she said her cousin would be charmed to see me; and she told me almost as many anecdotes about that place as her mother used to impart in former days. I observed, moreover, that Dennis cut her the favourite pieces of the beefsteak, that she ate thereof with great gusto, and that she drank with similar eagerness of the various strong liquors at table. "We Irish ladies are all fond of a leetle glass of punch," she said, with a playful air, and Dennis mixed her a powerful tumbler of such violent grog as I myself could swallow only with some difficulty. She talked of her suffering a great deal, of her sacrifices, of the luxuries to which she had been accustomed before marriage,—in a word, of a hundred of those themes on which some ladies are in the custom of enlarging when they wish to plague some husbands.

But honest Dennis, far from being angry at this perpetual, wearisome, impudent recurrence to her own superiority, rather encouraged the conversation than otherwise. It pleased him to hear his wife discourse about her merits and family splendours. He was so thoroughly beaten down and henpecked, that he, as it were, gloried in his servitude, and fancied that his wife's magnificence reflected credit on himself. He looked towards me, who was half sick of the woman and her egotism, as if expecting me to exhibit the deepest sympathy, and flung me glances across the table as much as to say, "What a gifted creature my Jemima is, and what a fine fellow I am to be in possession of her!" When the children came down she scolded them, of course, and dismissed them abruptly (for which circumstance, perhaps, the writer of these pages was not in his heart very sorry), and, after having sat a preposterously long time, left us, asking whether we would have coffee there or in her boudoir.

"Oh! here, of course," said Dennis, with rather a troubled air, and in about ten minutes the lovely creature was led back to us again by "Edwards," and the coffee made its appearance. After coffee her husband begged her to let Mr. Fitz-Boodle hear her voice: "He longs for some of his old favourites."

"No! Do you?" said she; and was led in triumph to the jingling old piano, and with a screechy wiry voice, sang those very abominable old ditties which I had heard her sing at Leamington ten years back.

Haggarty, as she sang, flung himself back in the chair delighted. Husbands always are, and with the same song, one that they have heard when they were nineteen years old probably; most Englishmen's tunes have that date, and it is rather affecting, I think, to hear an old gentleman of sixty or seventy quavering the old ditty that was fresh when HE was fresh and in his prime. If he has a musical wife, depend on it he thinks her old songs of 1788 are better than any he has heard since: in fact he has heard NONE since. When the old couple are in high good-humour the old gentleman will take the old lady round the waist, and say, "My dear, do sing me one of your own songs," and she sits down and sings with her old voice, and, as she sings, the roses of her youth bloom again for a moment. Ranelagh resuscitates, and she is dancing a minuet in powder and a train.

This is another digression. It was occasioned by looking at poor Dennis's face while his wife was screeching (and, believe me, the former was the more pleasant occupation). Bottom tickled by the fairies could not have been in greater ecstasies. He thought the music was divine; and had further reason for exulting in it, which was, that his wife was always in a good humour after singing, and never would sing but in that happy frame of mind. Dennis had hinted so much in our little colloquy during the ten minutes of his lady's absence in the "boudoir;" so, at the conclusion of each piece, we shouted "Bravo!" and clapped our hands like mad.

Such was my insight into the life of Surgeon Dionysius Haggarty and his wife; and I must have come upon him at a favourable moment too, for poor Dennis has spoken, subsequently, of our delightful evening at Kingstown, and evidently thinks to this day that his friend was fascinated by the entertainment there. His inward economy was as follows: he had his half-pay, a thousand pounds, about a hundred a year that his father left, and his wife had sixty pounds a year from the mother; which the mother, of course, never paid. He had no practice, for he was absorbed in attention to his Jemima and the children, whom he used to wash, to dress, to carry out, to walk, or to ride, as we have seen, and who could not have a servant, as their dear blind mother could never be left alone. Mrs. Haggarty, a great invalid, used to lie in bed till one, and have breakfast and hot luncheon there. A fifth part of his income was spent in having her wheeled about in a chair, by which it was his duty to walk daily for an allotted number of hours. Dinner would ensue, and the amateur clergy, who abound in Ireland, and of whom Mrs. Haggarty was a great admirer, lauded her everywhere as a model of resignation and virtue, and praised beyond measure the admirable piety with which she bore her sufferings.

Well, every man to his taste. It did not certainly appear to me that SHE was the martyr of the family.

"The circumstances of my marriage with Jemima," Dennis said to me, in some after conversations we had on this interesting subject, "were the most romantic and touching you can conceive. You saw what an impression the dear girl had made upon me when we were at Weedon; for from the first day I set eyes on her, and heard her sing her delightful song of 'Dark-eyed Maiden of Araby,' I felt, and said to Turniquet of ours, that very night, that SHE was the dark-eyed maid of Araby for ME—not that she was, you know, for she was born in Shropshire. But I felt that I had seen the woman who was to make me happy or miserable for life. You know how I proposed for her at Kenilworth, and how I was rejected, and how I almost shot myself in consequence—no, you don't know that, for I said nothing about it to anyone, but I can tell you it was a very near thing; and a very lucky thing for me I didn't do it: for,—would you believe it?—the dear girl was in love with me all the time."

"Was she really?" said I, who recollected that Miss Gam's love of those days showed itself in a very singular manner; but the fact is, when women are most in love they most disguise it.

"Over head and ears in love with poor Dennis," resumed that worthy fellow, "who'd ever have thought it? But I have it from the best authority, from her own mother, with whom I'm not over and above good friends now; but of this fact she assured me, and I'll tell you when and how.

"We were quartered at Cork three years after we were at Weedon, and it was our last year at home; and a great mercy that my dear girl spoke in time, or where should we have been now? Well, one day, marching home from parade, I saw a lady seated at an open window, by another who seemed an invalid, and the lady at the window, who was dressed in the profoundest mourning, cried out, with a scream, 'Gracious, heavens! it's Mr. Haggarty of the 120th.'

"'Sure I know that voice,' says I to Whiskerton.

"'It's a great mercy you don't know it a deal too well,' says he: 'it's Lady Gammon. She's on some husband-hunting scheme, depend on it, for that daughter of hers. She was at Bath last year on the same errand,

and at Cheltenham the year before, where, Heaven bless you! she's as well known as the "Hen and Chickens."'

"'I'll thank you not to speak disrespectfully of Miss Jemima Gam,' said I to Whiskerton; 'she's of one of the first families in Ireland, and whoever says a word against a woman I once proposed for, insults me,—do you understand?'

"'Well, marry her, if you like,' says Whiskerton, quite peevish: 'marry her, and be hanged!'

"Marry her! the very idea of it set my brain a-whirling, and made me a thousand times more mad than I am by nature.

"You may be sure I walked up the hill to the parade-ground that afternoon, and with a beating heart too. I came to the widow's house. It was called 'New Molloyville,' as this is. Wherever she takes a house for six months she calls it 'New Molloyville;' and has had one in Mallow, in Bandon, in Sligo, in Castlebar, in Fermoy, in Drogheda, and the deuce knows where besides: but the blinds were down, and though I thought I saw somebody behind 'em, no notice was taken of poor Denny Haggarty, and I paced up and down all mess-time in hopes of catching a glimpse of Jemima, but in vain. The next day I was on the ground again; I was just as much in love as ever, that's the fact. I'd never been in that way before, look you; and when once caught, I knew it was for life.

"There's no use in telling you how long I beat about the bush, but when I DID get admittance to the house (it was through the means of young Castlereagh Molloy, whom you may remember at Leamington, and who was at Cork for the regatta, and used to dine at our mess, and had taken a mighty fancy to me)—when I DID get into the house, I say, I rushed in medias res at once; I couldn't keep myself quiet, my heart was too full.

"Oh, Fitz! I shall never forget the day,—the moment I was inthrojuiced into the dthrawing-room" (as he began to be agitated, Dennis's brogue broke out with greater richness than ever; but though a stranger may catch, and repeat from memory, a few words, it is next to impossible for him to KEEP UP A CONVERSATION in Irish, so that we had best give up all attempts to imitate Dennis). "When I saw old mother Gam," said he, "my feelings overcame me all at once. I rowled down on the ground, sir, as if I'd been hit by a musket-ball. 'Dearest madam,' says I, 'I'll die if you don't give me Jemima.'

"'Heavens, Mr. Haggarty!' says she, 'how you seize me with surprise! Castlereagh, my dear nephew, had you not better leave us?' and away he went, lighting a cigar, and leaving me still on the floor.

"'Rise, Mr. Haggarty,' continued the widow. 'I will not attempt to deny that this constancy towards my daughter is extremely affecting, however sudden your present appeal may be. I will not attempt to deny that, perhaps, Jemima may have a similar feeling; but, as I said, I never could give my daughter to a Catholic.'

"'I'm as good a Protestant as yourself, ma'am,' says I; 'my mother was an heiress, and we were all brought up her way.'

"'That makes the matter very different,' says she, turning up the whites of her eyes. 'How could I ever have reconciled it to my conscience to see my blessed child married to a Papist? How could I ever have taken him to Molloyville? Well, this obstacle being removed, *I* must put myself no longer in the way between two young people. *I* must sacrifice myself; as I always have when my darling girl was in question. You shall see her, the poor dear lovely gentle sufferer, and learn your fate from her own lips.'

"'The sufferer, ma'am,' says I; 'has Miss Gam been ill?'

"'What! haven't you heard?' cried the widow. 'Haven't you heard of the dreadful illness which so nearly carried her from me? For nine weeks, Mr. Haggarty, I watched her day and night, without taking a wink of sleep,—for nine weeks she lay trembling between death and life; and I paid the doctor eighty-three guineas. She is restored now; but she is the wreck of the beautiful creature she was. Suffering, and, perhaps, ANOTHER DISAPPOINTMENT—but we won't mention that Now—have so pulled her down. But I will leave you, and prepare my sweet girl for this strange, this entirely unexpected visit.'

"I won't tell you what took place between me and Jemima, to whom I was introduced as she sat in the darkened room, poor sufferer! nor describe to you with what a thrill of joy I seized (after groping about for it) her poor emaciated hand. She did not withdraw it; I came out of that room an engaged man, sir; and Now I was enabled to show her that I had always loved her sincerely, for there was my will, made three years back, in her favour: that night she refused me, as I told ye. I would have shot myself, but they'd have brought me in non compos; and my brother Mick would have contested the will, and so I determined to live, in order that she might benefit by my dying. I had but a thousand pounds then: since that my father has left me two more. I willed every shilling to her, as you may fancy, and settled it upon her when we married, as we did soon after. It was not for some time that I was allowed to see the poor girl's face, or, indeed, was aware of the horrid loss she had sustained. Fancy my agony, my dear fellow, when I saw that beautiful wreck!"

There was something not a little affecting to think, in the conduct of this brave fellow, that he never once, as he told his story, seemed to allude to the possibility of his declining to marry a woman who was not the same as the woman he loved; but that he was quite as faithful to her now, as he had been when captivated by the poor tawdry charms of the silly Miss of Leamington. It was hard that such a noble heart as this should be flung away upon yonder foul mass of greedy vanity. Was it hard, or not, that he should remain deceived in his obstinate humility, and continue to admire the selfish silly being whom he had chosen to worship?

"I should have been appointed surgeon of the regiment," continued Dennis, "soon after, when it was ordered abroad to Jamaica, where it now is. But my wife would not hear of going, and said she would break her heart if she left her mother. So I retired on half-pay, and took this cottage; and in case any practice should fall in my way—why, there is my name on the brass plate, and I'm ready for anything that comes. But the only case that ever DID come was one day when I was driving my wife in the chaise; and another, one night, of a beggar with a broken head. My wife makes me a present of a baby every year, and we've no debts; and between you and me and the post, as long as my mother-in-law is out of the house, I'm as happy as I need be."

"What! you and the old lady don't get on well?" said I.

"I can't say we do; it's not in nature, you know," said Dennis, with a faint grin. "She comes into the house, and turns it topsy-turvy. When she's here I'm obliged to sleep in the scullery. She's never paid her daughter's income since the first year, though she brags about her sacrifices as if she had ruined herself for Jemima; and besides, when she's here, there's a whole clan of the Molloys, horse, foot, and dragoons, that are quartered upon us, and eat me out of house and home."

"And is Molloyville such a fine place as the widow described it?" asked I, laughing, and not a little curious.

"Oh, a mighty fine place entirely!" said Dennis. "There's the oak park of two hundred acres, the finest land ye ever saw, only they've cut all the wood down. The garden in the old Molloys' time, they say, was the finest ever seen in the West of Ireland; but they've taken all the glass to mend the house windows: and small blame to them either. There's a clear rent-roll of thirty-five hundred a year, only it's in the hand of receivers; besides other debts, for which there is no land security."

"Your cousin-in-law, Castlereagh Molloy, won't come into a large fortune?"

"Oh, he'll do very well," said Dennis. "As long as he can get credit, he's not the fellow to stint himself. Faith, I was fool enough to put my name to a bit of paper for him, and as they could not catch him in Mayo, they laid hold of me at Kingstown here. And there was a pretty to do. Didn't Mrs. Gam say I was ruining her family, that's all? I paid it by instalments (for all my money is settled on Jemima); and Castlereagh, who's an honourable fellow, offered me any satisfaction in life. Anyhow, he couldn't do more than THAT."

"Of course not: and now you're friends?"

"Yes, and he and his aunt have had a tiff, too; and he abuses her properly, I warrant ye. He says that she carried about Jemima from place to place, and flung her at the head of every unmarried man in England a'most—my poor Jemima, and she all the while dying in love with me! As soon as she got over the small-pox—she took it at Fermoy—God bless her, I wish I'd been by to be her nurse-tender—as soon as she was rid of it, the old lady said to Castlereagh, 'Castlereagh, go to the bar'cks, and find out in the Army List where the 120th is.' Off she came to Cork hot foot. It appears that while she was ill, Jemima's love for me showed itself in such a violent way that her mother was overcome, and promised that, should the dear child recover, she would try and bring us together. Castlereagh says she would have gone after us to Jamaica."

"I have no doubt she would," said I.

"Could you have a stronger proof of love than that?" cried Dennis. "My dear girl's illness and frightful blindness have, of course, injured her health and her temper. She cannot in her position look to the children, you know, and so they come under my charge for the most part; and her temper is unequal, certainly. But you see what a sensitive, refined, elegant creature she is, and may fancy that she's often put out by a rough fellow like me."

Here Dennis left me, saying it was time to go and walk out the children; and I think his story has matter of some wholesome reflection in it for bachelors who are about to change their condition, or may console some who are mourning their celibacy. Marry, gentlemen, if you like; leave your comfortable dinner at the club for cold-mutton and curl-papers at your home; give up your books or pleasures, and take to yourselves wives and children; but think well on what you do first, as I have no doubt you will after this advice and example. Advice is always useful in matters of love; men always take it; they always follow other people's opinions, not their own: they always profit by example. When they see a pretty woman, and feel the delicious madness of love coming over them, they always stop to calculate her temper, her money, their own money, or suitableness for the married life... Ha, ha, ha! Let us fool in this way no more. I have been in love forty-three times with all ranks and conditions of women, and would have married every time if they would have let me. How many wives had King Solomon, the wisest of men? And is not that story a warning to us that Love is master of the wisest? It is only fools who defy him.

I must come, however, to the last, and perhaps the saddest, part of poor Denny Haggarty's history. I met him once more, and in such a condition as made me determine to write this history.

In the month of June last I happened to be at Richmond, a delightful little place of retreat; and there, sunning himself upon the terrace, was my old friend of the 120th: he looked older, thinner, poorer, and more wretched than I had ever seen him. "What! you have given up Kingstown?" said I, shaking him by the hand.

"Yes," says he.

"And is my lady and your family here at Richmond?"

"No," says he, with a sad shake of the head; and the poor fellow's hollow eyes filled with tears.

"Good heavens, Denny! what's the matter?" said I. He was squeezing my hand like a vice as I spoke.

"They've LEFT me!" he burst out with a dreadful shout of passionate grief—a horrible scream which seemed to be wrenched out of his heart. "Left me!" said he, sinking down on a seat, and clenching his great fists, and shaking his lean arms wildly. "I'm a wise man now, Mr. Fitz-Boodle. Jemima has gone away from me, and yet you know how I loved her, and how happy we were! I've got nobody now; but I'll die soon, that's one comfort: and to think it's she that'll kill me after all!"

The story, which he told with a wild and furious lamentation such as is not known among men of our cooler country, and such as I don't like now to recall, was a very simple one. The mother-in-law had taken possession of the house, and had driven him from it. His property at his marriage was settled on his wife. She had never loved him, and told him this secret at last, and drove him out of doors with her selfish scorn and ill-temper. The boy had died; the girls were better, he said, brought up among the Molloys than they could be with him; and so he was quite alone in the world, and was living, or rather dying, on forty pounds a year.

His troubles are very likely over by this time. The two fools who caused his misery will never read this history of him; THEY never read godless stories in magazines: and I wish, honest reader, that you and I went to church as much as they do. These people are not wicked BECAUSE of their religious observances, but IN SPITE of them. They are too dull to understand humility, too blind to see a tender and simple heart under a rough ungainly bosom. They are sure that all their conduct towards my poor friend here has been perfectly righteous, and that they have given proofs of the most Christian virtue. Haggarty's wife is considered by her friends as a martyr to a savage husband, and her mother is the angel that has come to rescue her. All they did was to cheat him and desert him. And safe in that wonderful self-complacency with which the fools of this earth are endowed, they have not a single pang of conscience for their villany towards him, consider their heartlessness as a proof and consequence of their spotless piety and virtue.

A Note About the Author

William Makepeace Thackeray (1811–1863) was an English novelist, satirist, and illustrator. Born in India, Thackeray was sent to England by his mother at the age of four following the death of his father, a secretary for the East India Company. Educated at the Charterhouse School, a boarding school in Godalming, Surrey, Thackeray went on to study at Trinity College, Cambridge before abandoning academia in 1830. He spent the next few years traveling throughout Europe, visiting Paris and meeting the elderly Goethe in Weimar. In 1836, after squandering much of his inheritance on gambling and ill-advised investments, Thackeray at last settled down, marrying Isabella Gethin Shawe and embarking on a career as a professional writer. During this period, he contributed regularly to *Fraser's Magazine*, *The Times*, *The Morning Chronicle*, and *Punch*, while also publishing *Catherine* (1840) and *The Luck of Barry Lyndon* (1844), his first full length works of fiction. Despite his newfound success, however, these years were tragically marred by the decline of Thackeray's wife, who suffered from a debilitative case of postpartum depression that led to her institutionalization. Between 1845 and 1851, under the pseudonym Hibernis Hibernior, Thackeray produced illustrations in *Punch* that are now recognized as hostile to the Irish people and exploitative of their suffering during the Great Irish Famine. In 1848, Thackeray published *Vanity Fair*, a satirical novel examining the lives of England's elite during and after the Napoleonic Wars.

A Note from the Publisher

Spanning many genres, from non-fiction essays to literature classics to children's books and lyric poetry, Mint Edition books showcase the master works of our time in a modern new package. The text is freshly typeset, is clean and easy to read, and features a new note about the author in each volume. Many books also include exclusive new introductory material. Every book boasts a striking new cover, which makes it as appropriate for collecting as it is for gift giving. Mint Edition books are only printed when a reader orders them, so natural resources are not wasted. We're proud that our books are never manufactured in exce
quantity they need to be read and enjoyed.

Discover more of your favorite classics with Bookfinity™.

- Track your reading with custom book lists.
- Get great book recommendations for your personalized Reader Type.
- Add reviews for your favorite books.
- AND MUCH MORE!

Visit **bookfinity.com** and take the fun Reader Type quiz to get started.

Enjoy our classic and modern companion pairings!

Classic & Modern

Printed in the USA
CPSIA information can be obtained
at www.ICGtesting.com
JSHW082343140824
68134JS00020B/1854

9 781513 271996